Praise for Steven Womack and **Dead Folk's Blues:**

"A virtuoso performance."
—*The Virginia Pilot and Ledger-Star*

"A rising star among the current crop of American novelists."
—*Nashville Banner*

"There is a lot to like in Womack's hardboiled murder mystery—an engaging sleuth, a convincing setting, a passel of folks to distrust, and some good minor characters."
—*Publishers Weekly*

"A deft, atmosphere-rich novel: smart, funny, and filled with a sense of wry heartbreak. Steven Womack's Nashville stands out—it is a beautifully drawn backdrop."
—JAMES ELLROY

Also by Steven Womack
Published by Ballantine Books:

DEAD FOLKS' BLUES

TORCH TOWN BOOGIE

Steven Womack

BALLANTINE BOOKS • NEW YORK

Copyright © 1993 by Steven Womack

All rights reserved under International and Pan-American Copyright Conventions. Published in the United States of America by Ballantine Books, a division of Random House, Inc., New York, and simultaneously in Canada by Random House of Canada Limited, Toronto.

Library of Congress Catalog Card Number: 93-90511

ISBN 0-345-38010-X

Manufactured in the United States of America

First Edition: November 1993

Acknowledgments

My thanks to John Odom, a brilliant chemist, teacher, and arson investigator, who shared with me the finer points of catching people who set fires. If I've written it wrong, it's not his fault.

My everlasting gratitude as well to Joe Blades for his patience and support.

And as always, Cathryn.

Chapter 1

It was a magnificent fire, a marvelous fire, the kind of fire whose brilliance penetrates even closed window shades and eyelids. I'd been asleep barely an hour, had just plunged headfirst into the black hole that opened up before me right after I folded my paperback closed and snapped off the light.

I didn't consciously hear the sirens. Maybe they were incorporated into a dream. I only know that at some point I became aware of a dull red glow dancing around in the paisley blackness behind my shuttered eyelids. I drifted on in sleep, wondering where the glow came from and if it was real. But something about the light was pulling me up out of the hole, drawing me slowly upward. With each rising moment, my sense of trouble grew. Just before I broke the surface and opened my eyes, I rolled over in bed, away from the light, to throw my arm over her.

Only she wasn't there. I opened my eyes in a panic. I heard the sirens now, and felt around on the bed.

She was gone. But where? Then I remembered. We'd shared dinner and a decent bottle of Chilean cabernet, then had adjourned to what passed for the bedroom in my attic apartment above Mrs. Hawkins's house. We'd made passionate but quiet love, knowing full well that it was late enough for Mrs. Hawkins to have removed her hearing aids, but taking a certain naughty delight at being careful anyway. Like two teenaged kids necking downstairs while their par-

1

ents slept restlessly above them, we'd tussled and locked and
exploded together, then lay sweating with the cool autumn
air blowing over us through the raised window.

Then she went home. Didn't want to have to sneak out
ahead of Mrs. Hawkins, the early riser. I'd been sorry to see
her go, as always. But there was dinner to look forward to
tonight, this time at her condo over on the better part of town,
where one's overnight guests were one's own business.

The sirens grew louder. I shook my head, tried to focus.
Damn cabernet. Great stuff, but splitting a bottle between
two was about twice my usual ration. I couldn't think clearly,
not yet anyway. But I had sense enough to roll over, toward
the window.

This great and wonderful light show played through the
pulled shade, growing both in intensity and variety of colors
by the second. It had been all red at first, but was now punc-
tuated with bursts of blue and a steady, pulsating yellow. I
scooted across the bed and planted both feet on the floor,
then stood and raised the shade.

My eyes widened and I forgot that I was standing in front
of an open window stark flapping naked.

It was the house diagonally across the street. House, in
fact, was an understatement. Like so much of East Nashville,
the block I lived on was a strange hodgepodge of architec-
tural styles and price ranges. Mrs. Hawkins's home was brick
and stucco, a late 1930s cottage that by local standards was
still practically new, and immodestly cheap. But across from
her and down two lots was, by anyone's standards, a
nineteenth-century mansion. It was a grand survivor of the
great fire of 1914, the catastrophic firestorm my grandmother
witnessed before my father was even born; the one where
half the population of Nashville gathered on the banks across
the river and watched most of the other half burn to the
ground. But this convoluted, now somewhat seedy, Victorian
dowager had survived. She had weathered fire, tornado,

storm, blizzard, and a fleet of owners, tenants, children, pets, burglars, assessors, repairmen, as well as the deterioration of a once-proud neighborhood and its subsequent slow, painful gentrification. She had survived it all.

Until tonight. And now I stood transfixed in front of her, as naked as the day I was born, as she slowly became enveloped in brilliant orange and red and dancing white flame. Surrounded by the lime-greenish–yellow pumpers of the Metro Nashville Fire Department, the orange-and-white paramedic vans, and the blue on white squad cars of the Metro Police Department, she was the centerpiece of a grand kaleidoscopic opera, her death cries the crackling of century-old roof rafters, the screeching of collapsing floor joists, the popping of exploding electrical circuits. I stared ahead, unable to take my eyes off her.

As I awakened to the horror of the scene before me, my chest was heavy with sadness, but my head pounded with anger. Someone out there was having his own private Kristallnacht.

The East Nashville Arsonist had struck again.

Chapter 2 _____

I'm a private investigator, but arson's not my area of expertise. Come to think of it, I'm not sure I have an area of expertise. I haven't been at this very long. I've repo'd cars, skip-traced, done a couple of workmen's-comp fraud claims, and managed to fumble my way through one rather sensational murder case. Other than that, I don't have any idea what the hell I'm doing.

So it was more as a spectator than anything else that I climbed into my jeans, threw on a T-shirt and a pair of running shoes, and trotted out into the middle of the night to watch the god-awful biggest fire I'd ever seen firsthand.

A crowd had already gathered, held back by uniformed Metro cops with bullhorns and a few fire department non-combatants. I could have gotten a better view from my second-story bedroom window, but there's something about a blazing fire that compels one to get as physically close as possible. I wondered, as I cut across my neighbor's lawn to join the throng, if the old myth about arsonists was true: the cliché that arsonists were so enthralled with their own crime that they couldn't bear not to watch. I thought, as I wedged myself in between two other spectators, that the person responsible for this inferno could be standing right next to me.

Of course, it never occurred to me that this was just an ordinary house fire, that someone had gone to bed without

4

turning off the burner under the teapot or that the dog had kicked over a candle or that overloaded seventy-year-old, cotton-wrapped wiring had finally given way. There had been so many fires in East Nashville over the past year, with accompanying levels of paranoia never seen in this community before, that I just assumed the sicko was at work again. From the chatter going on around me, it was a good guess that everyone else thought the same thing.

"It's awful," a thin, wizened woman covered in hair curlers from the neck up said. "Nobody's safe anymore."

"Goddamn it," the guy next to her said. He was wearing a dirty undershirt and smelled of liquor so strongly that even the smoke couldn't cover it up. "I'd like to get my hands on the sumbitch."

I shuffled off to one side, to the thinner edges of the crowd, and stood behind two people, the gap between their shoulders flickering orange and leaping blue. Their silhouettes were black, only the barest shades of skin visible against the brightness of the fire. It was clear that the firemen were going to have trouble with this one.

Behind us, from Sixteenth Avenue, another pumper paired with a paramedic van roared past us, the whooping of the van punctuating the more traditional siren of the fire engine. There were four engines on the scene now, crowded into our high-density neighborhood so tightly they barely had room to maneuver. People were strolling up from blocks away to view the spectacle, some in bathrobes or pajamas, others in hastily donned pants and shirts, a few barely dressed at all.

The whole state was in the middle of a months-long drought. The autumn foliage turned early and quickly, leaving scattered, crisp orange-and-brown piles at the foot of bare trees. Naked limbs reached for the murky sky earlier than anyone remembered, and everything was as dry as dust.

Which had made the arsonist's work all that much easier. The heat from the house could be felt hundreds of feet away, and it looked as if the firemen were going to be lucky to save even the adjacent houses. Sparks wafted upward in great sparkling clouds, red dimming into blackness against the night sky. A crew of firemen to the left began spraying down the roof of the house next door. A couple of men encased in fireproof suits with oxygen tanks on their backs made their way up to the front porch and into the house, chopping through doors as if they were rice paper. I followed them into the house with my eyes, in awe of anyone who could walk into that inferno as if the gates of hell were the doors to paradise.

Then there was the sound of rushing wind from deep inside the house. A hundred throats sucked in great gulps of air just as every window in the house exploded with a dull *whomp*, blowing flame and tinkling glass crystals through the air. One woman screamed. The man next to me took a dive right on the grass. My heart jumped at the thought of the two firemen who'd just gone inside.

The interior of the house was engulfed now, the wind roaring out of her a raging firestorm feeding on itself, a miniature Dresden. Panic appeared to spread now even among the firemen, who rushed about with hoses, axes, pole hooks. A crew ran up the front porch, the man in front with a bullhorn yelling muffled instructions. Two men started up the concrete steps to the wooden porch, the roof of it totally enshrouded in brilliant red flame. The rest quickly followed. They stopped, the crowd of men straining to see inside, to get some glimpse of their comrades.

The lead man yelled again and pointed, then the crowd around me held its collective breath as the two firemen staggered out the front door through a pudding of thick black and boiling scarlet. One man held his partner up as the two stumbled into the arms of their comrades. The other firemen rushed forward and grabbed them, literally lifting the two off their feet and running for their lives.

As they scattered down the long walk toward the street, a great cheer rose from the crowd. Just as I opened my mouth to join the hurrah, the roof over the porch, which ran the entire width of the house, collapsed in a shower of sparks, exploding timber, and the suffocating tarry smell of melting shingles.

A quick dark silence settled in over the crowd as we realized how close we'd all come to witnessing catastrophe. There had been a dozen men standing on that porch. If they'd stayed two seconds longer, not one of them would have gotten out alive.

I felt queasy as the fire rolled and billowed out the windows up all four sides of the house. Anyone left inside was history. There was no way out now.

The long metal arm of a fire-department cherry picker rose in the air above and in front of us. Two men in the bucket grabbed a high-pressure nozzle just as water burst from it. Spray like jet exhaust filled the air with a misty fog. A great sizzle and huge clouds of steam erupted from the fire. Water streamed in great arcs on the house from at least four or five directions now, with more sirens on their way to the conflagration.

But it was too late, far too late. A roar rose from deep within the burning old lady, and with a tearing and a ripping the likes of which I'd never heard before, the roof of the mansion fell in on itself. A ball of flame fifty, maybe a hundred feet across erupted from the inferno and rose toward the sky. Like dozens of Cowardly Lions standing before the Great and Powerful Wizard of Oz, everybody took off running like hell—spectators, firemen, police, everybody.

The wind changed direction again, blowing smoke and sparks directly down on the crowd. The house to the right of the mansion, the one that hadn't been sprayed down yet, erupted like a wad of newspaper placed too close to a fireplace. I knew now what the term *spontaneous combustion* really meant.

I ran along with everybody else, stopping only a half block

away when I found a convenient wide oak to step behind. A fine shower of sparks and debris fell over the neighborhood. Squad cars screamed from all directions as police responded to a citywide call for help. I looked to my left, to Mrs. Hawkins's house. She was still in there, asleep. If the fire was going to send the whole neighborhood up, somebody better go get her. And fast.

I made my way back toward my own house in the direction of the inferno. The police had set up a blockade in a circle around the burning mansion perhaps a half block in radius. Unfortunately Mrs. Hawkins's house was inside the circle. An older black police officer laid a grip on my shoulder that would have jerked the ground out from under me if I hadn't stopped willingly.

"My landlady's in that house," I yelled over the noise, pointing. "She's deaf as a box of rocks. I've got to wake her up if you're going to evacuate!"

He looked at me for a second, then released me. "Okay," he said, his voice deep and streetwise, "but move your butt."

"Yessir, Officer. High gear."

I ran toward the house, my feet sliding on the grass that ought to have been slippery with dew, but was instead just slick with lifelessness. The blacktop driveway lay in front of me. I skittered around the back and up the rickety metal stairs to my apartment, where an extra key to Mrs. Hawkins's backdoor hung on a hook next to my coffee mugs.

I ripped the key loose from the wall, my nostrils burning with the acrid stench of fire. Burning insulation and tar were the worst, I knew, and the deadliest. As I stepped back outside, the fire illuminated the whole backyard. I heard yells and muffled cries, the roaring of engines, the crackling of burning wood. Even the ground beneath me seemed to shake.

Inside Mrs. Hawkins's kitchen, I switched on the light and shouted. I knew it was no good. I may as well have been screaming at the stove. All I could do was try to make enough noise and movement that she'd sense me coming and I wouldn't frighten her to death.

The living room was filled with flickering red, the colors dancing dimly on the walls. I extinguished them with the white of her overhead light and yelled for her once again. Her bedroom door was closed, a window air conditioner humming inside. I turned on the hall light and pounded on her door.

"Mrs. Hawkins!" I bellowed. No response. Oh, hell, I thought, the best I can hope for is that the old lady isn't sitting up in bed with a pistol aimed at the door, waiting for an intruder to burst in.

There was no choice. I jerked the door open quickly and stepped in, wiping my arm across the wall with a great sweeping motion to hit the light switch. The ceiling light flashed on, filling the room. My jaw dropped as Mrs. Hawkins shot up in bed, her eyes wide in horror. The sheet flopped off her, revealing a pair of sagging breasts that resembled two huge, empty wineskins tacked to her chest.

Holy Hannah, I thought, *the old lady sleeps in the buff.*

She screamed, a choked, gagging scream as she fumbled with the sheet and pulled it around her.

"What are you doing here?" she bawled, in a voice doubly loud from shock and deafness.

The sheet next to her stirred. I squinted, staring in surprise as another form rolled over.

Good heavens, it's Mr. Harriman. And he's naked, too.

Mr. Harriman lived three doors down. His wife was in Milwaukee visiting her sister, according to Mrs. Hawkins. It's a small neighborhood. The old-timers all know each other's business.

Mr. Harriman jerked up in bed, fumbling on the nightstand for his own hearing aid. He was mostly bald, a retired railroad engineer, with only the slightest suggestion of a paunch. Good-looking for his age.

"What's the matter?" he asked sleepily.

"Nothing much," I yelled. "Except the whole effin' neighborhood's burning down and we've got to get out of here."

Mrs. Hawkins went dark around the eyes as she got most of what I said by lipreading. Then she turned, noticing for the first time the prancing colors filtering through the window shade, and let the sheet drop down again. She fumbled around on the nightstand for her pair of hearing aids. Mr. Harriman swung his spindly bald legs around on the edge of the bed and reached for his pants. He reached over and jerked the shade down, then let go of it. It snapped upward with a crack and flapped around a few times.

"My God," he said. "It looks like a big one."

"The biggest. Now move, you two."

That's the last time I worry about Marsha being here overnight, I thought, spinning on the balls of my feet.

I ran out the back of the house and down the driveway just as the west wall of the mansion collapsed, which immediately brought down the whole edifice in a heap. One by one the walls toppled, the floors gave way, and the structure smashed down into its own cellar, its destruction complete and final. It was quite literally gone in a blaze of glory.

Chapter 3

For the second time in six hours light on my face brought me out of a deep sleep. Only this time it was sunlight. With the acrid taste of smoke in my mouth and a ticklish rattle in my lungs, I woke up feeling like I'd French-kissed an ashtray. How do smokers do it?

I'd forgotten to pull the shade when I fell face forward onto the bed just before dawn. The mansion by then was a heap of stinking, smoldering black ashes, with only a few scarred, bare timbers reaching for help that would never come. One by one the fire-department trucks had pulled away, their engines roaring, loudspeakers squawking. One pumper stayed behind in case the fire resurrected itself, with one squad car left to keep the locals from poking around before the investigators could get there.

I'd stayed for the whole shooting match, curious and fascinated. There weren't many left by the time the last flame was extinguished. After the walls of the mansion fell in and it was clear the fire was under control, the police barricades came down and people were allowed to trickle home. The last vision I had before climbing the stairs to my own bed was a couple of lone cops stringing the yellow tape with POLICE LINE—DO NOT CROSS emblazoned on it. By then, the party was long over.

Talk about a lousy night's sleep. I rolled over, still in my clothes, and dragged one eye open to view the clock:

10:20 A.M. I tried to remember if I had any appointments. Then it came to me. Today was Saturday. I started to drift back off to sleep when I remembered why I'd been up so late.

It seemed like a dream now. I rolled over and sat up on the edge of the bed. Out the window, just visible through the trees, there was a whole lot of empty space where the mansion had once been. So the night before had been real after all. There were two squad cars and four plain white Ford sedans at the curb in front. I hadn't been a detective long, but my years as a newspaper reporter had left me with the ability to spot an unmarked car a long way off. Not that that was such a highly refined skill to begin with.

I scraped a brush across my teeth, then buried my face in a hot washcloth. A cup of coffee later I was feeling like I might live. The day was cool, bright, the leaves in great drifts and piles all through the neighborhood. Mrs. Hawkins was, thankfully, quietly ensconced in the bottom of the house with no likelihood of showing her head anytime soon. I wasn't exactly sure how I was going to deal with finding Mrs. Hawkins in a—how did the Victorians describe it?— compromising position. . . .

These matters are better left alone. If she didn't bring it up, then neither would I. Please, God, I thought, let me keep a straight face the next time I see her.

I pulled a sweater on over my T-shirt, filled my insulated mug full of steaming coffee, and crunched through the leaves up the street. Autumn had always been my favorite season. Something about football weather, the holidays, whatever. Or maybe it was just one last chance to feel good before the wintertime blues set in.

There were a few people hanging around just outside the yellow tape, watching as the suited investigators searched the rubble, taking notes, collecting evidence, snapping photographs. I knew very little about arson investigations, but

I'd always heard that arson was a snap to spot. Finding the perp and proving it, though, was another matter.

I leaned against a thick maple, the bark rough against my back, just observing. Two local television-news camera operators were back a few feet filming into the hole that had once been a basement, but was now full of scorched wreckage. One investigator had some kind of device that looked like a Geiger counter, a box with a wand or something. He was poking around the edges of the wreckage. I assumed there were investigators down in the basement that we couldn't see from street level. I marveled at how big the house had been, how quickly it went up, how terribly it came down.

There was a shuffling on the edges of the pit. I squinted and noticed the top foot or so of an aluminum ladder that had been lowered into the basement. A head appeared at the top of the shiny metal, one hand on the top rung, the other held low and behind, as if the investigator were carrying something. The cameras backed away, filming the man as he ascended.

The climber wore thick rubber gloves that ran all the way up to his elbows. There was a grim look on his face. He came up the ladder a step at a time, his torso gradually coming into view, followed by his other hand, which was wrapped tightly around the canvas loop of a dark green body bag.

Something swirled in my gut. Suddenly the coffee wasn't sitting too well. The body bag slowly came into view, a blue-coated paramedic with the same heavy rubber gloves carrying the back end. The two men struggled up the ladder and laid the bag out on the lawn. The paramedic pulled off his gloves and turned to offer a hand to the person behind him.

My eyes grew wide as I recognized the person emerging from the charred basement. His clothes were streaked with soot, a long black smear down one side of his face. His jaw was set, his eyes weary. Sergeant Howard Spellman of the

Metro Nashville Murder Squad had been called out early
once again. He could kiss another weekend goodbye, and
the look on his face said he already knew that.

Two other paramedics pulled a gurney out of a medic van
and rolled it across the lawn. They gingerly picked up the
body bag, placed it on the steel frame, and got it into the
back of the van as quickly as possible. Out of sight, out of
mind . . .

I also recognized the first guy out of the basement, the one
in street clothes with the heavy rubber gloves. He was Charlie Hoover, a forensic investigator with the medical examiner's office. If Charlie was there, and Spellman was there,
then the next stop was the autopsy lab, where the woman I'd
found myself falling in love with would unzip that body bag
and begin a job so appalling and ghastly I could barely stand
to think about it. Marsha had great big brass ones, no question.

There was also no question that I'd lost my appetite. I
watered the maple with my coffee and turned for home. The
news junkies would have a lot to digest today.

After all, the East Nashville Arsonist had just become the
East Nashville Murderer.

I grabbed a copy of the afternoon paper on the way into
my office. Actually, *office* might be stretching it. I rent one
room on the top floor of a run-down Seventh Avenue building
that managed to survive the wrecking ball when the new
Church Street Center went up. The Church Street Center, an
enormous enclosed shopping mall right in the middle of
downtown Nashville, is the latest attempt to revitalize the
central city before everybody leaves for the 'burbs.

It isn't much, but it's the only office I can afford. Besides,
I like being downtown. Outside the parking hassles, it's convenient and close to a lot of lawyers, who might someday be
my clients. So I put up with the traffic and the crowds and

the late-night spookiness, and in return I get character and atmosphere. As much as I can stand.

I encountered my first bit of atmosphere when I turned left off the sidewalk and took the two steps up to the alcove to the locked door of my office building. A sleeping wino was splayed out on the bricks, a grubby brown hunting jacket smeared with heaven knew what wrapped around him, and an empty bottle of Wild Irish Rose cuddled in his arms like a faithful teddy bear. I stepped over him carefully, figuring he might want to sleep late on a Saturday morning, and slipped my key into the door. At the first click he shot awake with a squeal, terrified at the sight of a strange man standing above him.

"Chill, man," I said, holding my hand out palm down to soothe him. "I'm just going to work."

His eyes grew wide. He was looking at me, but it was only speculation as to what he was seeing.

"You okay?" I asked.

"Ah, ah, ah," he stuttered. I reached into my pocket and pulled out a wad of paper and loose change. I leaned down, set what was probably about three dollars on the filthy jacket. He stared in horror and tried to back away from his own lap, like I'd just laid of fistful of live copperheads on him.

"Go get some breakfast, man. 'S cool."

He shook his head, finally coming to grips with the realization that the dollar bills weren't slithering up his chest toward his throat. His face relaxed, and he settled back against the bricks. A shaking left hand appeared from behind him. He slowly swept the money off his torso and stuffed it into a floppy pocket.

"Yeah, Mike, thanks. Thanks, Mike."

I twisted the key in the lock and pulled the door open, wondering who the hell Mike was.

Upstairs, all was quiet. One of the reasons I came in on Saturday mornings was to have the whole floor to myself.

Ray and Slim, the two songwriters who ran a struggling music-publishing company out of the office down the hall, would be home sleeping off whatever it was they managed to get into last night. The other two offices on the floor were empty. One had been empty for months, since before I rented my office. The other had been rented to a psychic, who wasn't psychic enough to realize she wasn't going to be able to make her rent. She skipped out after eight weeks. The building manager, knowing that I was a private detective, asked me to track her down. Once I quoted him my daily rate, though, he figured she wasn't worth it.

The light on my answering machine was flashing one red blink at a time, so I hit the button and hung up my coat while my message played.

"So you're not in yet, eh?" I smiled, hearing Marsha's voice. Sorry. Can't help it. Great to feel this good about somebody again, especially at my age and with my track record. "Guess you had a rough night last night. I'm at the lab. Call me when you get in."

Her voice went into a fake falsetto: "Smoochie-smoochies, dumpling." Then a click, and the synthesized answering-machine voice was telling me that was the last message.

"Thank God, she's not serious with that dumpling stuff," I said out loud, relieved that no one was around to hear.

I carried my coffeemaker down the hall to the bathroom and washed it out, then made a fresh pot and sat at my desk to go over the mail that had built up over the last couple of days. A few bills—of course—and one check: $300 for the last four cars I'd helped my friend Lonnie repossess. Not much, but it would help. I was down to my last few hundred. Cash flow seemed a constant problem these days. I guess that happens when you have a midlife career change, especially when you weren't prepared for it.

I sipped my coffee and propped my feet up on the desk, then flapped open the afternoon paper, impressed with the bright color picture of the flaming mansion that filled half the front page above the fold. The two Nashville papers shared the same printing plant, which was one factor that kept this city a two-newspaper town. They upgraded the printing presses six months after I got canned—no connection, I'm sure, since my yearly salary wouldn't have paid for the ink they use every day—and the new graphics were incredible. Made me wish I was still on the street covering fires, although truth be told I hadn't covered a fire in years. That was for the young kids. I was a reporter on the hill, with a carpeted, air-conditioned press office and my own telephone line and fax machine. And cocktails every afternoon with legislators, if I'd been so inclined.

Today, the East Nashville Arsonist was the lead story once again, only this time the headlines screamed that he'd graduated from arson to murder. The police were pretty sure that the same guy had burned, at last count, nineteen houses in East Nashville. This was the first one, though, with a body found in it afterward.

I looked up from the paper and stared out my dirty window, thinking about what I'd seen the night before. There was some unusual perspective involved in being an eyewitness to a big event, followed by reading about it in the newspaper later. Since I'd left the profession, I had a greater understanding of the grief people give the media. Like this story, for instance.

The blaze last night didn't fit in at all with the pattern set in the other torchings. Only the reporter who'd written the story apparently wasn't savvy enough to pick up on that. All nineteen cases of arson had occurred in houses that were either completely empty, or temporarily vacant while being renovated. There was speculation among the police and the community that someone was torching gays, trying to save East Nashville from alternate-lifestyle infiltration. Because it had some of the cheapest housing prices in the city, combined with some of the oldest, classiest architecture, East Nashville was a prime target for young professionals, artists, and gentrifiers. And among this group was a fair number of gay and lesbian couples, who, by the way, make the best neighbors I've ever had. Only some of the local beer-can-and-undershirt crowd didn't feel that way.

This speculation increased after a gay and lesbian bar at an intersection called Five Points was firebombed last year. Thank heavens, it was after hours and the only people there were the cleaning crew, who crawled out through the back window. Only problem with the mad-arsonist theory was that they caught the guy who did it, a sixteen-year-old zit-plagued redneck idiot who somehow managed to inflict third-degree burns on himself while setting off a crude Molotov cocktail.

The police were never able to connect him to any other torching, though. I followed the case through the newspapers, and something about it was pretty stinko. They tried to hang a year's worth of arsons on the kid, but none of them would stick. I figured he was just a screwed-up punk of little intelligence who figured he'd impress his girlfriend enough to sleep with him.

Anyway, it became a moot point when three other houses were burned flush to the ground over the next month. And it was no quart Pepsi bottle full of gasoline and an old rag, either. Whoever was burning down East Nashville one house at a time knew what he was doing.

I focused back on the newspaper and continued reading. Second paragraph down, the reporter identified the owner of the home and the presumed victim. When I read the name, my jaw fell open and my feet plopped to the floor with a thud.

Dr. Will Elmore, Chairman of the Board and President of Psychology Associates, Inc., the largest psychological testing firm this side of Atlanta. His private practice drew the troubled elite of Nashville's political, show business, and corporate communities. The shrink to the stars, they called him. He was the same Will Elmore who'd made national news with his investigations into unethical Medicaid practices. The same Will Elmore who'd testified as an expert witness in over two hundred criminal trials.

And the same Will Elmore who'd been my ex-wife's therapist. And later, her lover.

Chapter 4 _____

Leave it to Lanie not to go to the local Doc-in-the-Box when she decided she needed help. No, not my Lanie, who wouldn't be caught dead in anything this side of a Volvo, and whose preferred mode of transportation is a Jaguar or a Mercedes. Not Lanie, whose idea of shopping on the cheap is to get the Super Saver fare to the Dallas Neiman-Marcus.

No, when Lanie decided she was unraveling, she went to the very best, or at least the best known: Dr. Will Elmore, whose hourly rates started at $150 and from there went up to whatever the traffic would bear. I know, because for a while I was that traffic.

Hell, I didn't have any idea he was my neighbor. Like most Americans, I don't even know who my freaking neighbors are anymore. Except Mr. Harriman, of course.

I finished the article, boiling it down to the relevant: Vanderbilt undergraduate, Stanford Ph.D., age forty-nine, adjunct professor of psychology at four different universities throughout his career. Only he'd given up the academic life for the big bucks of private practice and corporate consulting.

Divorced three times; two kids with his first wife, one with his second. The third, apparently, had sense enough to bail out when she could go as a single. He started Psychology Associates, Inc. in the early Eighties and had aggressively marketed himself and the company for the rest of the decade.

He was rich, respected, feared. Just the kind of guy somebody would want to ax.

Seeing his name brought back a lot of my old stuff. Lanie and I'd never had what you'd call an easy marriage. She was successful, aggressive, and I—well, I wasn't into designer clothes, Beemers, or spending my meager vacation time hot-air ballooning in the south of France. Compared with Lanie, and compared with what Lanie wanted, I was an ambition-less slug. I live cheaply, hate being in debt, and have a very low tolerance for that kind of phony, fatuous crap.

Funny, I feel vindicated now. When the Nineties flushed the Eighties down the dumper, Ivan Boesky, Charles Keating, and the legions of their yuppie admirers swirled right down as well. I may still be in the toilet, but at least my head's above the water.

When things fell apart for Lanie and me, at her insistence we went into marital therapy. She got the appointment with Elmore. We gave it our best shot. On the third visit he ventured his expert psychological opinion that I was blocking, locked down, or some such garbage. I can't even remember how he said it. But Lanie agreed with him, and a short time later we got our separation and divorce. The next time I heard of him, he shows up in the society column squiring my ex-wife to the Swan Ball, the biggest old-money do of the year.

Their engagement had been announced a month ago, a picture of the two of them appearing in the Sunday paper in the upper-left-hand corner of the first-announcements page, a place I knew was reserved for the most socially prominent. Over the past couple of decades the papers had attempted to treat engagement and marriage notices more equitably, but vestiges of the old society pages remained.

By that time I'd lost touch with her. During the separation, and for a while after the divorce, we kept in touch. We remained civil to each other throughout the process, as educated, sophisticated people do, with no hint of the boiling underneath. We checked in periodically, mostly over the phone, until the calls started coming at longer and longer intervals. When I saw the notice of her forthcoming nuptials, I hadn't spoken to Lanie in maybe six months.

Halfway through smearing peanut butter across a slice of whole wheat, I realized I'd forgotten to call Marsha. Guess connecting the fire with my ex-wife distracted me. I dropped the bread on the counter and crossed my kitchen to the wall phone.

This being Saturday, it wasn't likely the phone at the morgue—or as it's known in Nashville, the T. E. Simpkins Forensic Science Center—would get answered quickly. I was surprised then, when Kay Delacorte answered the phone on the second ring.

"Medical examiner's office."

"What are you doing in on a Saturday?"

As I expected, Kay recognized my voice. I'd been making a lot of calls to the morgue over the past few weeks. "Well, if it isn't Philip Marlowe himself. Or is it Sam Spade this week?"

"Naw, babe, this week I think I'll be Dick Tracy."

She smothered a laugh. "Yeah, I think I heard that. The Dick part, anyway."

I felt the color rising in my neck. Kay had a rather bawdy sense of humor once she got to know you. Apparently she'd gotten to know me.

"So what are you doing in today?"

Kay was the head administrator at the morgue. She processed bodies, did the paperwork, took care of about two gazillion things all at once. Occasionally she even assisted in autopsies, although she told me that activity no longer held quite the same thrill for her as it did when she was younger.

"Busy night. You'd have thought it was July. Three homicides, a couple of road kills, a suicide, and one very crispy critter.''

I whistled. "Rough night.''

"Yeah, they called in Dr. Marsh about six this morning. Only thing was, she was pretty sleepy. Like she'd been out late last night . . . Hmmm, how could that be?''

"Jeez, Kay, I don't know. It's not my week to watch her.''

" 'S not what I heard.''

"She around?''

"Yeah, she just finished cleaning up. She's pretty fried, though. So to speak . . .''

"I'll go easy on her.''

Kay laughed. " 'S not what I heard.'' Then I was on hold.

I rested the phone in the crook of my neck and stepped back over to my sandwich. I smoothed out the peanut butter, layered on some strawberry jam, and poured myself a glass of milk by the time Marsha got to the phone.

"Hey,'' she said. Her voice was weary, bone-dry.

"You okay, babe?''

"That's *Doctor* Babe to you.''

I smiled. "You sound beat. Let's just stay in tonight, okay?''

"Yeah.'' She sighed. "As long as you don't expect too much even then.''

"I'm kind of tired myself.''

"Good. We'll send out for pizza, open a cheap Chardonnay, catch a movie on the tube.''

"Go to bed early . . .'' I ventured.

"Sure, why not.''

"I was up most of the night myself. Even after you left.''

"Yeah?''

"The house that was torched last night? It was across the street and up a couple.''

"Yeah, I heard. Sounded like a big one.''

"Biggest one I've ever seen. We thought the whole neighborhood was going up. Don't want to pry, Doctor Babe, but did you do the victim?''

''Yeah. There's only two kinds that get to me. Child-abuse victims and crispy critters . . .'' Her voice took on a new edge of exhaustion. ''Yuck.''

I cringed, lowered my voice. ''Kay said that, too. How can you guys do that?''

''Do what?''

''That *crispy critter* stuff?''

Her voice tightened. ''You laugh or you go crazy.''

''So what time you getting off tonight?''

She paused, the sound of paper shuffling in the background. ''I've got another hour or so's worth of paperwork. Then I'd like to go home, take a hot shower, lie down for an hour or so.''

I looked at my watch. ''Okay, that'll put us around six. Since we're not going anywhere, why don't I pop over about seven? Give you some slack, clockwise.''

''Thanks. Appreciationwise.''

''Hey,'' I said as I sensed her hanging up.

''Yeah?''

''Keep it together. It'll be all right. I'll give you a long back rub.''

''You don't have to tell me that,'' she said irritably. ''I've been at this awhile, you know.''

''Didn't mean to offend you . . .''

A beat, then: ''I'll take the back rub, though. Gladly.''

''Later.''

A rare free Saturday afternoon stretched in front of me like a monthlong vacation. No chores to do, no work to interfere with the day's pleasures, and more importantly, the night's. Despite the rough night just concluded, I felt almost carefree.

I finished lunch and decided to visit Lonnie. On the way I

could go through the night deposit and stick the check he'd sent me in the bank.

Lonnie Smith is one of these people who, once you meet him, you're not likely to forget. I met Lonnie years ago, back when I was still working cityside for the newspaper. He'd given me some help on a story I was doing, a feature on repo men. Lonnie'd come here from Brooklyn to make it big in the music business and, like most, wound up doing something else. Despite never making it big time on the Opry, he'd stayed on and become as homegrown as you can get without having a birth certificate with a deep drawl stamped on it.

Lonnie had a—well, it was sort of a junkyard out off Gallatin Road, stuck back in a dreary neighborhood of auto-repair garages, pawnshops, motorcycle-gang headquarters, and what used to be the old Inglewood Theatre, which had been one of the grand old movie palaces of the Forties and Fifties, but was now a salvage store. You go left off the five-lane road headed out of town, then curve around behind the theatre. Lonnie's place is up there, but you kind of have to know where it is to find it. Doesn't matter much, anyway. Lonnie never has any customers, and that's the way he wants it.

I hadn't seen him in a couple of weeks, not since his work load piled up and he had about a half-dozen cars to pick up in two days. Lonnie works with a couple of fairly scruffy guys most of the time, but when things tighten up, he sends them out as a two-man team, then calls me to back him up. We picked up a three-month-old Nissan Sentra up Greenbriar, a little town near the Kentucky border, and had a bit of a scare when the redneck deadbeat who'd never made a payment came out on his front porch with a shotgun. It was one of the few times I wished I carried. As a rule I won't keep a pistol, figuring that having one makes you more likely to use it, and if you don't have it, you'll stay away from situations where you might need it.

This time I'd figured wrong, or at least that's the way it seemed at first. Sometimes Lonnie's almost magic, though. He knows how to take care of himself. I once saw him slap-jack a man twice his size as silly as a rat in a coffee can. But this time Lonnie just held out his hands and talked sooth-ingly. *Very* soothingly.

Next thing I know, my heart's beating like a trip-hammer, I'm covered in sweat, and I'm driving down I-65 in an almost brand-new Sentra, Lonnie following in the wrecker, laugh-ing his keister off at me.

Life's never dull around Lonnie.

I pulled into the drive-through window of my bank, stuck my ATM card in the slot, made my deposit, then drew out fifty dollars, just in case Marsha changed her mind about staying home. We've been pretty up-front with each other about this money situation; she knows my career change has left me living from one day to the next, and I know that even as a civil servant, a doctor's going to pull down some serious money. So we either split things most of the time, or if it's her idea, she picks up the tab. I try to remain as liberated as possible in these issues, despite feeling weird about it some-times.

I was halfway to Lonnie's before I remembered Shadow. If I showed up at the gate without a treat for Shadow, she'd never forgive me. And being never forgiven by Shadow might mean being torn limb from limb.

I U-turned in the middle of Gallatin Road and headed back toward town, the engine in my seven-year-old Ford Escort straining to keep up with the traffic. The Ford had been an-other buy-down in my lifestyle, but after my legal fees from the divorce and getting fired from the paper, it was the best I could do. With just over 110,000 miles on it and burning about a quart of oil every tankful of gas, I figured the heap had about six months on it before I could leave it behind the chain-link fence at Lonnie's for good.

I pulled off Gallatin Road and into Mrs. Lee's, the brakes on the Ford squealing at the effort of stopping. Okay, make that six months *if* the brakes last.

It was nearly three o'clock and the lunchtime crowd at Mrs. Lee's had dissipated. Mrs. Lee and her husband whip up the best Szechuan food I've ever tasted, and there had been many an evening when I'd popped in for dinner with clogged sinuses and left breathing like an Olympic athlete. Food so good it brings tears to your eyes. Literally.

Mrs. Lee was behind the counter, as usual, the sleeves of her flowered blouse rolled up to her elbows, her graying black hair pulled behind her in a tight bun. She looked up from the cash-register drawer and scowled at me.

"Oh, yeah, you get new gullfwend and we nevah see you no moah! Nice of you to dwop by evah now an' then." She slammed the drawer shut with a loud clang.

"That true, Harry?" Mrs. Lee's seventeen-year-old daughter, Mary, asked, stepping out of the kitchen through a pair of swinging doors. Every time I saw Mary Lee, my heart stopped long enough to fulfill the skipping-a-beat requirement. I hate to display an ingrained prejudice like this, but I've always considered Asian women among the most beautiful in the world. At their best, as Mary was, they are unutterably exquisite.

"You really find a new girlfriend?"

I stared at her, for once at a loss for a snappy comeback. "Well," I stuttered, "since I couldn't get you to go out with me . . ."

"Hah!" Mrs. Lee snapped. "You damn right, she won't go out with you. I snatch her baw-headed and cut you throat!"

But there was a glimmer of a smile on her face, and I knew Mrs. Lee wouldn't snatch her daughter bald-headed for going out with me. I didn't doubt for a moment, though, that she'd cut my throat.

"What you need today, lovahboy?" Mrs. Lee picked up her pen.

"The usual," we said simultaneously.

"Lissen, if I give it to you foah free, will you eat something besides Szechuan chicken?"

"I promise you, the next time I come in, it's something besides Szechuan chicken. In fact, I just need the chicken this time. Skip the veggies. To go, please."

She dropped the pad on the counter in disgust. "Oh, you too good to eat my food anymoah, but you don't mind taking it to Shadow."

I smiled at her. "You know what Shadow would do if I showed up without something from you?"

"The same thing I gonna do to you I catch you messing with my daughter."

"Mother," Mary said, embarrassed. "Don't talk that way to Harry."

"You hush up," Mrs. Lee ordered, "and go wash some chicken foah Shadow."

Mary pushed through the swinging doors with a look on her face that proved despite her beauty, she could do a teen-aged pout with the best of them.

"C'mon, Mrs. Lee, you know me better than that. You don't really think I'd do anything to your daughter besides admire her longingly, with the greatest respect—and distance."

"As wrong as you keep the distance . . ."

Mary brought a foam box out and laid it on the counter. Her eyes were still pouty, her lips curled out to die for, and she had what I interpreted as an apologetic look on her face.

"Here, Harry," she said. "Sorry about the bad attitude around here."

"Forget it, Mary. Believe me, if you were my daughter,

I'd want to watch out for you, too. What's the ticket, Mrs. Lee?''

"No chahj. Tell Shadow we said hi."

I smiled at her. Strangely enough, she smiled back. I'd have to start coming back here more regularly; there was too much grief to take when I didn't. Besides, Mrs. Lee was right. I hadn't been in much since Marsha and I started seeing each other.

Valves clattering and timing belt whining, I pulled back out onto Gallatin Road and headed away from town. The Saturday-afternoon traffic was in a lull, and I relaxed as I drove, the windows down, the cool fall air blowing over me. With the dull buzz of too little sleep taking the edge off, life seemed quite pleasant.

Suddenly the odor of burning leaves wafted across the road, and the hair on the back of my neck stood up.

I rounded the curve on the side street leading up to Lonnie's place, gave a quick wave to the four greasy bikers with raised cans of Pabst Blue Ribbon out in front of the Death Rangers' headquarters, and squealed to a stop in front of the chain-link gate.

Tires crunching on gravel brought Shadow out from behind the faded green mobile home with the brown rust streaks cascading down the side. Her limp in the back legs had gotten worse in the two weeks since I'd seen her. Old shepherds go fast, I've heard, when they finally start to go, even if they have got a good dollop of timberwolf in them. I wondered if she was suffering, and if she was, how long Lonnie'd let it continue.

"Shadow," I piped, "here, baby."

Her ears perked up. Her sight wasn't as good as it used to be, but her hearing was still sharp. She recognized my voice even before my smell got to her. Her tail switched back and forth; she knew what was coming.

I lifted the chain off the latch and pulled it up, pushed the fence door in a foot and a half, and slipped through. The box was in my left hand. I flipped it open, pulled the chicken pieces out and squeezed them into a tight ball, then crushed the box flat on the ground.

"Sit, Shadow. Sit." She stopped a few feet from me, went down on her haunches. I bent over, laid the chicken out on

30

the flattened box. Her eyes got bigger, darker, and her huge tongue hung out the left side of her mouth, dripping onto the ground. Her shoulders hunched forward, poised to go for it.

"No, Shadow! Sit!"

I stepped back a bit. She raised her head to me, gave me a look that said her patience was wearing thin.

"Shadow . . . go!" I snapped.

The chicken was gone before I got the words out of my mouth. In one quick leap she was on my shoulders, her hot breath in my face, smelling of Mrs. Lee's Szechuan chicken. I rubbed her back, talked baby talk to her for a minute. The door to the trailer opened and Lonnie stepped out onto the small wooden covered deck that had been nailed together precariously as a porch.

"You know how tough it is to get her to eat dog food after you bring that crap around?"

"I know how tough it'd be to get me to eat it," I said. Lonnie wore a pair of faded tight Levi's and a white T-shirt. Despite being almost a decade older than me, he was slimmer and tighter, and his hair—which he'd let hang a bit longer lately—had only the faintest trace of gray at the temples.

"C'mon in and wash that grease off your hands before she decides to rip your arm off and eat it, too."

I gave Shadow a last big scratch between the ears. As I hit the first step up to the porch, she dutifully trotted off to her nest behind the trailer.

"She's limping awful bad," I said.

"Yeah," he said, holding the door for me. "Vet says it's that hip thing. Not much to do about it."

"How long before . . . ?"

Lonnie looked at me darkly and bit down on the toothpick hanging out of the right side of his mouth so hard that it fluttered. "Don't know. Maybe a year."

"How old is she?"

"Twelve."

"Pretty old for a shepherd."

He slammed the door behind me. "She'll rip your face off, I give her the word. Can we talk about something else?"

I walked over to the sink and pumped a couple of squirts of liquid hand soap out of a bottle. The place was pretty neat and orderly, by Lonnie's standards. Lonnie had an apartment somewhere else, although I'd never been there. Most nights he worked and slept here.

There was a green metal box on the desk across the room, dials and knobs on the front, its guts all over the rest of the desktop. Tubes and resistors, capacitors and coils, lay around in disarray. I rubbed my hands together under the hot water, then pulled a couple of sheets of paper towel off a roll.

"What's that contraption?" I asked. My nose curled at the smell of burning solder.

"That? Just a hunk of war surplus I picked up. Communications receiver. I 'uz just screwing around with it, trying to modify it."

I walked across the room and plopped in a worn recliner. "Thanks for the check, man. I can use it."

Lonnie walked around the desk, sat behind the maze of electronic junk. "No problem. Thanks for the help. May use you again next week, business picks up again."

"Great. Give me a call." I shifted the wooden handle on the recliner and let the back slide down so that I was practically horizontal. "You see the news last night?"

He looked up from the metal tray, the soldering iron in his left hand pointed down toward a tube socket. "No, but I heard it on the scanner. Across the street from you?"

"Couple houses down. Pretty good fire."

Lonnie smiled. "Yeah."

I wondered what the smile meant. "What do you know about arson?"

He laid the tray down, slipped the soldering iron into its

holder. "Not that much, really. Why? You thinking about switching careers?"

"No. I guess having one go up that close to home's got my attention."

"This guy's been setting fires off and on for a year and a half, and you're just now noticing?"

"Just now noticing enough to ask you about it."

He leaned back in his chair, laced his fingers around his head. "Well, I can tell you this much—that crap you read in magazines and newspapers and see in the movies is a crock. All this about the possessed demonic pyromaniac setting fires, and getting the kind of sexual turn-on and stuff—that's a bunch of horseshit.

"Ninety-nine times out of a hundred," he continued, "you can solve the crime of arson by asking one question: *who benefits?*"

"What? You mean, like, arson's always insurance fraud?"

"Yeah. It's somebody burning his own house to collect the insurance money, to keep a divorced spouse from getting it, or something like that. And you can usually tell who did it right off."

"Really?" I pulled the chair into an upright position and planted my feet back on the floor.

"If the guns are gone, he did it. If the pictures are gone, she did it. If the guns and the pictures are gone, it's a conspiracy."

"What do you mean? Guns? Pictures?"

"Somebody torches their own house, they're always going to save one thing they can't bear to lose. With men, it's usually the guns. Women always save photo albums. There was one case I read about where the arson investigators found a photo album in the ashes of a burned house. Somehow it'd survived the fire. When they got it to the lab, they noticed the faded parts of the scrapbook pages didn't match the pictures that were pasted in. Turned out the woman replaced her precious snapshots with pictures she'd cut out of a magazine, then torched the house with the album in it so nobody'd suspect her."

I laughed. "Aw, man, get out of here."

"Regular pictures leave traces of silver when they burn. Magazines don't. People do some strange shit."

"What do you think about this guy? He fit that pattern?"

"How could he? One guy burns what is it, nineteen, twenty, houses? How can one guy benefit from all that? Maybe we do have a psycho running around. Then again, maybe it's not just one guy. Maybe it's a bunch of copycats."

"I saw this house burn last night. First time I've ever seen one up close. Whoever did it knew what he was doing. That house was gone from the first match. No way they could've saved it."

"That's what I heard over the scanner. Dude's a pro. Somebody passionate about his work. Say, did I ever tell you about that recipe I got that would improve the performance of a Molotov cocktail?"

"This the ersatz napalm?"

"No, man, this is much quicker. You take regular gasoline and mix in chain-saw oil. Makes the gas burn at a much higher temperature, harder to put out. Then you mix in roofing tar. Makes it stick to anything it touches."

I shook my head, sighed. "You're a truly dangerous man, you know that?"

"No." He brushed me off. "I just have an academic curiosity. You know there's a way you can pull the metal sockets off light bulbs by melting the glue? Makes a great container for the cocktail mix. Easy to throw, guaranteed to explode on impact. Much more dependable than a Coke bottle. See, first you . . . ."

Back at the house, I noticed Mrs. Hawkins's windows were all curtained off and the doors shut tight. She never went anywhere. I knew she must be inside. Normally all her curtains would be pulled back to let in the light and the windows cracked to allow for fresh air. I guess she was just suffering from a terminal case of embarrassment. I didn't want the old lady to spend the rest of her life avoiding me; maybe I'd better knock on the door and talk to her.

No, I thought, laughing to myself, let her sweat another day or two.

I had a couple of hours left before heading over to Marsha's. I plopped on the bed, grazed around with the remote control, and found an old Busby Berkeley musical on American Movie Classics. I drifted in and out, shuffling off to Buffalo in that half-asleep, dreamy, soft state between fully awake and dead to the world. Then the damn phone rang. I thought it was part of my dream. It rang again.

This time I thought it was part of the movie. Third ring, I finally picked the phone up, fumbling with it to plant it next to my ear.

"Yeah . . ." I muttered.

"Harry? Is this Harry Denton?"

"Yeah," I said, trying without much success to stifle a yawn.

"Were you asleep?"

"Yeah, but that's okay. I had to get up in a minute, anyway. Who's this?"

"It's me, Harry. Lanie. Has it been that long? You don't recognize my voice anymore?"

My eyes slid up to half-mast. "Lanie? Yeah, I recognize your voice. It's just been a while."

"Harry, I need your help."

I was still pretty far from complete consciousness.

"Lanie." I broke my sentence with another yawn. "Why me? We haven't spoken in months, and with good reason. Memory serves me, our last conversation was a doozy."

"I know, but that's all different now, Harry. I really need to talk to you."

"Okay, talk. What's the matter?"

"Not over the phone, Harry. Can you meet me? Downtown?"

I sat up in bed, dropped my feet to the floor. "What's going on, Lanie? Where are you?"

"I'm at the police station."

"What the hell are you doing at the police station?"

"Harry," she said, her voice choking in her throat, "the police think I killed Will."

Okay, I'm awake.

"Calm down, Lanie. Are the police holding you? Have you got a lawyer?"

"No, they said I could go for now." Her voice broke again. I'd rarely heard Lanie cry. I probably cried more about our marriage than she did. "But it's awful, Harry. They think I killed him. They—"

I reached up and rubbed my temples, my hand opening to squeeze both sides of what was rapidly becoming a pounding headache. Jesus, I need this like I need a hole in the head.

"All right, Lanie," I said. "Give me twenty minutes."

Chapter 6

I knew Lanie was distressed; otherwise she never would have agreed to meet me at my old hangout, the Gerst Haus. The Gerst was East Nashville funky at its best: German food cooked Southern style—deliciously greasy meat and over-cooked vegetables. Great stuff, but over the past few years I've developed a certain appreciation for my arteries.

The place is especially popular among politicians when the legislature's in session. Certain times of the year, you can't get a table at lunchtime for all the cigar-smoking fatcats cutting deals between orders of sauerbraten and Wiener schnitzel and far too many frosty mugs of the dark, thick Gerst Haus draft. I loved the place back when I worked for the newspaper. I got more insider stuff from one meal at the Gerst than from two dozen press conferences at Legislative Plaza. Since I got myself fired, though, it hasn't been the same.

On the other hand, it was much more my turf than Lanie's. Ordinarily she wouldn't be caught dead at the Gerst Haus. The trendy Green Hills cafés and *grilles* were more her style.

I made it through the yellow light just before the freeway entrance ramp, then watched through my rearview mirror as six more cars ran the red. The National Transportation Safety Board says Nashville, Tennessee, is the deadliest place in America to drive—worse than New York, worse than Chicago, worse than L.A. We're real proud of that down here. Most people think our only claim to fame is picking guitars.

Five-thirty on a Saturday afternoon. The Gerst Haus parking lot was almost empty. It was still too early for the dinner clientele, too late for the lunch crowd, leaving only the afternoon beer drinkers to fill the hard wooden booths.

I parked the Ford next to the entrance steps and managed to get the door shut on the second try. Behind me, up the hill next to the smelly Dempster Dumpster, a red Alfa-Romeo Spyder with the top up occupied two parking spaces far away from the other cars. Lanie always was careful with the Alfa.

When you walk into the Gerst from a bright, sunny afternoon, you have to be careful for a few seconds. Otherwise you'll trip over a table in the darkness and break something you might need. Over the bar, a dim bulb strained to illuminate the glossy wood through a plastic, fake Tiffany, hanging lampshade. A bored blonde in a white T-shirt stood behind the bar absentmindedly wiping glasses as the television behind her blared coverage of a stock-car race. A fat guy in khakis and red suspenders sat nursing a mug of Gerst and staring silently at the tube, the only bar customer on a slow Saturday afternoon.

A couple of tables in the middle of the restaurant were occupied, but none by my ex-wife. I squinted in the dim light. In the booth farthest away from me I caught a glimpse of a stockinged foot with a shiny black high heel dangling off the big toe. Had to be Lanie; she's the only one I know who'd dress to kill for a police interrogation.

I made my way to the other end of the bar, past the glass display case with the electric train, beyond a series of booths with high partitions, and came up behind her. I sat down quickly and slid as far over against the wall as I could.

"You know where they got the name, don't you?" I joked. "*Gerst* is German for grease."

It was the same line I used the one time I'd brought her

here when we first married. She hated the place immediately, refused to touch a bite, and swore she'd never return. Somebody forgot to tell her never to say never.

"Jesus, Harry," she snapped, then rolled her eyes. "After all I've been through today, you can make jokes?"

Despite what she'd been through today, Lanie looked great. Lanie always looked great. That was part of the problem.

"Sorry, Lanie," I said, rubbing my burning eyes with the thumb and middle finger of my right hand. Despite the scarcity of patrons, a thin blue pall of cigarette smoke hung throughout the room at eye level. "It hasn't been the peachiest day for me either. The fire kept me up all night."

She fingered the collar of her silk blouse nervously, her hand brushing against the dangling string of pearls that were almost certainly genuine.

"You were there?"

I stared at her a second, trying to recall how many months it had been since we last spoke. "You didn't know?"

She brushed a lock of brown hair out of her face and past the frame of her designer glasses. Her hair was cut shorter than I remembered, more businesslike, perhaps even stern.

"Know *what*?"

"Lanie, I live across the street from Will Elmore. I didn't realize it, though, until I read his name in the paper."

She sighed and rubbed her face, then checked her finger for mascara smears. "You mean we were almost neighbors?"

I smiled and chuckled despite myself. "Yeah, only you'd have been living in a mansion while I rent an attic apartment."

"Well, we wouldn't have been living there long. I'd already talked Will into putting that dragon of a house on the market."

"Don't insult East Nashville, Lanie. It's my home now. Truth is, I'll take it over Belle Meade any day."

She stiffened and glared at me in the dim light. The waitress ambled over with a couple of menus and slid them down on the table between us.

"Glenlivet on the rocks," Lanie ordered without looking up at the middle-aged woman with the bad bleach job. "Clean glass, if you've got it."

"A what?" the waitress asked in a deep drawl that stretched the word *what* into about three syllables.

"The lady means she'd like a Scotch and soda, and please excuse the rude remark about the glasses. I'll have a Coke, extra ice. And thank you."

The waitress scribbled our orders, picked up the menus, and strolled off.

"I see grief hasn't dampened your inherent snottiness."

That seemed to let the air out of her, and she slid further down in the seat. Lanie was about five-four, maybe a hundred and fifteen, with a presence that made her look taller and more imposing. But just then, she seemed swallowed up by the seat.

"I'm sorry," she said, with apparent sincerity. "It's been a hideous day, Harry. And if I don't exactly seem grief-stricken, it's only because it hasn't sunk in yet that Will's really . . ."

She waited a second, as if expecting me to finish her sentence—or to do something, anything, that would keep her from saying the word herself. I felt for her; my ex-wife had a value system that wasn't exactly my cup of tea, and priorities that were largely incompatible with mine, but she wasn't a bad person. She certainly didn't deserve this hand, but it had been dealt to her irrevocably.

"I know," I said soothingly. "It's hard to comprehend. I woke up this morning, after finally getting to sleep around dawn, and thought it was all a dream. Until I smelled the smoke in my curtains."

Her eyes teared up and her face screwed up in anguish.

"Oh, God, Harry, it's so awful. To think of him, of Will, in that dreadful—"

"Stop," I said as the waitress set two glasses on cocktail napkins between us. "That's not going to do any good. Whatever he went through, it's over now." I reached across and took her hands. "The important thing is for you to deal with this and get past it. Will's gone and you're not, and nothing we can do is going to change that."

She squeezed my hands back and her face relaxed a bit. She pulled away, picked up the drink, and watched as the waitress headed to her perch at the back counter. Then Lanie lifted the drink to her lips and downed half of it in one gulp.

"Careful," I said. "That's not Glenlivet. And you're not used to it even if it were."

She let the glass plop back down on the wet napkin as the beginning of a glaze settled over her eyes. "Harry, they think I had something to do with it. I know they do."

"Tell me about it," I said. "Tell me everything."

She picked up the glass again and took another long sip, leaving only a trace of brownish liquid at the bottom of a glassful of ice. "You heard we were going to be married."

"I only know what I read in the papers."

"Two weeks." She sighed. "Two more weeks and we would have been together for good. There was so much going against us, so many people against us."

"Like who?"

"Oh, God, the kids. The first wife . . . Even his office manager hated me. I don't know, just so many. . . ."

Her voice drifted off. Lanie never could hold alcohol very well.

"Lanie, when did you last see Will?"

Her voice brightened. "Last night. We had dinner at Arthur's." Located in the old, renovated Union Station, Arthur's was one of the only four-star restaurants in town. I'd only been able to afford to take Lanie there about once a year. Now she probably had her own waiter and a weekly reservation.

"Then we stopped in Mère Bulles on Second Avenue for a nightcap and some jazz. About eleven I drove him back to his house. I was tired, had some errands to run this morning, so I decided to go on home."

"Good thing," I murmured, aware of what I'd be feeling now if Lanie had spent the night at Elmore's.

She ignored me and went on, leaning out first to motion to the waitress for another drink. "The first I heard was when I woke up this morning and the police came while I was drinking my coffee. I was sitting at the table with my laptop, making some changes in my résumé—"

"Your résumé? You looking for another job?"

"Oh." She shook her head wearily. "You didn't know. I got laid off last month."

My mouth dropped in shock. "You? How could they lay off a vice-president?"

From the moment she stepped through the door, Lanie had been the fastest-rising star at the city's oldest ad agency, Adams & Charrin.

"It's this recession, Harry. Nobody's ever seen anything like it. Agencies and PR firms are cutting back all over town. A and C's about to go into chapter eleven."

If Adams & Charrin was about to declare bankruptcy, the corporate world was falling apart. They'd been around since the Thirties.

"So anyway, you were updating your résumé."

"Yes," she said, nodding thanks to the waitress as she handed her the fresh drink. "They told me about the fire, about the body in the fire. God, Harry, they said they hadn't even been able to identify it yet. That the medical examiner would have to perform an autopsy. But even then, they're convinced it's Will."

I learned a long time ago that it's not what you know that's important, it's what nobody else knows that you know. I kept my mouth shut about Marsha, and the fact that the woman I was dating had finished the Elmore autopsy about three hours earlier.

"They said they just had a few questions for me. They were real nice, Harry. Two perfect gentlemen. But when I got down there, there was this awful room. So cold, so dirty. They weren't so gentle anymore. They practically accused me of . . ." She paused to bolt down another slug. "They had already talked to Will's kids. They had to have. Otherwise they wouldn't have made such nasty implications."

"What implications?"

She put the drink down and looked me directly in the face, the film over her eyes reflecting brightly the dim light, as if the mixture of tears and Scotch had worked its way to the surface. "Harry, Will was a wealthy man. He'd done well over the years. The wedding was coming up. We'd both made wills, and he had changed his life insurance."

"Making you the beneficiary, no doubt," I said.

"And the will left almost everything to me. Before we did it, Will met with the kids to tell them. They're taken care of. Trust funds and all that. But almost all the money, the property, the company came to me. There was a terrible row."

I thought of Lonnie's question about the crime of arson: *who benefits?*

"Lanie, can I ask you a personal question?"

She pulled the drink away from her lips. "You want to know how much there is?"

"No." I shook my head. "That doesn't matter. What I want to know is if there was a prenuptial agreement?"

Her eyes darkened. "Yes," she said, her voice low and soft. "Will insisted on it. This *was* going to be his fourth marriage, after all."

"And the prenuptial agreement gave you something if the

marriage broke up, but not anywhere near what the will provided for.''

She set the glass down a little too hard. Scotch and soda sloshed on the table, and for the first time, fatigue and alcohol were evident in her voice.

"What's that supposed to mean?" she demanded, the faintest trace of a slur growing around the edges.

"I'm just trying to think like the police. And from where I sit, the police see a murdered man who was about to be married to a woman fifteen years younger than him, with a taste for nice clothes and nicer cars, who just lost a prestigious and well-paying job, one that's not likely to be replaced, given economic realities. She'll inherit a bundle if he dies, but won't get squat if the marriage breaks up. The question is—who benefits? And the way the police see it, you're the big winner.

"They don't know you like I do, Lanie," I continued. "I know you didn't kill Will. But in the eyes of the police it's damn lucky for you that somebody did."

With that, the porcelain finally cracked, and the woman whose composure I'd never been able to break—no matter how hard I tried—fell face forward onto the table and sobbed like a brokenhearted child.

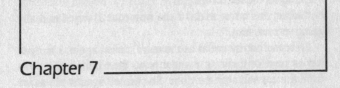

Chapter 7

I pulled the Alfa into the turning lane in front of Lanie's condo and drummed the steering wheel irritably.

"C'mon, give me a break," I muttered at the oncoming traffic on Hillsboro Road. It was nearly 6:30; I had to get Lanie in, then call a cab to take me back to the Gerst for my own car. Marsha was expecting me around seven. She'd just have to wait.

"I could have driven myself, you know," Lanie complained. The slur in her voice was gone now, but she'd nodded off briefly on the freeway.

"You've had a bad day. No need to compound it with a DUI."

She moaned. "I don't drink very well, do I?"

I smiled as about a two-second break in the traffic gave me the chance to shoot into the parking lot. "Not cheap Scotch, anyway."

We drove through the lot of the condo complex, past the Mercedes and the Jags, the Cadillacs and the Alfas, and parked in front of the entrance to what had once, and briefly, been our home. I crawled out of the two-seater and crossed around in front to open Lanie's door. First one leg came out, then the other, in that incredibly sexy way women with great legs have of emerging from low-slung two-seaters; then she grabbed my hand to pull herself up.

She moaned again and leaned her head into the crook of

45

my neck. She still wore the same perfume, which was now being rubbed into the fabric of my shirt. Rather like a cat marking its owner, I thought.

"What am I going to do?" she whined. "Harry, I'm really going to miss him."

I felt wet on my collar as the tears started again. I hugged her as comfortingly as I knew how, then pulled her away from the car and shut the door. She leaned against me as we walked up the stairs.

"I know," I said. "Tell me, what was he like?"

She pulled away in front of her door and fumbled in her purse for the keys.

"It's funny, Harry," she slurred. "A lot of people didn't like Will, but I found a side of him that was real lovable." She twisted the key in the lock, then opened the door quickly and punched the security code into the burglar alarm. I stepped through after her and closed the door behind me. It was dark, the curtains pulled to on the French doors that led out onto the balcony. She switched on the lights and turned to me, bleary-eyed.

"People didn't understand him," she continued. "You don't know the toll it takes, listening to people's problems, day after day, year after year—their anxieties, frustrations, neuroses, all the sick little scared parts. I think that's what drove him to distance himself from his patients. You have to have that detachment. Otherwise it'll drive you crazy."

I thought of what Marsha'd told me about autopsying dead kids and burn victims.

She kicked her heels off, then tossed her purse onto the sofa. "Can I get you a drink, anything?"

"No, just let me call a cab."

"Oh, hell, Harry, I'll take you back."

"That's not a good idea."

"Then just take my car. I'm not going out tonight. Bring it back tomorrow."

I thought for a second. "That's not a good idea either."

She turned to me and put her arms around my neck. "I wish you'd quit being such a boy scout."

"What are you up to, Lanie?"

She dropped her arms to her side. "I'm sorry, Harry. I'm not trying to start anything. I need somebody to hold me, but that's all. And it's not your job to do it. I appreciate your talking to me, listening to all this. I know you didn't like Will very much. You certainly had no obligation to come to my rescue."

"I didn't come to your rescue. Of all the people I've ever known in my life, you're one of the least likely to ever need rescuing."

She smiled and turned, then walked into the kitchen. "Flatterer." I heard the water running, then she stepped back out with a glass of water.

"What do you want from me, Lanie?"

She stared over the top of the glass in a daze, her eyes dark and heavy with fatigue and grief. "Help me, Harry. Find whoever killed Will. . . ."

East Nashville to Green Hills, then back to East Nashville, then out again—my quiet, carefree Saturday afternoon had become an extended trip into automotive hell. To make matters worse, a tractor-trailer had overturned on the Silliman Evans Bridge, turning roughly two tons of tomatoes into tomato paste dripping slowly into the Cumberland River. By the time I pulled into the parking lot of Marsha's condominium complex, I was harried, tense, and forty-five minutes late for dinner.

Marsha opened the door on my second rap. She stood there, a head taller than me, dressed in a sweatshirt and a pair of workout pants, no makeup, jet-black hair pulled back in a ponytail. Pleasure rolled over me like a storm surge.

"Oh, no," she said. "The traffic again?"

"Wreck on the Interstate."

"Well, my dear, it *is* Saturday night."

"Yes," I said, sliding into her open arms, "and I'm glad we're in for the duration. Care for a little cocooning tonight?"

I bent my neck backward to reach her lips. Marsha Helms was the first woman I'd ever dated who was taller than me. Thin, small-breasted, angular, she'd had her fill of basketball-player jokes about a hundred years before we ever met, so I was careful to spare her whenever possible.

We kissed gently for a long time. I'd been mindful of getting too attached to this—we had, after all, only been dating a couple of months—but truth was, it was getting more difficult by the day. She had become an important part of my life altogether too quickly.

"Sorry to be so late," I said, my arms around her waist loosely. "It's been a longer and tougher day than I expected."

She kissed me briefly on the cheek. "Let me get you a glass of wine."

"You're on. And then I'll fill you in."

She crossed the living room, then went down the hall to her small kitchen. I hadn't realized until that point how similar Marsha's condo was to Lanie's. Guess I have a thing for smart, professional women who buy condos.

She walked back in with two tall wineglasses full of buttery yellow. "A great California Chardonnay, as promised," she said, handing me the one from her left hand. We clinked glasses.

"To the end of a long day," I said.

"And the beginning of the evening," Marsha offered.

"This is wonderful," I said, meaning it. I didn't drink a lot of wine, knew even less about it. But Marsha was a budding oenophile, even subscribed to a couple of expensive wine magazines. I'd learned a lot just being around her; about wine, that is.

"That autopsy you did this morning?" I asked. "The burn victim?"

"Yeah?"

"My ex-wife's fiancé. She called me after the police got through with her."

Marsha smiled and sidestepped past me and over to the couch. "Guess that explains the perfume."

I sat next to her. "Yeah, small world, ain't it?"

Marsha sipped the wine, then set her glass down on the table in front of the sofa. She hooked her elbow around the back of the couch and turned to me. She spoke cautiously, almost nervously.

"So why did she call you?"

"I'm not sure. Except that she needs help. She seems to think the police suspect her."

"*Do* they now?"

I thought for a moment. "Probably. If the estate probates cleanly, Lanie stands to inherit—even though she and the good doctor weren't married. They'd already written new wills and changed their life insurance."

"How convenient," she said, turning away from me.

I reached out and laid my hand on her shoulder. "What's that supposed to mean?" I asked. "C'mon now, Marsh, you're not getting weird on me, are you?"

"Well," she said, then sniffed as if trying to calibrate her response. "I guess not. All my lovers get called by their ex-wives when the police drag them in for questioning."

"She wasn't *dragged* in for questioning. She hasn't been charged or anything. They let her go home."

"So what does she want from you?"

"She wants me to find out who murdered her fiancé."

"Oh, great," Marsha said, exasperated.

"Marsha," I said, squeezing her shoulder with what I

hoped would be interpreted as affection. "If—*if* I do get involved with this woman, it will be strictly on a business and professional basis. I'll be glad to help her, at my standard per diem rate."

"Besides, how does she even know he was killed?" Marsha asked.

I sat for a moment, watching her, wondering what was going on inside her. After years of knowing her casually, and two months rather more closely, I found her in many ways still a mystery. I hoped she always would be.

"That's right," I said. "Only you and the police know that."

"That's right."

"Well?"

"Well what?"

"*Was* he murdered?"

Marsha pursed her lips, reached over, and picked up her wineglass. "You know I can't tell you that."

"I don't want details. Just curious. Everything will be in the papers tomorrow anyway."

"I don't know. I—"

She was in midsentence when I was struck with an overwhelming compulsion to kiss her.

"You're trying to bribe me," she whispered. I leaned over to kiss her again, softly, sweetly.

"Shamelessly," I whispered back. "Bribery's not the right word, though. I was overcome by an attack of spontaneity. Sorry."

"No need to apologize," she said, shifting in closer to me and resting her head in the crook of my arm. Her hair held just a trace of dampness, with the clean fragrance of being freshly washed.

She stretched her long legs out across the table. I crossed my legs between the sofa and the table and let the weight of my knee press against her thigh.

Marsha Helms felt very good to me.

"And he *was* murdered." She sighed, nuzzling in closer. I felt her mouth open, the wet, light touch of her lips on my neck. Something deep inside me lit up, an electric sensation that spread throughout my core.

"Murdered, huh . . . ?" I said, my voice drifting off, woozy.

"Blunt instrument," she whispered into my ear, taking my earlobe gently between her teeth.

"Wow, that's terrible."

"Bashed in the back of his skull," she continued between nibbles. "Then the fire got him. Tox screen results won't be back for a couple of weeks. Don't know what the tissue samples will show."

I let my hand fall to her leg and rest lightly between her knees. "Bet that was awful." I moaned as she sank her teeth into the side of my neck. My shoulders shook unconsciously. No control. Swear to God, couldn't stop it.

"Oh, yeah," she gasped as I rubbed the inside of her thigh. "Human body has a lot of fat in it, especially middle-aged bodies. Get 'em near an open flame . . . just like burning a pot roast."

I brought my other arm around her waist and gently pulled her over on top of me. Her weight pressed down on me like a warm blanket, and I felt myself becoming dizzy.

"It's amazing what survives, though. You can tell a lot from a hot body," she continued.

Just before my lips met hers and my eyes closed, I muttered something to the effect of "No kidding . . ."

Chapter 8

The message light on my office answering machine blinked relentlessly as I wandered in around 9:30 Monday morning. It had been a warm, slow weekend and I hated to see it end. I wound up staying both Saturday and Sunday nights at Marsha's, something I'd never done before. By the time I got home, changed clothes, showered, and set off for the office, the morning was half-gone.

I punched the button. Lanie's voice, tense, raspy, shot out of the speaker: "Harry?" it demanded. "Harry, where are you? Call me. Right now, damn you!"

Not exactly sweetly persuasive, but then again, when Lanie wanted something, she didn't tap-dance around. I punched her number and she picked it up on the second ring.

"Lanie?"

"Where have you been, Harry? I've been trying to call you for over an hour and all I get is that blasted answering machine." If anything, she sounded even more strung out.

Take a breath, woman, I thought. It's going to be a long week.

"What's up, Lanie? Police back at your door?" I didn't mean it to come off smartass, but I guess it did.

"No, damn it. The police aren't back at my door," she snapped. "I have to see you. Right now. Can you sit tight, right there in your office, until I get down there?"

"Sure, Lanie," I said, trying to soothe her nerves. "I'll be here. You know where—"

"I'll be right there." Then there was the distinct electronic bang of a phone slamming.

I pulled off my coat in the stuffy office and raised a window. Outside, the morning traffic was thinning out in preparation for rising again at lunchtime; the ebb and flow of noise and exhaust smells brought a rhythm to my day that was almost a comfort in this chaotic world.

There were no other messages. Ordinarily I'd have kicked back, drunk coffee, read the paper for a while. If the phone didn't ring by lunchtime, I'd be off to Mrs. Lee's for my usual Szechuan chicken, then on to Lonnie's to see if he had any skip tracing for me to do. Maybe a repo run that night. I'd had to shuck and jive pretty lively the past few months to make a living. But my expenses were as low as they'd ever been, and I'd found there were lots of advantages to adopting a simpler life.

I was finishing up the comics when I heard the tapping of high heels on the steps of the landing leading up to my floor. There was usually very little visitor traffic in this building. Intrusions in the silence were hard to miss. The tapping was coming my way, so I folded the newspaper, tossed it on my desk, and just managed to get my feet back on the floor when the door jerked open.

"I might have guessed you'd be in a building without an elevator," she snapped.

"Good morning, Lanie," I said. "How nice to see you again. Recover from the other night?"

I stood up, motioned toward my one visitor's chair. She looked at it like I was inviting her to park it on the slag heap.

"Barely," she said as she slid into the chair and placed her purse tightly on her lap. She wore a black-and-white-checked suit, the jacket cinched tight in the middle, the skirt just above the knee with black stockings and black patent-leather pumps. Her hair was pulled back sternly and she had on her professional makeup. Job interview, perhaps?

"What's up?"

"I've got something that may not only clear me, but will blow this whole mess wide open. I'm just afraid, Harry, that if I give it to the police, they won't believe me. They'll think I made it up, to divert suspicion away from me."

I looked at her directly. There was a thin sheen of perspiration—make that sweat—across her upper lip, and it was beginning to soak through to the armpits of her jacket. But her eyes were solid, unblinking, unyielding. Maybe she was lying to me. I'd been lied to before.

Not this time, though. At least I didn't think so.

"What are you talking about, Lanie?"

She looked down at her lap, at the closed black purse with the short gold chain that was entwined in her fingers like a knot of rope. She closed her eyes and sighed deeply, as if trying to center herself, then opened them again and snapped open the purse resolutely.

"This," she said, retrieving a long white envelope and handing it to me. "It came to my post office box this morning. I was there early this morning, to see if I'd gotten any answers from my résumés."

I took the envelope from her. It was a plain white number ten, the kind of generic business envelope you could get at any grocery store or office-supply house. Typed across the front was the name ELANIE HERRINGTON and a post-office-box address.

I looked up at her. "When'd you go back to your maiden name?"

"Damn it, Harry. That doesn't matter. Read the letter."

I looked back down. No return address, mailed last Friday—the day of Elmore's death—with the zip code on the cancellation indicating the downtown post office.

I turned it over. Lanie'd already opened it, carefully and

neatly. Her usual style. I reached in and unfolded the letter.
I didn't count the pages, but there must have been three or
four.

A line centered across the top of the first page read, in
bold capital letters: TO THE PATIENTS OF DR. WILLIAM EL-
MORE.

Below that, a series of single-spaced block paragraphs with
intermittent stripes of black filled the page.

"What?" I asked, confused. I looked up at Lanie, who
sat there blank and silent.

"Just read it," she whispered.

I turned back to the page.

*This letter is being sent to the patients and former pa-
tients of Dr. William Elmore. Elmore's continued violations of the ethical provisions of his profession regarding
conduct, client confidentiality, and business affairs have
made this letter necessary. For the past several years Dr.
Elmore has been able to quash and suppress investigations
into his conduct, and he has been able to silence the complaints brought forth by both former and present clients
against him. It is the feeling of the writer of this letter that
all of Dr. Elmore's clients, both present and past, must be
made aware of his conduct and the complaints against
him. Among these complaints are:*

*1) Illegal and unethical business practices, including
tax evasion, establishing business relationships with clients, and other violations of the ethics provisions.*

*2) Ongoing breach of patient confidentiality. In other
words, your darkest secrets become fodder for cocktail-
party chatter. . . .*

3) Sexual misconduct with patients.

*4) Insurance fraud, and conspiracy to defraud both
insurance and Medicare through the mails.*

If after reading what Dr. Elmore has unethically and

illegally revealed about you to others—usually in the context of entertaining stories at parties—you feel he has violated your rights, contact the Chief Investigator, Ethics Division, State Licensing Board.

My palms began to sweat and the room seemed unusually stuffy, even with the window open. I looked up at Lanie; she sat in the chair and stared at the wall, her gaze unfocused, her lips tight. My eyes returned to the page, where a Magic Markered black stripe extended across the first two inches of the next paragraph, obscuring what looked like a name.

██████████—*Your sexual escapades with teenaged boys have made you the laughingstock of the Belle Meade cocktail set for years. Elmore says the only reason you haven't been arrested and sent to prison yet is that your father's position as a circuit-court judge has been able to keep you out of the grand-jury room.*

██████████—*Elmore says that secretly you just want to be a whore. Only problem, he adds, is that he's tried you and he thinks you'd starve to death.*

██████████—*You have an insatiable desire for oral sex, Elmore announced at his Christmas party last year, and that* ██████████ *divorced you because she got tired of you falling asleep and leaving her unsatisfied after you'd gotten your rocks off.*

██████████—*Your attempts to evade taxes by skimming cash off the top of your business is laughable, Elmore says. If he had any respect for you at all, he'd show you how you could steal even more. But why bother . . . ?*

██████████—*Dr. Elmore thinks your marital infidelity is hilarious, calling you a nympho and a pitiful alcoholic.*

██████████—*Elmore says he thinks your bulimia is cute, that it's admirable when a dried-up old broad still cares what she looks like. But, he adds, your compulsive use of*

*laxatives probably means you'd like to, as he puts it, get
butt-fucked.*

██████████ *—Elmore says your affair with* ███████████
probably will wind up getting you both thrown out of the
███████████ *Country Club. The incestuous details of your
childhood are also good for a few laughs at his parties.*

I had to put the letter down. On and on it went, for three
more pages single-spaced. Tales of indiscretion, a disgusting
breach of patient confidentiality, and almost a cruel delight
at the sufferings of others would be the legacy of Will Elmore. If, that is, the letter ever got out and the writer was
telling the truth.

"Jesus Christ," I whispered.

"Yeah, heavy stuff," Lanie agreed.

"You know what the blacked-out names are?"

She knotted her hands together. "I held it up to the window and was able to make out a few of them."

I turned to my desk and opened the center drawer. Inside
was a large magnifying glass—my one concession to Sher-
lock Holmes. I took it out with my right hand, then grasped
the first page of the letter in my left. I stood up, leaned over
my desk lamp, and tried to get the reflection just right.

"Holy moley," I muttered. "This is the head of the largest
church in Nashville."

"How about that? Teenaged boys, no less."

"And this one. Roy Padgett. Why, he's the head of the
Chamber of Commerce, isn't he?"

"And local coordinator for the Jerry Lewis Labor Day
Telethon."

"Get out of here," I said, turning to her.

"No, really," Lanie said matter-of-factly.

"An old guy like that?" I turned back to the paper, twisting my head and the glass to get the reflection just right. You
had to read through the black ink, below it, to the actual

impression the typewriter keys made on the paper. It was tough; sometimes you had to guess a letter or two; sort of a psychotic *Wheel of Fortune*.

"Wait a minute," I said. "This can't be true. Not Nancy Weeks Johnson. A bulimic? She's as healthy as a horse. And head of the arts commission."

"Oh, Harry, grow up. These are the Nineties, you know. Nobody's normal."

"My God, Lanie, *this* one's the mayor!"

I heard her get up behind me and step over to the desk. She put her right hand on my shoulder and leaned into the light.

"Yeah, I saw that. Only I couldn't make out the name of the woman he's having the affair with."

I squinted and strained my eyes. "M-A—can't make out that one—G-A-R—Margaret. Yeah, that's it. Margaret. R-U-T-L—"

"Oh, my God," Lanie whispered. "Margaret Rutledge."

I turned and looked at her, my eyes gaping wide in shock.

"Our deeply Republican, right-wing, ultra-conservative mayor is having a sleazy affair with—" I stammered.

"The head of the local branch of the American Civil Liberties Union," Lanie finished for me.

I couldn't help it. I broke apart laughing, helplessly, and dropped into my seat.

It took an hour to go through the rest of the letter and decipher the names. That hour also included the compulsive rereading, with a kind of fascinated horror, of what was one of the most explosive letters I'd ever seen. If it ever became public—

No, no way. It couldn't. Not ever. You've got to understand: Nashville, Tennessee, has the better part of a million people in it. We're a major airline hub, one of the few cities in the country with three interstate highways intersecting in its downtown.

But we're still a small town. People talk about the Reverend Jewell P. Madison of the Old Hickory Evangelical Church of Christ as if they just had dinner with him. We see his commercials every night as we eat dinner in front of reruns of *Cheers* on Channel 19, pushing the love of God like it came with a dealer rebate and an air bag. He leads the largest church in a city that has more churches per capita than any other place in the nation. If the people of this city ever learned that the head of the Old Hickory Evangelical Church of Christ had a thing for teenaged boys . . .

I don't want to think about it.

And the mayor; jeez, the mayor. Mayor Terrence Durrell, whose only previous notable achievement was two terms in the state legislature, where he headed the House Subcommittee on Traditional Values. He'd fought like the Looney Tunes Tasmanian Devil to defeat George Turner in the last election. Turner was decent and capable, but a man of little passion and, frankly, great listlessness. His speeches were not exactly inspiring; in fact, they were dull as cold dishwater. He ran the city honestly and competently, and he'd been defeated in a typical Republican whirlwind exercise in character assassination, ethnic slurring, and divisiveness.

I never met Durrell. He'd won the election a few months after I lost my job at the newspaper. But if he was having an affair with Margaret Rutledge—the heir to an insurance fortune, local Democratic party behind-the-scenes power boss, militant feminist, and head of the local ACLU—then the world really had gone topsy-turvy.

And what of Margaret? I'd met her in my capacity as a journalist and found that I had great respect for her. Unlike many other children who inherit $75 million on their twenty-first birthday, she'd gone on to make something of herself. She'd done undergraduate work at Pembroke, then come home to attend law school at Vanderbilt. She was a lady of taste and sophistication, in her late forties, divorced, and one of the few intelligent liberal voices in the community. How could she be doing the dirty deed with a hypocritical red-baiter like Durrell, who got elected primarily through proposing legislation like abortion gag orders on local public-health clinics? Like there weren't enough teenaged girls having babies in the public-school rest rooms already . . .

One thing was for sure: we'd gone from having one suspect in Will Elmore's death to three pages of them. The question was what to do with it.

"Do you have any idea who wrote this letter?" I asked.

Lanie leaned back in her chair, then sighed deeply, out of either frustration or resignation. "I know a few of those people in the letter, but nobody that I think would do something like this."

My eyes burned from squinting into the light. I rubbed them hard with the thumb and first two fingers of my right hand, the pressure almost a delightful release.

"Maybe somebody in his office," I speculated. "After all, it had to be either someone who saw him socially in these situations or it had to be somebody who had access to the files."

"Maybe it was more than one person," she said.

I shrugged. "Maybe."

She put her elbows on the arms of the chair and leaned forward, then rubbed her own tired eyes. "God, Harry, you know what the worst is? Or at least feels like?"

"No, what?"

She hesitated, the words caught painfully in her throat. "I wonder what he was telling people about us."

That hit me. Lanie and I were fairly normal, as middle-class, neurotic professional couples in the middle of marital deterioration go. No whips, no chains, no twisted infidelities and cheap motels. But there were secrets we didn't want to share with anyone else, and thought we weren't.

"No, not a chance," I said, hoping to reassure her. "We weren't socially prominent enough. After all, everybody in this letter winds up in the society columns at least once a month, if not more often."

She smiled. "You're just trying to make me feel better. I appreciate it. Crazy thing is, though, I was going to marry him."

Lanie sighed again, turned her gaze out through my dirty window. "Maybe I didn't know him as well as I thought I did."

"Nobody ever does, Lanie. Everybody's got a dark side they'd rather not have anyone see."

"That's the hard part. Apparently he didn't mind sharing his dark side. I mean, I knew he could be difficult, demanding. When you caught him on his off days, he could be cruel. But this? I don't know. Makes me wonder if my judgment isn't impaired."

I'd never seen Lanie doubt herself. This was a new one.

"We have to figure out what to do with this letter. That's the important part."

"I don't want to take it to the police," she said. "They'll think I fabricated it."

"That's not what I'm worried about," I said, hesitating.

"What?" she asked.

"What scares me is that once the powers that be discover the letter and its contents, it'll disappear faster than a Vanderbilt football fan late in the fourth quarter."

"What do you mean?"

"There are still a lot of good old boys in this town who take care of each other. I'm afraid that once they got hold of this letter, there'd be a ton of pressure to nail this on somebody, anybody, just to get it buried."

Lanie stared at me a second, her brow furrowing, the reflection off the thin film of perspiration on her face shining. "That somebody could be me," she whispered.

Chapter 9

I rolled my chair over next to her and did something I hadn't done in a long time: I took her hands in mine and held them. Somewhere in the back of my mind was the notion that maybe I was playing with fire. Not a good metaphor under the circumstances, perhaps, but an accurate one. Lanie and I had once been on fire, but that was over a long time ago. Maybe it was curiosity on my part, wondering somewhere if the embers were still glowing. Anyway, I was concerned about her. She was in deep on this one. We once cared for each other. The decent thing was for me to help her as much as I could.

"Elaine Herrington," I said. "I want you to listen to me."

She did. I almost never called her Elaine unless I was really trying to get her attention.

"We've got to find you an attorney, and fast. He'll know what to do with the letter."

I thought she was going to crack again, but she swallowed deeply and brought herself under control. "I've got this problem, Harry."

I smiled. "You mean another one?"

She nodded. "I always thought my job at the agency was solid. I was happy there, worked hard there. Figured, especially being married to Will, that I sort of had it made . . ."

"And?"

"And so, I spent everything I made. All of it. No big deal

when you've got those fat checks coming in every two weeks. Then the bottom fell out.''

''So now you're . . .''

She bit her lower lip and nodded. ''Haven't got a penny. I'm a month behind on the condo payment, and the leasing company's threatening to pick up the Alfa. I can't afford a lawyer.''

I let go of her hands and slid back in my chair. ''This throws a new light on things,'' I said.

''More than anything else, Harry, I'm embarrassed. I never thought the ride would be over.''

''So did every other yuppie.'' I said. ''Welcome to the Nineties. It's a brave new world out there. Fast-food managers have advanced degrees.''

''What am I going to do?''

I spun my chair around facing the wall, away from her, and leaned back as far as it would go, resting my feet on the corner of the desk. I wanted to offer solace, but I was drawing a blank. If she couldn't afford a lawyer, then she couldn't afford me either. That was definitely going to throw a kink in the tow rope.

''Wait a minute,'' I said, plopping my feet back on the floor. ''You said you and the doc had already changed your wills, right?''

''Yes.''

''And the kids are taken care of in trust. The rest goes to you.''

''Okay, but I can't get any of it now. Not with the murder investigation going on.''

''How was Will's company set up? Legally, I mean?''

Her forehead wrinkled again. ''It was a PC, you know, one of those corporations set up by health-care professionals.''

''A professional corporation, okay. Any partners?''

"No, just Will. He owned all the shares in the PC, and the PC was the company. It even owned the building."

"He had to have a lawyer. Right?"

"Sure, Marvin Shapiro. He's a double-dipper, a CPA as well as an attorney. He kept the company books, everything. Will used to call him Marvelous Marvin."

I stood up. "Well, my dear," I said, reaching for my jacket, "let's go see Marvelous Marvin."

EAT IT, DRINK IT, SMOKE IT, AT MOSKO'S the sign over Mosko's blared. I hadn't been down to Elliston Place, known affectionately among the locals as the Rock Block, in quite a while. Elliston Place was, I guess, the closest Nashville was ever going to get to having a Greenwich Village, but it was sure trying its best.

The last time I was in Mosko's was a couple of months ago, after a bean burrito and a couple of drafts at the Gold Rush. I'd wandered across the street into Mosko's and spent about an hour browsing among the off-color, bawdy greeting cards and the rows of magazines. Marvelous Marvin Shapiro's office was on the second floor of the same building, which struck me as decidedly odd—what passed for a Nineties version of countercultural retailing right below an attorney's office.

I lucked out; a Vanderbilt student in a Land Rover that cost as much as I made the last two years had just pulled out of a parking space. I coasted the Alfa into the slot and braked. I'd wanted to take my own car, but Lanie had insisted I drive hers one more time before the repossessor got it. I smiled to myself as I crawled out of the car, wondering if I'd get to be the guy doing the repossessing.

"Upstairs," she said, pointing.

We took the outside flight of white-painted concrete steps up to the second floor, then down a breezeway to a glass-fronted retail shop that had been converted to office space.

In the crash of the late Eighties/early Nineties, a raftful of retailers had gone under and you could just about do anything you wanted with the space, as long as you mailed the check in each month.

I pulled open the heavy chrome-and-glass door and held it as Lanie walked in ahead of me. The inside of what had once been a store was now covered in dark law-office paneling, with a pale green carpet on the floor. At a desk behind a counter a middle-aged woman with tired eyes sat hunched over the green screen of a computer.

"Hello, Nancy," Lanie said. The woman stared darkly at us for a second, then finally spoke.

"Oh, hello, Miss Herrington," she said nervously. "I'm so sorry to hear about—"

"I know, Nancy. I appreciate that."

Nancy bit the end of her pencil and stood up. "Marvin's waiting for you. Go on in."

I stepped back from the counter so Lanie could go in first, then followed her into Marvelous Marvin's office, which had no windows, dark paneling, and walls that looked like they'd been framed up out of nowhere just to shut him off from the pedestrian traffic.

Marvin Shapiro sat behind his desk as we walked in. It was hard for me to tell because he didn't get up, but I took him to be about five-eight, maybe one-eighty, midforties, black hair thinning and combed straight back, with the makings of a pretty good spare tire bulging beneath his white shirt.

"Hello, Elaine," Marvin said somberly. "How are you?"

He motioned for us to sit down. He sat way back in one of those imposing rolled-leather high-backed executive chairs. This was his turf, much as the Gerst Haus was mine, and he wanted us to know it.

"I'm fine," she said, taking the seat to his right. I sat across from his desk on the left. "Marvin, this is Harry

Denton. He's a private investigator who's doing some work for me.''

"Hi," he said, nodding toward me.

"Pleased to meet you," I offered.

"Marvin, you know the police have questioned me about Will's murder."

"I know," the lawyer interrupted, "and I can't believe they'd contemplate any such thing. It's slanderous."

"Oh, no, it's not," Lanie said wearily. "Frankly I'd suspect I did it myself, except for one thing. I know I didn't."

"And so do I," Marvin said. "I'll do anything I can to help you."

"That's why we're here," she continued. "My understanding is that with Will's death, Psychology Associates will belong to me."

"Well, yes, that's true," Marvin said carefully, "although there are a number of other matters to settle first. Not the least of which is a potential battle in probate with the ex-wives and children."

"But unless I'm convicted of murder," Lanie said flatly, "it's probably going to be mine."

"That's about it."

"Good. Then I want to borrow against the assets of the company in order to retain your services."

Marvin Shapiro sat up. "Wait, I'm not sure I can—"

"There are no other stockholders," Lanie said, her voice turning sharp. "I control the company, or I will in a matter of a few weeks. You represent the company. You can represent me."

"I'm not a criminal lawyer," he sputtered. "I've never taken a criminal case."

"This isn't a criminal case. Not yet, anyway. I'm asking you to be my attorney for the time being, specifically to give me advice and to establish an attorney-client privilege. I want to be able to discuss matters with you under the assurance that everything will be confidential.''

"What about him?'' Marvin asked, motioning in my direction.

"The problem is that this state doesn't recognize privilege in the case of private investigators working for individuals,'' I said. "However,'' I offered, "if I'm in the employ of an attorney—say, you—then that's an entirely different matter.''

"Besides the fact that I'm having a slight cash-flow problem,'' Lanie said, "the money really has to come from you. I would, of course, reimburse you for your expenses as well as time. And I'd expect you to put a pass-through charge on Harry's bill to compensate your processing it for me.''

Marvin lifted an eye. He had to be thinking what I was thinking, which was that Lanie was either on her way to the women's prison in Joelton for murder, or she was going to be a wealthy and lucrative client. I could see the wheels turning in his head.

"What's your daily rate?'' he asked me.

"Two-fifty plus expenses.''

He whistled. "How much would you expect as a retainer?''

"Do whatever makes you comfortable,'' I said.

"Things have been a little tight around here lately, too, you know. Would two days be enough to hold you?''

I smiled. I hadn't expected that much out of him.

"Fine. As soon as you hand me a check, I'm yours.''

He leaned over and picked up his telephone receiver. "Nancy? Cut me a five-hundred-dollar check to the order of—what was your name again?''

"The Denton Agency.''

"The Denton Agency,'' he continued. "And post it to the Psychology Associates account.''

A couple of minutes later Nancy walked in and presented a check. I folded it neatly and stuck it inside my jacket pocket.

"There," I said, "you just bought yourself an investigator. Now, Marvin, look at this." I reached inside my other jacket pocket and handed him the letter.

"What's this?" he asked, reaching across the desk. A bright gold Rolex and tufts of forearm hair peeked out from the cuff of his white shirt.

"That came in my post office box this morning," Lanie explained.

"Actually," I said, reaching back into my pocket again, "this one might be easier. I made a copy of the original and wrote in the names that are blacked out on the copy. Might make it more intelligible."

"How did you figure out the names? They're all blacked out."

"Trade secret," I said.

He laid the original down on the desk, then unfolded the copy. I looked across to Lanie, who sat on the edge of her seat, tight as a clock spring. She turned her head stiffly in my direction as Marvin read. I leaned back, tried to look as if I could relax, and then quietly winked at her. Her thin, compressed lips broke into a slight and temporary smile.

"Oy," Marvin groaned. "The mayor . . ."

"Yeah," I said.

"And, *my God, it's Harvey Watts*!" Marvin gasped. Harvey Watts owned a chain of department stores that, over the years, had gone from being a regional force in retailing to a national player. The Watts Foundation, formed by his parents just before their death in a 1984 plane crash, was also one of the regional heavies in philanthropy. Harvey and his wife, Pooky, had parlayed the family foundation into a ticket to every major social obligation on the calendar.

"Harvey Watts likes to tie people up?" Marvin asked, his voice lifting up at the end in questioning surprise.

"Ride 'em, cowboy," I said.

Marvin looked at me sternly. "You know, this really isn't funny."

"I agree. It's freaking *hilarious*. But it's also dangerous. We have to figure out what to do with this letter."

"I don't know," Marvin admitted. "I'm not a criminal lawyer. I do books, tax returns. I close real-estate transactions. On one hand, this may be evidence in a criminal case. On the other hand, everything in this letter is highly privileged and confidential doctor-patient communication."

"Which takes precedence?"

"I'll have to figure that one out."

I was beginning to wonder if Marvin was going to be much help to us. He may have had a law degree, but he sounded to me like a guy who'd taken the H&R Block course and was now trying to figure out how to do Ross Perot's taxes.

The phone buzzed in the outer office, and I heard, through the thin paneling, Nancy's voice answering.

"I can get us some answers this afternoon," Marvin said, a little more forcefully. "For the time being, let's just sit quietly. There's certainly no hurry."

Suddenly the door to Marvin's office flew open. Three heads whipped around.

"Dr. Elmore's office manager," Nancy announced. "The police are there with a search warrant. They want files, records, everything."

"Oh, Jesus," Lanie said. She turned to Marvin. "We've got to stop them."

Marvin's face darkened and he seemed to stare at some point about six inches over the middle of his desk. I watched him for a few seconds, wondering what was next. If the police got those records, it would be like kicking a live hornet's nest.

"Line two?" Marvin asked.

Nancy shook her head about five seconds longer than she

had to. Marvin jerked the phone to his ear and punched the button for line two.

"Who am I speaking to?" he demanded, his voice suddenly stern and authoritative.

"Well, Julie," he continued after a moment, "you did right to call me. Who's the officer in charge there?"

Another pause. "Okay, you put him on the phone with me." Marvin turned to Nancy. "Get Judge Dore's office on the other line. Quick."

Nancy disappeared into her office. Sweat broke out like a storm on Marvin's forehead. I was beginning to get a little steamy myself inside the closed, windowless office. I looked over at Lanie; her jaw was set, her eyes dark.

"This is Marvin Shapiro, attorney for Psychology Associates, Inc., PC, and executor of Dr. William Elmore's estate. In that capacity I am ordering you off the property immediately, pending a ruling on a motion to quash your search warrant which is being filed right now."

Marvin's voice was rigid but controlled. Maybe I underestimated the guy.

"No, you don't understand, Detective," Marvin all but shouted. "Doctor-client privilege and confidentiality, under Tennessee code and federal law, supersedes all other considerations unless you have specific evidence and probable cause to indicate that one of Dr. Elmore's patients was involved in his death. Otherwise you're on a fishing expedition and that's not allowed. I'll have an injunction against your search warrant over there within the hour, and unless you want to incur the wrath of the court, I'd hold off. This is *not* a request. There will be severe legal consequences if you proceed with the execution of this unlawfully issued warrant."

Well, Marvin, I thought, you're a lawyer after all.

Marvin hung on to the phone for another few moments, then grunted something and slammed the phone down. The moment the handset hit its cradle, he went completely ashen gray.

"Incur the wrath of the court?" I said lightly. "Jeez, Marvin, after that performance he better be more worried about hacking you off."

"Great job," Lanie said.

"Holy Jesus," Marvin squeaked. "I never talked to a cop like that before. Something tells me I'm going to start getting a lot of traffic tickets."

I laughed and stood up, stretching my arms. "Now that that's over," I said, "I've got work to do. Ride back to my office, Lanie?"

Nancy stuck her head in the door. "Judge Dore's on line one."

"I forgot about that," Marvin gasped. "Oh, Jesus, what if I piss him off, too?"

I turned for the door, with Lanie right behind me. I got one last look at Marvin as he stared at the phone like it was going to bite him if he touched it.

"Knock 'em dead, Perry Mason," I called from his waiting room.

Chapter 10

My beat-to-death, oil-burning Ford Escort was quite a change from the Alfa, but strangely enough, almost a welcome one. I drove out Gallatin Road past the funeral home and the Taco Bell with a paper sack full of Szechuan chicken from Mrs. Lee's on the seat next to me. The sky was clouding over, the threat of rain in the dry early-autumn months a welcome one.

I was thinking about all the politically powerful and socially prominent people who'd been mentioned in the letter; all the little peccadilloes, weaknesses, imperfections, addictions. Not to mention the perversions, the dark secrets, the hidden places . . . I'd always heard nobody's chain lay straight, but this stuff was right out of a Victorian erotic novel—tales from *The Pearl* with a Music City twang.

Truth is, I never could figure out why my own chain wasn't any more twisted. Straight-up heterosexual coupling with fairly normal women is about the best I can do. Maybe there's something wrong with me.

I put all such naughty ruminations out of my head as I tried to figure out what to do next. I'd squirreled away a copy of Lanie's letter in my own files, but I had a feeling that was less useful to me right now than some other things could be. To begin with, I had to find out whether the torching of Will Elmore's mansion last Friday night was really the act of the East Nashville Arsonist, or was it some kind of copycat burn-

ing perpetrated by a disgruntled patient, employee, business
associate, lover, ex-wife, fill in the blank. I figured the best
way to do that was to find out what the investigators knew. I
also figured out my chances of getting the police investigators to talk to me were about as good as Sinead O'Connor's
chances of getting an invite to the Vatican. That meant I had
to turn elsewhere.

The Death Rangers' clubhouse was quiet as I made the
curve past it and pulled to a stop in front of the chain-link
fence that surrounded Lonnie's junkyard. Bikers don't get
out much on Monday afternoons.

The Ford's squealing brakes brought Shadow out immediately. She was loping badly today, her hip sliding to the left
as she dipped with each step. I nuzzled her through the fence,
then opened the gate and stepped in. We went through our
tap dance together with the ball of chicken, then I sent it into
the air in a low arc toward her. For the first time in my
memory, she didn't nab it at the top of the curve. It was like
she started up and the leg gave way, so she just settled back
down and let gravity do the work. It broke my heart, but she
was having a great time lying on the ground chowing down.
I squatted down in front of her and dug my nails into the stiff
fur between her ears on top of her head.

"Hey, Shadow," I cooed. "Hey, babe. Where's your old
man?"

"Her old man's in here," a voice came from inside the
trailer.

The door to the trailer was cracked open.

"Be there in a minute," I said loudly, raking my finger-
nails down her back. "He sounds kind of cranky today," I
whispered. Her huge brown eyes looked up at me, shiny,
wet, as if to say, "Yeah, be careful with the old SOB."

I stood up after a moment and walked the fifteen feet or
so over to the trailer, then took the wooden steps in one jump
to the door. Lonnie was sprawled across a couch in the front

room next to his desk, dirty T-shirt rumpled up from his waist, greasy blue jeans a shade darker than normal.

"What got into you?" I asked. "You look beat."

He sighed, stretched on the couch. "Aw, man, I feel like I been shot at and missed, shit at and hit."

"Late night?"

"All night," he said. "Me and Carl went up to Kentucky to pick up a ninety-one Taurus. Farm up near Bowling Green. Guy comes out of his house like a crazy man, jumps Carl from behind. So I jump on the guy. We all three wind up rolling around on the blacktop for a while."

"You have the guy popped?"

Lonnie gave me that another-stupid-question look. "Hell, yeah, I got him popped. County sheriff's holding him on aggravated assault."

"Carl okay?"

"Few bumps and bruises. He'll live. Guy pulled a knife on him, but Carl got it away and bit the fire out of him doing it."

The thought of Carl biting somebody made me wince. He had teeth that made Shadow's look like a Belle Meade cheerleader's. I sat down in the worn vinyl chair behind his desk. "Tell me something. How can I find out what insurance company had the policy on Will Elmore's house?"

Lonnie stretched, then settled further into the couch. Part of his right arm had a long, nasty scrape up one side.

"And then what?"

"I want to talk to the investigator."

"Good luck," he said.

"Maybe I'll need it, maybe I won't."

He thought for a moment. "Registrar of deeds, maybe. They'd have the lien holder on the house."

"Okay," I said, reaching for his phonebook. "I'll give it a shot."

After about ten minutes on hold-slash-ignore with the local deed office, I discovered the mortgage holder on Elmore's house was Chemical Bank in New York City. I called a toll-free number and waited through ten rings before somebody answered.

"I'm calling from Nashville, Tennessee," I said to the operator. "I live next door to a house that just burned down last Friday night and did considerable damage to mine. In fact, the owner of the house was killed. I'm trying to find out who his insurance company is so I can contact them about the damage to my place."

"You can just give that information to your own agent and he'll take care of it," a New York voice said.

Oops, I thought. No good. "Uh, well, ma'am," I said, throwing on a deep Southern accent, "you see, my house's paid for and I ain't got no insurance on it no more. Don't need it. It's done paid for."

"Oh," she said, after a moment's incredulity. "I've never met anyone who's paid off a house before, let alone dropped the insurance."

"Aw, ma'am, down here we do it all the time," I drawled. "My pappy passed this house on down to me afore he died."

"If you'll give me the address and owner's name," she said, "I'll pull up the account on the computer."

"Aw, shucks, ma'am, ya'll done got them com-pooh-ters and ever'thing up there now, ain't cha?"

Lonnie sat up on the couch with a grin pasted across his face. "Don't overdo it, asshole," he mouthed.

I gave her Elmore's name and address. I covered the mouthpiece with my right hand and leaned back. "I'm on hold."

Lonnie got up, crossed the room, and sat on the corner of the desk. "Goddamn it, you sound like something out of *No Time for Sergeants* when you do that."

"Hey, whatever works," I said. "Just another phone scam."

"You keep that up, I'm going to put you back to work skip tracing."

"Things don't get any better for my bank account, you'll have to. By the way, I picked up five bills on a retainer today."

"Good," Lonnie said. "You can pay me back that six-pack of beer you've guzzled over the past couple of months."

"It hasn't been a whole six—" I began, when the operator came back. I clicked my ballpoint pen and scratched a note across a piece of paper. "Thank you very much," I said properly, then hung up.

"She's going to think you're schizo."

"She's right. Listen, the insurance company's Tennessee Mutual."

"Tennessee Mutual," he said. "That's going to be Rick Eberhart."

"Never heard of him."

"He's an independent, works for a bunch of different companies. Smart guy, knows his stuff. I met him a few years ago. Want me to make a call?"

I grinned. "How much's it going to cost me?"

"How about that six-pack?"

"Yours," I said. "You got it."

"Make it Market Street," he said, reaching for the phone. "I like the local stuff."

Ten minutes later I was petting Shadow goodbye on my way to meet Rick Eberhart at what was left of Will Elmore's mansion.

The yellow police tape flapped brightly in the autumn afternoon sun, the light hitting it at just the right angle to make it shimmer against the brown and gold of the leaves. I coasted the Ford to a stop against the concrete curb and behind an old Jeep parked in front of the skeletal remains of Will Elmore's great mansion. What few timbers were left were blackened and cracked, swaying gently in the wind for a little while longer before they, too, collapsed into the concrete pit that had been the basement of the house. The smell of ash and burned insulation still hung in the air.

The stone foundation of the house was blackened as well, ugly streaks of black and gray soot like spray-painted graffiti on the sides. In the yard, at random intervals, the twisted metal of unidentifiable cremated household furnishings littered the yard. Here a chair; there a lump of melted plastic and glass that was once a portable television, or perhaps a computer. Who could tell? Junk everywhere; the possessions of a lifetime, of a fortune, incinerated like yesterday's garbage.

I stepped out of the car, wondering if Eberhart was already here. I couldn't see him anywhere, although he could be in the back behind the house next door, which was itself scorched and dirty over the entire third closest to the old mansion. The firemen had managed to get that fire out before it brought the house down, but the water damage had been great and it seemed to me it was going to take a lot to restore it.

I walked up the concrete walk, up the slightly sloping expanse of well-manicured front yard. I'd always heard one of the rules of real estate was never have the best house in your neighborhood; Elmore had violated that one for several neighborhoods around.

A short man, tanned, wrinkled, and stooped over, stepped out from behind the house next door, a 35mm camera in one hand and a large canvas bag slung over his shoulder.

"Mr. Eberhart," I called.

He came around the side of the house and stared up at the roof where the shingles had spontaneously erupted. He shook his head as if confused, then aimed the camera upward and snapped off a few.

"Mr. Eberhart," I called again.

He turned, as if he'd just heard me for the first time, and stared at me suspiciously. I took a few quick steps toward him and stuck out my hand.

"I'm Harry Denton," I said. "Lonnie called you about me."

He looked at me through eyes so brown they were almost black. He had the withered look of a man prematurely aged about him, as if he'd had some hard days and some equally hard nights.

"Oh, yeah," he said, clearing his throat and turning his head to spit. He let one fly against the cinderblock foundation of the house, then turned back to me. "Private investigator, huh?"

"Yes, I've been retained by Dr. Elmore's fiancée to investigate his death."

"I hear the police think she may have something to do with it," he said. His voice sounded like he either had a throat full of loose gravel or he was a lifetime smoker. An arson investigator who smokes, I thought, how appropriate.

"There has been some indication of that," I said carefully. "Although it certainly isn't true."

He stepped past me toward the ruins of Elmore's house and walked over to within five or six feet of the edge of the basement. Above us, the blackened framework of a wooden wall stood unsupported. It was the most complete piece of the house left standing, and it could have been carted off in a wheelbarrow.

"I coulda told them that," he said, then hacked and spit into the hole. "Listen, I ain't supposed to be talking to you. But Lonnie says you're a straight guy, so that's okay by me. Anybody asks, though, we never met."

"Fair enough," I agreed.

He wore an old flannel shirt with black stains on it and a pair of brown corduroy pants that looked beyond washing. I don't know what he had in that bag, but he looked to me like it was a burden he'd carried for a long time.

"So what do you think of all this?" I asked.

He turned to me, his dark, filmy bloodshot eyes taking me in as if I were just another piece of the house.

"Just got here," he said. "Haven't had a chance to go over everything thoroughly. But I can tell you one thing. . . ."

"Yeah?" I asked.

"This was one hell of a fire."

"I know," I said. "I saw it?"

He turned back to me. "You saw it."

"I live over there." I pointed to Mrs. Hawkins's house and my second-story bedroom window.

"You might be able to help me, then," he said. "C'mon."

I followed in his steps as he looked first at the ground around the house, then at the remains of the house itself.

"My job's usually a two-parter," he explained. "First I figure out whether or not the fire was set. Then I try to figure out how. First part's easy in this one."

He paused to hack up some phlegm, then turned away and let fly another one toward the street. I swiveled my head away from him just as the gob flew past me, hoping the wind didn't shift direction.

"So it was arson for sure," I said, knowing the answer to that one myself.

"What else could it be? This is a rapid-response zone in a large city. No accidental house fire would burn this fast and this completely before the firemen could get it under control."

He stopped and bent down in the grass, combing it with his fingers and coming up with a few shards of broken glass.

"Hmmm," he said. "Windows were open."

"How can you tell?"

"The way the glass broke," he said absentmindedly.

"Doesn't look like smashed glass. Either somebody opens the windows or the fire blows 'em out. These were opened."

We stepped around the charred remains of a sofa that was half in, half out of the house. When the second floor collapsed onto the first and the walls gave way, it had tossed furniture and bookcases and objects about like confetti. Eberhart maneuvered to get closer to the pit as we walked. I stood on tiptoe to look over his shoulders; over in one quadrant of the house, part of the subflooring and the floor joists below had survived, blistered and singed but relatively intact. Eberhart raised his camera and started shooting pictures.

"What's that mean?" I asked. "How come that part over there didn't burn as completely?"

He lowered the camera. "You look for patterns of heat," he said. "Subtle shades of black and white, alternated with shades of gray. If you catch the patterns and get a feel for how the fire moved, you can trace it back to the point of origin and literally map the entire thing."

I thought for a second. "I've never seen one go up like this before. I've seen a couple of house fires. Even saw a car catch fire once. Never seen anything like this, though."

"Went up quick, did it?" he asked. I shook my head yes. "Almost as if it were three or four fires at once, right?"

I thought back to the middle of the night, when I'd been awakened from a deep sleep by the sirens and the dancing colors.

"Yeah," I said, excited. "You're right. Almost as if the fire didn't really progress at all, but started in five or six places at once."

Eberhart shook his head, but didn't say anything. He turned away from me and walked on. He stopped carefully in front of a metal box on a sooty metal pole. The shattered globe of an electric meter lay on the ground next to it.

"Careful," he said. "That could still be hot."

We were around the side of the house now, a part of Elmore's house that would have been shaded from my view by a line of trees. This was where the electricity and the phone came into the house, the ripped cables still lying haywire on the ground just as they'd been left Saturday.

Eberhart got down on his knees in front of the jumble of wires and metal, set his canvas bag down, and opened it. He took out a multimeter and separated the leads, then gingerly tested the line from the street to see if it was still hot. Apparently the current had been turned off at the street, because the next thing I know, he was cutting off a piece of the wire and dropping it in a plastic bag, then taking some scrapings from the metal and dropping them into a second bag. He took the slivers of glass that he'd been carrying around and dropped them into a third bag, then took a felt-tipped pen and labeled all three.

For the next hour we traipsed wordlessly around the house, collecting samples, taking pictures, the only communication from Eberhart coming in short grunts and non sequiturs. I followed him wordlessly, giving up after a while on getting answers to my questions. After three more rolls of film and about two dozen plastic bags full of burned junk, he turned to me and grinned. His teeth were brown, tobacco-stained, in terrible shape. He might be the most brilliant arson investigator in history, but he needed to get a handle on personal hygiene.

"Okay," he said. "I've got everything I need for the preliminary. I'll probably be back later, but for now, I'm outta here."

"Great," I said, frustrated. He's got what he needs, but I don't have a clue what I need, let alone how to get it.

"C'mon back to the car. We'll talk."

I followed him down the walk, then around the front of the Jeep and into the passenger's seat. The Jeep, I noticed, was in about as good shape as Eberhart's laundry. This guy's wife, I thought, puts up with a lot.

"Let me give you an idea how this stuff works," he huffed, slinging the camera and the canvas bag into the back of the Jeep. "What you've got here is a very unusual kind of fire. I haven't seen too many like this, and I've seen a shitload of fires. For instance, it's weird to see floors damaged to the extent that they were here. Fire goes up, not down. So if you start a fire on the floor, it's going to want to climb the walls to the ceiling, not through the floor to the basement."

"Okay," I said, nodding my head. "Is that what happened here?"

"Yeah, I mean the whole gawl-durned house collapsed into the basement. That's the other thing. Most arsonists don't understand the chemistry and the physics of a fire. If they did, my job'd be a lot harder."

He leaned over in front of me, popped the glovebox door, and withdrew a pack of unfiltered Chesterfields. He fumbled with the pack and finally got one out, bent and wrinkled, and lit it with a cheap disposable butane.

"Fire's very predictable," he said, inhaling deeply on the cigarette. "So are arsonists. Arson's usually a crime of opportunity. Mostly jerks throwing Molotov cocktails. No planning, no strategy. Just light a bottle, throw it, then run like hell."

"But not here," I offered.

"Oh, hell, no." He laughed. The laugh broke something loose in his chest, and it rumbled around echoing in his lungs until he coughed, brought it up, and sent it flying out the window onto the sidewalk. Having a bit of a weak stomach, I tried hard not to watch.

"No, I'd say the arsonist here probably spent several hours putting this one together, and when he set it off, it went down like a Fourth of July fireworks display. I mean, usually you've got studs and rafters and beams that survive, even if the house is totally involved. You look for your arrows and pointers—''

''What?'' I interrupted.

''Patterns of the fire, the information you get from the surviving studs, like that. The pattern of the fire is revealed by the heights of the remaining studs. You can trace it all the way back to point of origin, just like a road map.''

''Only there were no remaining studs here,'' I said. ''Or very few.''

''That's right. Not enough to even get a sense of differing temperatures. Everything was hot, the whole house. You want my opinion?''

''That's what I'm here for.''

''Whoever set this planned it out to the extent that he had accelerant on each floor. He may have even punched holes in the drywall or the plaster and poured it down inside the studs from floor to floor. House that old probably didn't have firebreaks in between the studs. Codes didn't call for it back in the nineteenth century. Then he opened all the windows. That's what convinced me more than anything. Ventilation, that's the secret. Probably eighty percent of the insurance fraud in this country's residential arson. If fire starters understood that it takes as much air as it does gasoline, problem'd be a lot worse.''

''I guess that's why they didn't find much of Dr. Elmore,'' I said, thinking back to Lanie and her anguish over what had happened after she left that Friday night. ''I understand he was pretty well burned up.''

''I'm surprised they found anything. My source in the homicide squad told me they found him in the basement. That'd explain it. If the killer had left him on the top floor, there would've been nothing left but his fillings.''

''What I want to know, though, is whether or not this was a copycat arson. Was this the same guy who's been starting all the other fires, or did somebody take the opportunity to do Elmore and make it look like an arsonist?''

Eberhart looked off toward the ruins. ''You notice the smell?''

''Smell? You mean the burned stuff? Sure.''

''No, not that. Beneath that, just beneath the burning wood and insulation and roofing tar.''

I shook my head. ''No, what?''

He turned back to me, a thin gray line of cigarette smoke curling up from his lips and drawn into his nose. ''I've got my samples to take back to the gas chromatograph, so I'll know pretty quick. But I'd be willing to bet I already know.''

''Know what?''

''The accelerant. The stuff the burner used to keep the fire going. I've seen it before, but only with a pro. It's a mixture of gasoline and either diesel fuel or something like chain-saw oil.''

''What's that do?'' Lonnie'd already told me, but I wanted to hear it from the expert.

''Gasoline makes a great fire, but it's over quick. Mix it with diesel fuel in the right mixture, it gives you the high temperature of the gasoline with staying power. That's prob-ably the best. Easy to spot, but what does this sumbitch care? He's not trying to hide that it's arson. Matter of fact, he's probably proud of it.''

''But what you still haven't told me is whether or not it's the same guy who's done, what, the other nineteen fires over the past year and a half.''

''I can't answer that for sure,'' Eberhart said. ''I've inves-tigated twelve of those fires for insurance companies. This makes the thirteenth. I can only draw my own conclusions.''

''And what are they?'' I asked impatiently.

He hesitated before speaking. ''Arsonists almost always fall into three categories—profit seekers, revenge seekers, or the psychologically disturbed. Clearly the perpetrator of this series of fires is in the third category, which is a real small minority. But this fire is different. It was too thorough, too planned. Either the guy who did this is the East Nashville Arsonist who decided to take extra care on Elmore, or we've got two profoundly dangerous psychotics loose in this city, one of whom is smart enough to be a chemist.''

"Okay," I said, trying to muster more calm than I really had. "What else can you tell me about him?"

Eberhart looked me over from head to toe. "How much do you know about this series of fires?"

I shifted uncomfortably in the seat. "Only that there's some speculation the arsonist is targeting gentrifiers, renovators. Maybe gays."

Eberhart smiled. "It ain't speculation. It's dead on. This nut, whoever he is, has really got it in for gays. I mean, it ain't my cup of tea either. But I believe in live and let live, you know? Every one of the houses has belonged to either a gay or a lesbian, mostly older gay guys. Every one. If Elmore wasn't gay, then he was the first that wasn't.''

"Okay, but he wasn't. He was engaged. Had kids, been married a couple, three times before."

"Since when does that mean anything?" Eberhart asked, raising an eyebrow.

"Point taken," I conceded. "But I still don't think so. Just doesn't fit."

"I tell you what else doesn't fit," he said. "On a statistical basis, a lot of your pyromaniacs, your for-real psychos—"

"Yeah?"

"A fairly high percentage of 'em are gay men," he said, with his brown-toothed grin spreading slowly across his face.

Chapter 11

I slowed to make the curve where Riverside Drive changes names just before it intersects Gallatin Road. It was a little after four in the afternoon, the early drive-time traffic just picking up and a few last straggling school buses slowing the whole works down.

"No," I said aloud. "Can't be." I just couldn't buy the notion that there was a statistical correlation between sexual preference and pyromania; that is, in fact, if pyromania was something we were dealing with here. Eberhart *seemed* to know what he was talking about, but did he? There are a lot of ways to be nuts.

The more I pondered all these events, the bigger they seemed. My ex-wife was suspected of murdering her fiancé, who was our marriage counselor, and who apparently was sufficiently guilty of indiscretion with his patients that somebody was out to destroy his reputation even before he was killed by an accomplished and professional arsonist, whose knowledge was so thorough that, as Eberhart said, he might even be a chemist. Too much to deal with . . .

I tried to think logically, despite the distractions of looking for a parking space in the Inglewood Kroger supermarket parking lot. It seemed clear to me that if Lanie was a bona fide suspect, she wouldn't be one for long. There was nothing in Lanie's background to suggest she'd have any comprehension of the science of fire starting. As far as I knew, she never even took high-school chemistry. When we were married, she couldn't even get a fire in the fireplace lit right. It just wasn't her style.

Then again, it might take more than that to clear her. I have the greatest respect for the local police and the district attorney, but I know they consider their job unfinished until they get a conviction. Prosecutors have been known to go for second best. The system isn't perfect. Just ask the guy who starred in *The Thin Blue Line*.

I parked the car next to a decades-old Chevy pickup that actually made the Ford look good. People streamed in and out of the automatic doors of the supermarket, heads down, no eye contact. I melted into the stream, and before I knew it, I was wandering down the frozen-food aisle looking for dinner. A couple of nukeable gourmet dinners, a six-pack of soda, coffee, and milk for the next morning, and I was all set. Just keeping it simple.

The express line was crowded, as usual, with people who didn't understand that ten items or less meant, damn it, ten items or less. Not twelve, not fifteen, and not, as the old lady in the fright wig two places in front of me figured, a whole freaking basketful. I sighed irritably and resigned myself to the wait, wondering if anyone would mind if I passed the time by sneaking a look at the latest *Enquirer*. Then I decided I'd had enough sleaze lately and settled back into reverie, staring ahead at nothing.

Two guys were in the line in front of me; crisp shirts, ironed pants, haircuts straight out of the salon, one dark-haired, the other sandy blond, both with a single earring. The dark guy held a red basket with a couple of small items; the other stood next to him chatting. They were young, good-looking, bodies still tight, lean. The blond, whose trim mustache looked nearly perfect, leaned over to his friend and whispered something; they broke out laughing, sharing some private joke. Then I noticed out of the corner of my eye, where no one else could see, that the blond guy brushed his left hand discreetly along the outside of his friend's right thigh.

I thought about my friend Alice back at the paper, a young woman maybe five years younger than me, who moved here from New York City to take the job at the paper. She used to complain that you could always tell gay men: they were better looking, better dressed, better groomed, better kept, smarter, wittier, and they knew how to treat you on a date.

"You heterosexual slobs," she'd say, "you're just not worth it."

And I thought back to when Lanie and I were breaking up, the marriage all over but the paper signing, and I had a late-night conversation with one of my fellow reporters at the paper, Clayton Johnson. Clay worked the lifestyle section, wrote features on the side, and was a damn fine writer. At the time I was one of the few at the paper who knew he was gay. Later on, when he came out of the closet and wrote an article about it, the paper refused to run it. Clay then told them, in effect, to take this job and shove it. I don't know where he is now.

Anyway, Clay and I were the only ones left in the city room one night, and I was sitting around drinking a cup of coffee because I didn't want to go home. Clay walked in; we started talking. Next thing you knew, we were having a real heart-to-heart.

"You know, Clay, I look at gay people and I think to myself, 'Hey, these guys have got the world by the ass—' "

"So to speak," he interrupts.

"Right—no emotional entanglements, no nasty divorces. You party, have a great time, great sex, then it's see you later, babe. Sweet and simple."

"Oh, yeah," he said. "Sweet and simple. No problems. As long as you discount herpes, AIDS, rampant homophobia, armed rednecks, Republicans, and other assorted right-wing idiots, bigots, fundamentalist zealots, and Pat Buchanan types. And one other thing, bucko. When I break up with a lover, I hurt just as bad as you do.''

"I'm sorry, Clay," I said after a moment. "I usually hide my ignorance better than that.''

My mind back to reality, I watched these two kids in front of me, amazed at the apparent carefree ease with which they seemed to be enjoying each other's company. I thought of Clay and wondered what had happened to him. One other time, in that short period between my divorce and my departure from the paper, he had asked me out on what amounted to a date. But I am, alas, boringly, hopelessly, and terminally heterosexual.

The lady with the full basket put the last of her groceries on the black conveyor belt just below the sign reading 10 ITEMS OR LESS ONLY. The checker, a late twenties/early thirties guy with chipmunk cheeks, greasy black hair, and the last vestiges of acne, ran a can of coffee over the scanner, punched up few numbers, said, "That'll be forty–sixty-three, please," then grimaced as the woman handed over a book of food stamps.

He checked her out with a scowl on his face. His name tag, I saw, read TOMMY S and below that PROUDLY SERVING YOU_YEARS. The number _10_ was inked in on the black line.

God, I thought, ten years of checking out groceries. You'd think they'd give the poor guy time off for good behavior.

The lady loaded her four brown sacks into the basket and pushed it away. The blond guy in front of me reached into the basket, still held by his friend, and put a six-pack of beer and two deli pizzas on the conveyor belt. Then he took the basket out of his friend's hand and walked down to the end of the conveyor.

Tommy S, the cashier, glowered at the two of them and

began quickly sliding their stuff over the scanner. His jaw muscles were tight and set, his eyes dark and focusing intently on the cash register in front of him.

"Twelve–ninety-five," he announced, after punching the last of the buttons.

The dark-haired young man pulled out his checkbook and a pen, then began scribbling. He tore off the check and handed it to the cashier. Tommy S took the check gingerly between his thumb and index finger, as if it had been pulled out of a septic tank still wet, and laid it down on the counter.

"Driver's license," he said coldly. The young man patiently pulled out his driver's license and held it out. Tommy S yanked it out of his hand and stared down at it. He copied the number while leaning over, then handed the license back to the man without looking up at him. The blond had already sacked the groceries, so they booked out of there as soon as Tommy S handed them the receipt.

My turn now; I stepped up and dumped my soda and frozen dinners in front of the scanner. Tommy S looked up at me and seemed to thaw a bit.

"Good afternoon," he said, almost pleasantly.

"Mine's okay," I said, "but it looks like you're having a rough one."

"I can't help it," he spat, slinging my groceries across the scanner. "I think that's disgusting." He motioned his head toward the two who'd just left.

"C'mon, man, chill out. Different strokes for different folks."

"Hmmph," he mumbled, "disgusting perverts. God'll take care of them."

I paid cash and sacked my own groceries to get out of there quickly, before I got into a real argument. I thought of the people whose homes had been burned, whose safety and security had been shattered, their lives disrupted, all because somebody else didn't like what they chose to do in their spare time in the privacy of their own homes. In a world full of deep doo-doo, people were wasting time and energy worrying about what other people were doing with their own genitalia and their own hearts.

Go figure.

Speaking of hearts and genitalia, Mrs. Hawkins was in the front yard raking leaves when I pulled into the driveway just as the sun started going down. I hadn't seen her in days, since the night of the fire.

Since the night I caught her in bed with Mr. Harriman from three doors down . . .

I parked the car in back, then walked around front, still carrying my grocery sack. Mrs. Hawkins was over near the front left corner of the yard, near the street, her bamboo rake flying with an intensity that belied her age. I walked in a wide arc around her, approaching her from the side, knowing that if I sneaked up behind her, I'd scare her to death.

"Mrs. Hawkins," I yelled, crunching some leaves loudly. The rake stopped and she seemed to freeze. Then she slowly turned to me, nervously avoiding eye contact.

"Oh, hello, Harry," she stammered. Poor dear, I thought. She was, no doubt, a genuinely Victorian lady who saw getting caught naked in bed with a man as a sin tantamount to mass murder.

"Mrs. Hawkins, I'll be glad to rake the leaves this weekend," I said.

Her right hand flew to her ear and she adjusted her hearing aid. "What?"

"I said I'll rake the leaves this weekend. I thought the yard work was my job."

"Oh, that's all right," she said. "I need the excercise."

It occurred to me that Mrs. Hawkins was getting all the exercise she needed already. But I refrained from saying so.

"Well, I'm not going to knock you down and take the rake away," I said, smiling as broadly as I knew how. "But if you want me to do it, I'll be glad to."

She grinned just a little, the straight white of her dentures like a row of corn kernels. "I feel like doing it," she said. "It's a nice day."

"Okay, then. Have a good time. I'm going to go eat an early dinner."

I turned and walked away, the leaves crinkling and rustling brittlely underfoot.

"Harry," she called from behind me.

I turned. "Yes, ma'am?"

Her eyes had softened a bit, her voice steadier. "I appreciate the offer. You're a good boy."

"Thank you, dear. I appreciate that," I said. I knew then that we'd made peace.

The upstairs apartment I rented from Mrs. Hawkins was furnished with appliances that dated from the late Forties. They still worked, though, and I thought lent a little art-deco funkiness to the place. The phone rang just as I got the last frozen dinner stashed in the Kelvinator.

Marsha's sweet voice was on the line. "Harry?"

"Hi, there."

"What's going on?"

"Just got home. Decided to call it an early day, although I brought some work home."

"What're you working on?"

"Arson do's and don'ts. I caught up with an insurance investigator today as he was doing an on-site at Elmore's house. I learned a lot."

"So now if detecting doesn't pan out, you'll have a skill to fall back on."

"Yeah." I laughed.

"Listen, dawlin', I just wanted to hear your voice and say hi. I don't know whether I want company tonight or not."

"Hard day?"

"Mostly paperwork from the weekend, but that's what always drains me." She paused for a moment. "You see your ex-wife today?"

So that's what all this was about. "Yeah, she came by the office this morning and we went over to her attorney's. Took care of some things, got me on the payroll. Technically I'm retained by the lawyer as executor of Elmore's estate. I'll be paid on a company check."

"Oh," she said. Then an avalanche of silence.

"Listen, Doc, you don't have to feel threatened. I'm quite helplessly crazy about you, for what that's worth, and anything that happened between Lanie and me was over long ago. People do have ex-spouses, you know. You can't avoid them forever."

"I know." She sighed. "It's not exactly threatened. It's more like . . . Oh, snot, Harry, I've been alone for ages. Never been married at all, except to my work. I'm not used to this."

"So what? You, like, want to stop?"

"Not at all. I'm just not accustomed to this . . . turmoil."

"C'mon, we're having fun, aren't we?"

"Probably more than we should."

"I don't believe that," I said. "Not for a second. Don't get shaky on me. We're going to be okay."

"Yeah," she said without conviction. "Right. Listen, I got to go now. More paperwork."

"You going to be home later?"

"Yeah, but I think I'll take a long bath, call it an early night."

"Can I call you? Say before ten . . ."

"Yeah," she said after a moment. "I'd like that."

We rang off and I popped a frozen chicken Florentine into

the zapper. Jeez! Mrs. Hawkins, Marsha, my ex-wife—for a guy who likes to keep his life as simple as possible, I sure was juggling a lot of women all at once.

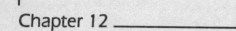

Chapter 12 ───────────

I called her again that night just before the ten o'clock
news. We small-talked, then made a Wednesday-night dinner
date. As soon as we hung up, I forgot what we'd even talked
about. My mind was somewhere else.

I kept going back to the letter. I unfolded it again as I lay
in bed sipping a diet soda and waiting for the local news to
begin. Did the police already know about the letter? Was that
why they wanted to get into Elmore's office for those files?
One thing was certain: as soon as they did find out about the
letter, even Marvelous Marvin wasn't going to be able to
protect Elmore's confidential files. I was no legal genius, but
I surmised that the letter lying in my lap was probable cause
for about a dozen of the wealthiest people in Nashville.

I debated calling Lanie, but didn't want to miss the local
news. Tomorrow was Elmore's funeral. The police news
conference announcing the autopsy results had been held at
noon. Both were bound to make it to the tube.

I fought the heaviness in my eyelids until I saw Margot
Chambers, the local news anchor, come on over the credits
of the network show that was just concluding. I grabbed the
remote control and turned the sound back on.

"Police investigators confirmed today that prominent psychologist Dr. William Elmore was indeed murdered," her
earnest voice said. "More on *Nashville at Ten*, coming right
up."

I muted the set again during the commercials, then closed my eyes for a moment. I started to drift off, then snapped back to just as the opening logo for the local news came on. I hit the mute button again as the anchorwoman's lips started moving.

"Police announced today that preliminary autopsy results indicate prominent Nashville psychologist Dr. William Elmore was beaten to death with a blunt instrument. And they now speculate that the Saturday-morning fire in his East Nashville mansion was set to cover up the murder. For more, let's turn to reporter Sandy Rice."

Cut to a film obviously made earlier, during daylight, of the reporter standing in front of the Criminal Justice Center down on the James Robertson Parkway. The reporter got right to the point. "Police announced today that Dr. William Elmore's skull was crushed by a blunt instrument and his body dragged to the basement of his East Nashville mansion before the murderer deliberately torched the mansion to cover his crimes."

How did they know it had been dragged to the basement? I wondered. The screen flashed to a tape of Elmore's house burning. "It was one of Nashville's most spectacular residential fires in recent history," the voice-over said. "Area residents say it reminded them of the great East Nashville fire of March 1916. It was only with the greatest effort that fire fighters were able to keep the fire contained to Elmore's house. But even then, two houses on either side of Elmore's received some fire damage, as well as smoke and water damage."

Cut back to the courthouse now. "Police have also obtained a search warrant for Dr. Elmore's confidential files, but early this afternoon lawyers for Elmore's estate sought and received a preliminary injunction, claiming that Elmore's patient files are confidential and protected."

I sat up in bed as the camera cut to a nervous and self-conscious Marvelous Marvin Shapiro. "Yes, that's correct," he said as someone stuck a microphone in his face. "We maintain that Dr. Elmore's patient files are strictly confidential and that this privileged material is absolutely protected."

A reporter in the background shouted another question.

"Yes," Marvin answered. "It's absurd for the police to speculate that any of Dr. Elmore's patients are involved in this horrible crime. They're on a fishing expedition and that's simply not allowed. We'll be seeking a permanent injunction to bar the police or anyone else from ever obtaining those files."

Then Margot Chambers was back on. "Thank you, Sandy. Late this afternoon Judge Martin Dore ordered Elmore's files sealed, pending resolution of the request for a permanent injunction. Dr. Elmore's funeral will take place at three P.M. tomorrow at the Old Hickory Evangelical Church of Christ in Lakewood. Internment will follow at Mount Olivet Cemetery here in Nashville. When we come back, a six-car pileup on I-24 near Hickory Hollow Mall sends eight people to the hospital and ties up traffic for hours."

So the Reverend Jewell P. Madison would be preaching the eulogy for his murdered therapist. This ought to be good.

The program broke to commercial and I hit the mute button again. I debated flicking the set off and trying for sleep. Funny, my body was tired, nearly exhausted, but I couldn't click my brain off. I kept picking up my copy of the letter, staring at it as if it contained some secret I hadn't figured out.

"Talk to me," I whispered. "Which one of you—"

The phone went off next to my ear like a fire alarm. I grabbed for the receiver; it jumped out of my hand and clattered to the floor.

"Damn it," I muttered, fumbling for it until I got it next to my ear. "Yeah?"

"Harry?"

"Oh, hi, Lanie. Sorry. I dropped the phone."

"Did you see it?"

"Yeah."

"Are you going to the funeral tomorrow?"

I thought of the good Reverend Madison. "Wouldn't miss it."

"I wonder if I can keep it together with that awful man preaching."

"You'll have to, Lanie. Nobody can know that we know what we know. Especially since we don't even know that what we think we know is true."

She paused. "I *think* I understood that. Which kind of worries me."

"Lanie, the more I dwell on that letter, the more I think I should take a look at those files myself."

She drew in a deep breath. "You're crazy. You can't see those files."

"I can if you let me."

"Oh, no," she said, her voice rising. "Don't get me caught in the middle. I'm already in enough trouble with Will's family and the police."

"I've got a feeling the police are going to wind up with the files anyway."

"Not if we can stop them."

"Lanie, my gut tells me something in that letter is the key to all this. The only way we'll ever know is to get a look at those files."

"Have you considered one other thing?"

"What?"

"Say one of the people in that letter killed Will, somebody who was willing to go that far to protect whatever they had to protect. What makes you think they won't do it again?"

"What do you—"

"I mean, Harry, you could wind up getting hurt. We're not exactly each other's favorite person anymore, but I wouldn't want to see that happen."

"Neither would I. But looking at those files isn't going to get anyone in trouble if nobody finds out."

"But how are you going to keep them from finding out? I spoke with Will's office manager today. For the time being, the staff is being kept on. The psychological testing aspect of the business is continuing as always. How are you going to look at Will's private files without having an office full of people finding out about it? Besides, the files are sealed."

I settled back into the pillow. "I don't know, Lanie. I only know that I've got to see what's in those files. One way or another . . ."

She sat quietly for a long moment. "Okay, tell you what. Meet me in Marvin's office tomorrow. Say around ten?"

"Oh, no, that's crazy!" Marvin yelled. "Those files have been sealed! I'm not going to be a party to screwing around with a court order. At the very least, it's contempt. At the very most, disbarment and criminal prosecution."

"I didn't mean I wanted to *take* the files," I protested. "Just take a look at them. Maybe—maybe make a few copies here and there."

Lanie sat in the chair to my left. Marvin turned to her. "What do you want me to do?" he asked, almost pleading.

"It's the letter, Marvin, the letter. I think Harry's right when he says if the police find it, they're going to get those files. Why can't we take a look at them first?"

"You're both crazy. The judge has sealed those files. If you wait until they're unsealed, then maybe you can get a peek. Until then, forget it."

"All I want is some indication of what we're dealing with here, Marvin. You know as well as I do that some of the people named in that letter have enough pull to deep-six this whole investigation. And don't think for a second they won't, especially if they think Elmore's files will hurt them, murder investigation or not. I only want a head start so that if something happens, say, and it looks like somebody's going to take a fall for the murder, we've got some leverage.''

"Take a fall for the murder?" Marvin asked. "You're insinuating the police themselves might frame somebody!"

"Not in so many words," I said, "but innocent people have been prosecuted before. The innocent party in this case just might be Lanie."

Marvin leaned back and ran his thick fingers through his thinning hair. "You know, I had a nice, stable, safe law practice until you two walked into my office. Close a few real-estate deals, file a few tax returns, doctor a set of books here and there . . . Life was simple. Now my mother is calling at ten o'clock at night telling me she saw me on the news. My mother, for God's sake. You know what late-night phone calls from my mother are like?"

Marvin held up an imaginary telephone to his ear and mimicked an operator's voice: *"Hello, collect call from hell. Will you accept the charges?"*

"C'mon, Marvin," I said. "It's not that bad."

"No, *you* c'mon. I'm serious as a heart attack. I'll tell you the law, which is that when a judge seals a file, it stays sealed until he unseals it or a judge above him unseals it. Until then, you don't mess with it. Understand?"

I knew I was beaten, at least for the time being.

"Okay, Marvin, you've made your point. How about when the judge lifts the seal?"

He looked over at Lanie. She nodded yes.

"What are you *yessing* me for?" Marvin demanded. "Until the estate's probated, you technically don't have any say either."

Then Marvin settled back in the chair, resigned. "But as executor of the estate, I can act in accordance with what your wishes will be after probate. Keep this in mind—you're opening yourself up to liability questions here. Elmore's patients find out you're looking at his files, they can sue you. Not only to block your seeing them, but possibly for damages as well. I'm not sure it still wouldn't be illegal.''

''Then what should happen to the files?'' Lanie asked. ''I mean, after probate, after the investigation.''

''Legally and ethically medical records belong to the patient. The records should either be returned to the patient or forwarded along to whoever takes over their case.''

''My God,'' I said, ''I'm terrified what will happen to these people when they hear what Elmore was writing about them. Especially if they've seen the letter.''

''Me too,'' Marvin Shapiro said wearily. ''The best thing that could happen to those records is that they should be destroyed.''

''How long will it be before the judge unseals the files?'' I asked.

''Judge Dore set a hearing date of next Wednesday.''

''*Next* Wednesday? That's nine days off.''

''The wheels of justice grind slowly, my friend,'' Marvin said. ''Thank God.''

Chapter 13

There were a few hours left to kill before Will Elmore's three o'clock appointment with the eulogist. I eased the Ford into the garage on Seventh Avenue and started up the spiral concrete ramp looking for a parking space. I got lucky; on level five, a car was pulling away near the elevator. Not even a bad walk this time.

My karma didn't hold, though. As I stepped off the elevator one of the brown-shirted attendants accosted me before I could get away. "Mr. Denton?"

I turned. Uh-oh . . . "Yes?"

"Mr. Denton, the boss just saw you pulling in. He says I had to come stop you. He says you're a week late on your monthly bill. He says you got to pay up today or you can't park here no more."

I patted my suit-coat pocket and studied the name sewn on the front of his shirt. "Andy, I don't have my checkbook on me right now, but it should be up in my office. How about if I stop off with a check when I pick the car up."

"Well, okay, I guess. But boss says you got to pay today." Andy's head bobbed up and down as he spoke, and a gob of saliva appeared in the corner of his mouth.

"Great, I'll be back here in an hour or so. Okay?"

"Well, I—" he began, but by that time I was walking away.

I really did have a check up in my office, and strangely

enough I had the money in my account to cover the check, thanks to the five bills Marvin had awarded me yesterday. My only decision was whether or not it was worth the fifty bucks I owed the parking lot to retrieve the Ford.

What the hell, I thought as I dodged the traffic and jay-walked across the street to my office. It's the only game in town for me. Until I could afford better, the oil burner would have to do. With the mileage it had on it, I was surprised the heap ran as well as it did.

I heard the yelling as soon as I hit the landing just below my floor. There were a couple of voices at work, but the most distinctive was Ray's. In the midst of it all, he let loose with a Rebel yell—"Eeeee-*haaahhh*!"—that must have felt like a Volkswagen locking up its brakes in the back of his throat.

Okay, I thought, stop in and say hi. No beer, though, not this early. Matter of fact, seems kind of early for Slim and Ray to be celebrating.

S&R ENTERPRISES the gold letters on black plastic read on their door. Things must be going well; last time I talked to Ray, he and Slim couldn't afford a sign. Struggling songwriters usually don't have much extra cash. In fact, they usually don't even have a roof over their heads.

I rapped on the door twice, just hard enough to be heard over the medley of laughs, howls, and whistles coming from inside.

"Yeah!" Ray's dulcet tones.

I opened the door and stepped in. Like my office, they had no waiting room: just one big space with a couple of desks, along with a maze of tape recorders, stereo equipment, guitars, a fiddle, and a synthesizer.

"Harry, you rascal!" Ray yelled, throwing his scrawny arms around me. I hadn't seen these guys in a couple of weeks. Slim, the quiet, younger one, even wore a big smile.

"Hey, Harry, how you doing?" My jaw dropped; coming from Slim, that was a soliloquy.

"Fine, Slim. How's it going with you guys?" I slapped Ray on the back, then disengaged myself from his wiry bear hug.

"What the hell you think, boy?" Ray yelled. "We just got the call! The Garth-man is putting one of ours on his next album!"

"Garth Brooks?" I asked in amazement. "*The* Garth Brooks?"

"We don't think it'll be the single or anything, you know," Slim said. "But it's something."

"Aw, listen to him," Ray squealed. *"But it's something. . . ."*

"I don't know much about the songwriting business," I said, slipping into my best Molly Ivins Texas drawl. *Sawng-writin' bidness.* "What's it mean when you sell a song to somebody like Garth Brooks?"

Ray threw back his head and horse-laughed. "It mostly means we won't be in this dump of a building much longer."

"Hey, c'mon, man," Slim said.

"I'm sorry." Ray laughed. "Hell, Harry knows I don't mean nothing by it. We'd all like to be in a building with an elevator and decent air-conditioning in the summertime. Wouldn't we, Harry?"

"Got that right, Ray," I answered, figuring if I ever got out of this building, it would be just ahead of the wrecking ball. "How long's it take for an album to get made?"

"We don't know," Slim said carefully. Of the two, I got the feeling Slim was the only one who wasn't already counting his chickens. "Now that the Garth-man's a daddy and all. He says he's going to slow down a bit."

"Might even take a year or two," Ray said, grinning. "But that's okay. 'S worth waiting for, believe me. This's the break we been looking for."

"Great, guys, I'm really happy for you. Ya'll ought to celebrate. It's not every day you get a phone call from Garth Brooks."

" 'T weren't exactly from Garth Brooks hisself," Slim said. "It was one of his people. Said they were working up the contract now."

"Harry's right," Ray yelled, punctuating his joy with another "Eeee-haaah!" "We ought to go celebrate! Harry, why don't you join us? Le's go get a bucket of beers."

I laughed. "Naw, you guys go on. Knock yourselves out. I got too much work to do. Believe it or not, I got a case this weekend."

"Hot damn!" Ray said. "I hope it's a good un!"

"It'll be a few days' retainer." I opened the door and started back out into the hall.

"I just hope," Slim said quietly, "we don't find no more dead bodies outside. Not like that last time."

Ray slapped his thigh and laughed loudly. "Damn, boy, what you trying to do, throw cold water on the parade? Let's get out of here before the phone rings again and we have to fly to Hollywood to star in a movie."

This time, it was my turn to laugh. If bullshit was music, Ray'd be the Grand Ole Opry. "Don't worry, Slim," I said, "ain't going to be any dead bodies on this one."

"At least not any more, I hope," I whispered to myself as I walked down the hall.

Lonnie either wasn't in or he wasn't answering his phone. I left a quick message on his machine, then rummaged around in my desk and, after about five minutes, managed to find my checkbook. I scribbled out a fifty-dollar check to the order of Downtown Parking, Inc. I wondered how long it would be before I got tired of being fashionably poor and gave up this line of work for something else. I'd been a detective less than a year, barely ten months, in fact, and I enjoyed the freedom and weirdness of it all. There was still something delightful about meeting people casually and saying something like "Yes, I'm a private investigator. Have my own firm . . ." and then, when they didn't believe me, whipping out my license and the shiny gold badge that cost me twenty-five bucks mail order through Law Enforcement Supply House.

That was the fun part. The downside was that I'd taken in exactly $800 so far this month; $600 of it was already gone for rent and parking, and I still had the utilities on my apartment to deal with. Thank God the office utilities are covered in the rent. Pretty soon I was going to be the only private investigator in Music City on food stamps.

Now there's an idea: I could hang a sign on the door, maybe lift one from the neighborhood market, that says WE ACCEPT FOOD COUPONS. Then I could start taking the real low-life business. Your wife cheating on you while you're out of work? Fine, two coupon books will buy three days of my time, as long as I don't have any expenses.

Oh, well, I thought as I locked my office door behind me and started back to the parking lot, it beats wearing a paper hat and asking the multitudes if that was eat in or take out.

I pulled out into the afternoon traffic on Seventh Avenue and realized that if I was going to make it to Will Elmore's funeral on time, I'd have to hustle. I maneuvered down to the James Robertson Parkway and crossed the river between the courthouse and the police station, then caught the Ellington Parkway through East Nashville all the way to Madison. The EP kind of peters out in a residential neighborhood, changes names, then wanders past Memorial Hospital to the infamous Old Hickory Boulevard. It's a measure of the influence of history on the South that this city had chosen to name every other road on the map after Andrew Jackson.

I managed to make it to Gallatin Road in about twenty-five minutes, then sat at the long light for five more. I sneaked through under the yellow, then watched this time as six other cars behind me ran the red—a personal record, I think.

The road separated into four lanes divided by a median at that point, so the traffic pushed up to about sixty and I was soon crossing the river again by the Du Pont plant, out in a section named, appropriately enough, Rayon City.

I slowed considerably—this part of town is a notorious speed trap—and searched for the street off to the left that would take me to the Old Hickory Evangelical Church of Christ. I spotted the sign just past the next light, then turned off Old Hickory Boulevard onto a quiet, residential tree-lined street that was home to the largest church in the city, and one of the fifteen or so largest in the country.

The Reverend Jewell P. Madison had built the place practically by himself; with, of course, generous help from the collection plate and the multimillion-dollar fund-raising effort that supported the church, the syndicated television show, the private jet, the highly publicized food-for-the-homeless program, the blah, blah, blah, on and on. I'd never met the Reverend Madison, but we all kept an eye on him at the paper. We figured the only reason Madison escaped the fate of his fellow evangelists like Jim Bakker and Elvis's distant cousin down in Louisiana was that he only paid himself a modest $75,000 a year and kept his pants zipped up.

Now it would appear from the Lanie letter that we were wrong on at least one count.

I'd been to more funerals in the past year than ever before, which had done little to diminish my aversion to them. My gut tightened as I made the curve around to the right and the Old Hickory Evangelical Church of Christ rose into view in front of me.

The pictures I'd seen didn't do it justice. When Madison took over the church in 1972, it had been barely more than a cottage, a small neighborhood church that, if anything, was shrinking in size due to the inevitable dying off of its parishioners. But the dynamic and ambitious Jewell P. Madison had taken it upon himself to bring the Gospel to the masses. In doing so, he had demolished the small brick church, ripped out the centuries-old red oaks and maples that dotted the property, and replaced them with a glass-and-chrome monstrosity surrounded by acres of parking lot that was probably hated by the locals not only for its ugliness, but for the traffic problems it created three times every Sunday and on Wednesday night.

I don't mean to sound prejudiced or critical, but I've never been able to figure out why a church needs a satellite dish and transmitting tower. If the Second Coming occurred tomorrow, Christ Almighty would have to get a license from the FCC.

The ten-thousand-seat auditorium was full up to about the fourth row, and the rest was a cavernous, curiously hollow, brightly lit empty space. I tried not to gape as I walked in the front doors, through the entranceway, and into what amounted to a small domed stadium. Two young boys, maybe fifteen or sixteen tops, stood stiffly at attention at the central doorway, handing out printed programs for the services and directing the people forward to the front of the church.

I couldn't help but wonder if they were friends of the reverend's. Different strokes for different folks was one thing, but not when you were talking jailbait.

In the balcony above, two camera crews from local television stations filmed the proceedings for the evening news. I settled into a seat by the aisle and shivered in the dry, cold institutionalized air. On a pedestal at the front of the church, between a gigantic gold cross perhaps thirty feet high mounted on the wall behind where the choir sat, Will Elmore's massive bronze closed coffin lay under a pall of red roses and baby's breath. On the first row closest to the coffin, a line of people in black sat, heads forward, voices muffled. The family, I guessed. On the first row across the aisle sat

Lanie, in black, alone except for her mother and father. I
started to go up, then decided I didn't belong there. Chances
are her parents didn't want to see me any more than I wanted
to see them.

I looked around, mentally reviewing the letter and wondering if any of Elmore's prominent patients were here. I
looked for the Mayor, Harvey Watts, Padgett, Nancy Weeks
Johnson, Margaret Rutledge. . . .

Nothing. Nobody. Surely Lanie wasn't the only one who
got a copy of that letter. It was, after all, addressed to "the
patients and former patients of Dr. William Elmore." Maybe
that's why they weren't here, among the maybe fifty or so
mourners who had gathered to tell what was left of him goodbye. Maybe just knowing he was dead was enough. Maybe
they figured if they were seen here, people would think they
were patients, especially if they showed up tonight as the
lead story on Channel 4. Psychotherapy had made great
strides over the years in the direction of respectability, but
there were still plenty of people out there who thought getting
therapy was shameful and reflected a lack of character.

I pulled up my coat sleeve and checked my watch: five
more minutes to go. I pulled a small notepad and a pen out
of my pocket and started doodling. I drew a house, then blue
ink flames peeking out the upstairs windows, then the roof,
until my hand spun on the paper and the whole house was
engulfed.

The faint first notes from the organ slowly filled the church,
then grew into a somber fugue that permeated the hall and
seemed finally to shut out all thought. Inappropriately loud
and overwhelming, the music crescendoed just as the Reverend Jewell P. Madison took the stage and strode across in
front of Elmore's coffin to the podium. He moved like a cat
and wore a gray suit, a single rose and a sprig of baby's breath
in his lapel. His salt-and-pepper hair was blown dry, styled,
sprayed to keep it in place. His eyes were dark, intense, but

his face was soft, its edges rounded with lines that seemed from a distance vague. He was shorter than I expected, less imposing. How could he fill an auditorium?

Then he spoke, and I realized the source of his success. His sonorous voice leaped out as if it came from ten men.

"A helper," he intoned. "A healer . . . A man who cared deeply about others and their problems. A man who touched lives with sensitivity and concern. This was the life of Dr. William Elmore. We are here to celebrate that life. In this troubled world, he was a man who listened with sympathy to the deepest and darkest secrets of the people he touched, those same people who grew to love him as much as he loved them."

Yeah, and maybe one of them loved him enough to crush his skull, then barbecue him like a side of beef.

As the eulogy went on I found myself drifting almost subconsciously into believing the words I was hearing. But then I thought again of the letter. Blast it all, who wrote that damn letter?

And what of the files? Whatever secrets there were had to lie hidden and sleeping in Elmore's files. Locked in a sealed filing cabinet was a clinician's dry and objective psychological profile of a killer.

The files . . . I've got to see those files.

Chapter 14 _____

I'd never done anything like this before. I mean, I'd pushed an envelope or two in my time, but never anything like this.

Elmore's funeral was over in thirty minutes. I sneaked out the back without even saying anything to Lanie, and I wasn't about to follow the long funeral procession all the way across town to the cemetery. No, there was too much to do.

This is crazy, I thought. Not only was I going against the direct wishes of my client, but almost certainly breaking the law on a felony level as well. If I actually went through with it, that is. And I didn't know if I could.

I made a left at the light off Charlotte Avenue toward Centennial Park, a beautiful, central-city urban park surrounded by hospitals, the university, office buildings. Behind the park, nestled in between two larger buildings, was a small four-story office building of gold-tinted glass and metal. I pulled into a slot in the parking lot farthest from the front door and killed the engine.

The building belonged to Will Elmore. His company, Psychology Associates, took up the entire fourth floor. The rest of the building was rented commercially. A canvas awning stretched out from the center of the building, over the front door and out to the parking lot. A glassed-in entrance alcove jutting out from the building itself provided a little protection from the weather.

I got out of the car and walked calmly toward the front door. Fortunately my coat and tie, gray pants, and recent haircut rendered me inconspicuous. I tend to be that way, anyway, which was something I learned to appreciate as a reporter. No need to stick out in a crowd if you don't have to.

The entrance to the alcove had a building directory and an intercom system. The building was mostly doctors' offices, and if you were coming there after hours, you could punch a button on the intercom and be buzzed in. Over in the corner, though, a discreet panel about the size of an index card sat unlabeled. I'd seen that kind of keyless entry security system before; you just hold a special plastic card up to the panel and a sensor opens the door.

I decided to scout the building out. I checked my watch: 4:15. I could probably wander around the place for a half hour or so without raising suspicion, so I took the hallway all the way to the back of the building on the first floor. An entrance at the rear opened onto the back of the parking lot. It, too, had the keyless entry system, but no intercom.

I took the stairs all the way up to the fourth floor. As I hoped, there were no locks on the fire doors for each floor. That way, if the elevator's turned off, I can still get where I need to be.

I can't believe I'm thinking about doing what I'm thinking about doing.

The heavy metal door made a rushing sound as I pushed it across the thick carpet on the fourth-floor hallway. The hall led down to a double oak door with gold letters on it, which read:

PSYCHOLOGY ASSOCIATES, INC., PC
DR. WILLIAM ELMORE

A large, smoked plate-glass window looked out over the park. The building was plush and well furnished. Elmore had done very well for himself.

The locks in the door were standard cylinder locks—nothing special, although that didn't mean I could do anything about them. I paused in front of the door for a second and collected myself, then pushed the door open and walked into a large waiting room.

A woman sat at a desk behind a high counter. I looked around the room for a moment, especially at the walls next to the door, then walked up to the counter.

"May I help you?" the well-dressed, middle-aged woman asked.

I looked over the counter at her desk, the wall behind her, next to her. Nothing.

"Yes, ma'am, I hope so. I'm kind of turned around. I was looking for Dr. Peterson's office. I thought the building directory said fourth floor."

"Oh, no, sir," she said pleasantly. "Dr. Peterson's on the line right above us on the building directory. That's how you mixed it up. This is Psychology Associates. Dr. Peterson's on the second floor."

"Oh, I'm sorry," I said. "Thanks for your help."

I turned away from her and started toward the door, my eyes scanning every square inch of the room I could see.

Nothing.

I stepped back out into the hall and checked once again. Then I smiled and headed for the elevator.

The offices of Psychology Associates, Inc. did not have a burglar alarm. Now if I could just figure out some way to get in that front door.

Mary Lee was behind the counter, her jet-black straight hair pulled back in a ponytail. Her dark, almond eyes made me go weak in the knees.

"Hi, Harry," she said brightly. Her voice made me go weaker.

"Hi, Mary Lee. Light crowd tonight." I looked around. There were only two other people in the whole restaurant and it was nigh on to dinnertime. "Where's your mom?"

"Not feeling well," she said. "Business has been off lately, so she decided to take the evening off."

"You're not here by yourself, are you?" I asked. This wasn't the greatest neighborhood in the world under the best of circumstances. If Mary Lee was here alone tonight, I just might have to put on my white hat and keep her company.

"My dad's here. He's in the back. My brothers will be here a little later, too."

So much for the white hat. "How do you find time to get your schoolwork done and still work here in the restaurant?"

She sighed, leaned against the stainless-steel counter. "Sometimes it's tough. Toward the end of the week we're all pretty tired."

Mrs. Lee had started closing the restaurant on Sunday. The strain of seven days a week was proving too much, I suspected.

"Marry me, Harry, and take me away from all this." She was only joking, but I felt a twinge in my chest.

"You shouldn't say things like that," I said solemnly. "Somebody might think you're serious."

"I don't have to worry about that. Nobody ever takes me serious."

If you were a few years older and I'd never met Marsha . . .

"Don't worry," I said. "Your day'll come. How about the usual?"

"With a little extra on the side for Shadow?"

"Sure, thanks."

Over the past ten months of my diminished lifestyle, Mrs. Lee's had become kind of a second home to me. There was something about the place, some connection, that made me feel like I was a part of their life in a way that I had absolutely no reason to expect was real. I'd never been to their house, never seen them anywhere outside of the restaurant, knew relatively little about them. Maybe that's the way people make connections today, with families scattered, communities shot to hell, everyone suspicious of neighbors and strangers. The world feels as if it's growing more dangerous and threatening by the hour, and yet we all still want to make that jump between being alone and not being alone.

When Mary brought my plate full of Szechuan chicken, I ate it there at the counter, standing up, making small talk with her. I stood there for a half hour and not a single other customer interrupted us. This was bad. If Mrs. Lee had to close down her restaurant, as so many others had already done, it was going to be a hard adjustment.

Where would I get Szechuan chicken for Shadow?

The wad of chicken wrapped in a paper towel sat in the seat next to me as I scooted out Gallatin Road toward Lonnie's. The sun was almost down now, the orange sulfurous glow of the streetlights driving the last of the dusk away. I'd talked small talk with Mary, played little idiot games inside my head, all to avoid thinking about what I was reasonably certain I was going to go ahead and go through with, depending on what Lonnie said. I'd need his help, but it was real important to me not to get him involved any more than I had to.

Shadow and I went through our little routine quickly this time, and I left her licking her paws on the yard in front of Lonnie's trailer.

He sat inside, legs over one end of the couch, a cold beer can perched on the table in front of him. "You bring that six-pack you owe me?" he asked as I opened the front door.

"I forgot it. But I'll get it later."

"Where have I heard that before?"

I sat down in an easy chair opposite the couch. Lonnie read the look on my face, then sat up.

"You got something on your mind, haven't you?"

"Yeah."

"Sounds like some kind of heavy."

I reached into my pocket and pulled out my copy of the letter Lanie'd been mailed, the copy where I'd penned in the names of the patients.

"Anybody ever finds out I showed you this, there's going to be hell to pay for both of us."

He stared at the letter for a second. "Okay then, nobody ever finds out."

I flipped it across to him. He picked it up and unfolded it, then leaned over and flicked a light on next to the sofa. His forehead wrinkled as he read. He stopped once or twice, looked up at me in amazement, then went back to the letter. When he finished, he laid it down gently on the coffee table.

"Wow," he said softly.

"Anybody ever tell you you're the master of understatement?"

"How many people have seen this letter?"

"Your guess's as good as mine. My ex-wife got the letter in her post office box yesterday. Probably everybody who's in it's seen it."

"How'd Lanie wind up getting a copy of it?"

I scrunched down in the chair. "We were seeing him for marriage counseling before we called it quits."

Lonnie's eyes widened. "Then *they* were going to get married?"

"Yeah. One of life's little curveballs, I guess."

"You never told me about that," he said.

"You never asked."

Lonnie reached over, grabbed the beer can, and took a long swig. "So what are we going to do about it?"

"Funny you should use the term *we*. The police got a search warrant to search Elmore's patient files."

"And?"

"The court quashed the search warrant and sealed the files. Now it's going up for a hearing next week. I don't know whether the police have seen the letter or not—that'll come out at the hearing. I want to see those files first."

Lonnie sat there stone-faced. Nothing ever fazed him, short of having somebody put a ding in his favorite pickup truck.

"You check the security yet?"

"Keyless entry on the building, one of those card sensor things. Standard cylinder lock on the office door. No burglar alarm."

"So what do you want me to do?"

"You're the security whiz. Help me get in, then you split. I don't want you in any trouble. I'll stay behind, photocopy the files, then get out myself."

Lonnie whistled. "Might take some doing."

"I know."

"You get popped, you're in deep shit."

My stomach flip-flopped. "I know."

"It's that important?"

"I think so."

Lonnie got up, walked across the room to the refrigerator, and grabbed another can of beer. "You better *know* it's that important. Don't be no thinking about it. You're talking about felony B and E here, my man. Ain't no parking ticket."

"All I want to do is look at the files," I said. "Not take them. I get in, get out—nobody ever knows I was there."

He studied the can of beer for a moment, then stuck it back in the refrigerator without opening it. "*We* get in," he said, "and *we* get out. And nobody ever knows we were there."

Lonnie cut the lights on the black pickup as we crested the hill behind the park and started on the downhill side toward the office building. The truck's interior lights were off; the only sound the faint drum of the engine and the muted speaker noise of the police scanner.

I wore black jeans, black T-shirt, generic running shoes; my best Pink Panther getup. Lonnie, next to me, wore a dark green running suit and a pair of Nikes. Said that if he had to take off, at least he could pretend to be jogging through the park.

We turned left into the parking lot, then continued on around back to the rear entrance. Lonnie pulled next to a Dumpster and killed the engine. I looked out the back window of the truck; a single overhead light illuminated the steps and the awning that led up to the back entrance. There were no other security lights in the parking lot, which gave the whole area a decidedly creepy feeling.

This wasn't exactly my area of expertise. In fact, I never expected us to make it this far.

"What do we do now?" I asked. "Knock out the light?"

Lonnie swiveled his head around, checked it out. "Maybe not. Depends on how fast we can get in. Listen, this is how it's going to go down. You stay behind me until we get to the entrance. Then I'm going to pop that panel and see if I can't short the sensor. I've studied how these systems work, but I won't know until I actually get up there and check it out."

"Okay," I agreed.

"When I get the door open, you hold it for me while I pop the panel back together. Then we go in the building. We'll have to feel our way until we can get away from the windows. I don't want any flashlight showing outside."

"Right."

"I'll have the radio with me, so if the cops get called, we'll have about two minutes to beat it out of here. Don't go to the truck; just leave it there. Make like a pedestrian. We'll

split up, meet back in front of the West End Amoco as quick
as possible. Got that?''

"Yeah. But why not the truck?''

"They see the truck pulling out of the parking lot, we're
pulled over sure as hell. If they just see it in the lot, they'll
figure somebody left it there overnight.''

"Okay," I said nervously. "You get us in the building,
I'll get us up to Elmore's office.''

"One last thing. We run into anybody inside, you can take
'em out with one of these.'' He reached under the seat and
grabbed something, then came back up with his palm open.
Inside lay a small black plastic box about the size of a beeper.

"Stun gun?'' I asked.

"Yeah.''

I thought for a second. "No, man, this is crazy enough
without taking even the remotest chance of hurting somebody. I'd rather get caught.''

He slipped the stun gun back under the seat. "I knew you'd
say that. You ready?''

"Yeah.''

"Let's do it.''

Lonnie eased the driver's-side door open, the interior of
the cab remaining dark. We each wore a pair of latex surgical
gloves; I carried an empty briefcase, Lonnie a small toolbox.
A portable police radio—don't even ask me where he got it—
hung from his belt, the volume turned down to the barely
audible level.

I softly pushed my door shut and latched it as quietly as
possible. The night air was dry and cool, with just a hint of
impending winter. Behind us, the distant late-night traffic
along Charlotte Avenue whooshed by. On the other side of
the avenue, we heard in the distance the metallic clanging of
boxcars banging together as a freight train prepared to move.
I glanced down at my watch in the darkness; the luminous
green dial read two A.M.

We padded silently over to the door, hurrying as we got into the corona of yellowish light cast by the bulb over the doorway. Lonnie squatted down on the concrete and set his toolbox down. I came up behind him and scanned the area around us. There may have been some kind of night ghoul creaturing in the darkness around us, but I couldn't see it.

Lonnie worked swiftly, quietly, the orange plastic of his small toolbox opened like a doctor's bag. He pulled a heavy screwdriver out of the bag, wedged it in behind the panel that held the scanning device, and with a sudden, quick thrust popped it loose from the wall. He pulled a small penlight out of the toolbox and flicked it on, running it around inside the maze of wires and bare circuit boards. I looked briefly over his shoulder at the jumble of electronic stuff; good thing he knew what he was doing, because I sure as hell didn't have any idea what any of it was.

I wasn't made for this sort of thing. I suddenly realized I had to go to the bathroom. Big time.

The door buzzer went off as the lock unlatched. I jumped about a foot grabbing for it. It sounded like it could be heard in the next county. I pulled the door open, held it. Lonnie put the panel pack against the wall and slapped it flat-palmed back into its mounting. Then he gathered up his tools, snapped the box shut, and stepped through ahead of me.

I sensed the movement and heard the hissing of the door closer as the door shut behind me. I had walked through a door that, in a sense, I could never go back through and be the same. I had broken the law, stepped over the line, lost another illusion about myself. Something grabbed my chest deep inside; there was within me a brief and terrible moment of panic.

Then I relaxed and took a deep breath. It was only my heart beating fast.

Chapter 15

"You got to what?" Lonnie hissed.

"I can't help it, man," I whispered back. We'd just stepped up out of the stairwell onto the fourth floor down the hall from the offices of Psychology Associates.

He stopped, leaned against the wall. "Well, for God's sake, man, don't flush. If there's anybody in this building, they'll be on us in a New York minute."

I pushed open the men's room door and stepped into a dark, cold room. I set down my briefcase, fumbled for the lights, snapped them on, then squinted in the dazzling white fluorescent light. A minute later I hit the light and plunged the room back to black. Lonnie was leaning against the wall outside, down on his haunches, the toolbox in front of him. He looked poised, wound tight, ready to bolt at the slightest danger.

"You all right?" I whispered.

"Yeah, just let's go, okay?" He grabbed the toolbox and pushed himself up the wall.

We walked down the carpeted hall quickly and stopped outside the office doors. Only the red glow of the exit signs at either end of the hallway illuminated the area. Lonnie squatted down and opened the toolbox again.

"You ever gone to the bathroom wearing a pair of surgical gloves?"

122

Lonnie looked up, a wry look on his face. "Nope. Can't say I've tried that one."

I bent down next to him. "It's a major thrill. Try it sometime."

He handed me the penlight. "I'll remember that," he said as he fumbled around inside while I held the light on target. He pulled out a small, zippered leather case about the size of a wallet and opened it. Inside, a collection of small black metal picks lay strapped together inside the case.

"Cylinder locks are pretty easy," he whispered. "Most of the time, anyway."

He extracted a thin metal blade twisted in the shape of an *L*. "Tension wrench," he explained. "You take the short end of the blade and slip it into the lock, then gently grab the long end and put just a tiniest bit of tension on the cylinder. See, like this?"

I shone the penlight on the lock. The thin long part of the *L* was bent at just a slight angle. "Then you take one of the picks—I usually start with a raker, sometimes a diamond—and you slip it in beside the tension wrench, then feel for the pins."

He inserted the pick all the way to the back of the lock. "Then," he continued, "you just gently rake the pins, trying to get them past the shear line, and when you do it just right, the tension wrench—"

He pulled the raker pick out once, very slowly, then twice, then a third time. The bent part of the tension wrench suddenly spun the cylinder clockwise.

"There you go," he hissed. He pulled the pick out, used the tension wrench to spin the cylinder a bit more, then stood up and opened the door in one smooth motion.

"Jeez, you're good," I said in a normal voice.

"Shhh," he hushed, "c'mon. I'll teach you how to do it. That way, if things don't work out in the detecting business, you can always become a burglar."

I cleared my throat. "In case you haven't noticed, bud, I already have."

The waiting room was pitch-black, with only the faintest dim green glow coming from a computer screen at the reception desk that had been left on overnight.

"First thing," I said, shining the light around the room, "is get our bearings. No lights on, though."

"Right," Lonnie said, pulling a second penlight out of his toolbox and switching it on.

There were two doors on either side of the room. I did a quick eenie, meenie, minie and opened the door to the left. It led into a narrow, carpeted hallway.

"C'mon," I said, leading the way.

"We don't even know what we're looking for, do we?"

"William Elmore's office."

"So what happens when we find his office?"

"We hope his files are in there. If not, we'll just have to keep digging."

The suite of offices was laid out like a horseshoe, with the open end of the horseshoe being the two doors leading into the reception room. Down the left hallway, doors to other therapists' and examiners' offices were unlocked and open. Farther down, an employee break room had the usual refrigerator, cabinet, communal microwave oven. Another closed door led into a room holding office supplies, then just past that, staff washrooms. Past that, a door led into a large room with desks and filing cabinets scattered about in busy confusion.

"If Elmore kept his files out here," Lonnie said, "we're screwed. It'll take days to find them."

"Yeah, but look," I said. "None of these files are sealed. If they were Elmore's personal files, wouldn't they have a court seal on them right now?"

"Okay," he said, "so you're not a complete boob."

We threaded our way past the desks, computer printer cabinets, filing cabinets, stacks of printout four feet high in places, to the other side of the room. A closed door, isolated from the rest of the staff and the other shrinks, bore a sign:

DR. WILLIAM ELMORE
PRIVATE

"Locked," I said, twisting the knob unsuccessfully.

"Well, let Doctor Lonnie have a look at it."

I stepped aside as Lonnie got down on one knee and took out his set of picks again. This time he popped it on the second try.

"Nicely done, Doctor," I offered.

"Elementary, my dear Denton." He opened the door and stepped into Elmore's private sanctuary.

"Elementary, your ass," I said. "We get caught up here, you can pick our way out of the slammer."

"Don't be such a pessi—"

He stopped midstep and backed up against me. "Lights down," he spat. I killed the flashlight and walked in behind him. Elmore had a window, a tall plate-glass window the full width of his office, that looked out onto the back parking lot and the field behind. We walked over to the window just as the white-and-blue of a Metro police car pulled into the lot, its headlights scanning the area like searchlights at a prison camp.

"Oh, Jesus," I hissed.

"Shhh, back up."

We stood against the wall, in the shadows, so even if there were enough light to see us from the ground, we'd be out of the way. I leaned over and peeked out. The squad car had stopped, its headlights like a soft glow over Lonnie's black pickup. The officer opened his door and stepped out slowly, a long black baton flashlight in his left hand, his right clearly resting on the strap of his holster. We were right above him, staring down, waiting.

He walked over to the truck and seemed to relax as he shone his light in, relieved to find it empty.

"He's going to figure one of the employees left it overnight or something," Lonnie said. I heard the faint hissing and popping of static as he turned the volume up on the portable police radio. "Especially since he didn't have sense enough to put his hand on the hood and see the engine's still hot. If he calls it in, we'll hear him."

"Then what?" I asked.

"Then we're up to our pelvic regions in reptiles."

We stood there for an intolerable couple of minutes, my bladder starting to beg once again for relief, sweat breaking out inside the latex gloves like a fourteen-year-old on his first date. Finally the cop walked back to the car, sat inside, made a few notes on a clipboard, then backed the car around and pulled away.

"Let's move," I said.

"Yeah, time's a-wastin'."

"Maybe I should pull these drapes."

"Sure," Lonnie agreed, "just make sure you remember to pull them back when we leave."

I found the cord in the darkness and pulled the drapes to. Behind me, Lonnie flicked on his flashlight. I turned mine on, and together we scanned the room.

"Nice place," Lonnie said of the leather chairs and couch, the Queen Anne butler's table on the center of a Persian rug, the custom-made oak bookcases that lined the walls. Also on the walls were pictures of Freud, Jung, Elmore's doctoral diploma, and his framed state license.

"Yeah, but no filing cabinets."

"That door?"

I looked behind me, to where Lonnie shone his light on a door in the farthest corner of the room, to the left of the window. I stepped over quickly and opened the door into a large walk-in closet. Inside the closet, two four-drawer steel filing cabinets were pushed against the wall. They were locked, and down through the front of the filing cabinets, looped through the handles of each drawer, was a broad yellow tape that read POLICE EVIDENCE—DO NOT REMOVE over and over.

"Bingo," I whispered. Lonnie stepped into the closet behind me and shut the door behind him. I fumbled for the light switch and clicked it on. We both groaned immediately.

"Was that necessary?" Lonnie demanded, rubbing his eyes in the harsh light.

"Yes."

I studied the two filing cabinets. Labels on each drawer identified the contents. The top drawer of the second filing cabinet was labeled CURRENT/ACTIVE CLIENTS.

"What are we going to do about the tape?" he asked.

"Peel it off," I suggested. "Carefully."

Lonnie grabbed my arm just as I was reaching for the cabinet. "I don't mean to break up this little party, but I want you to think about this. Right now we're in the stew, but given our lack of criminal records, we probably won't take too bad a fall. But this, this is some serious sewage, man. You hack off a judge, you can get locked away indefinitely."

I hesitated for a moment. "You take off if you want, but I've come too far to ease off now."

He stared at me for a second. "Be careful not to wad the tape up. We've got to put it back on just like we found it."

I took a deep breath and slowly peeled back a piece of the tape, then unraveled it a bit at a time, weaving it in and out of the handles so as not to tangle it up. When I had a few feet loose, Lonnie took the end and held it for me, while I continued stripping the tape off.

My breath came in short gasps, my gut in a knot, as I pulled the last bit of tape off.

"There," I whispered. Lonnie looped the tape into a manageable bundle and laid it gently on a shelf behind us. Then he opened his picks for the third time that night and popped the lock on the filing cabinet.

I pulled the drawer open. If the number of files was any indication, Elmore's current, active caseload was small. Of course, the guy could afford to be choosy, to take only the most interesting cases or the most prominent people. Who'd pass up the chance to do therapy on the mayor, a famous country-music star, or somebody else like that?

I counted the files; Elmore had only twenty-two active patients. Some of the files I recognized immediately: Reverend Madison's, Mayor Durrell's. Others I didn't. The files were thin, each one having only a few pieces of paper. Still, there'd be over a hundred pages to copy if I wanted to really know what Elmore had written about each person.

"What if it's an inactive patient?" I asked. "We can't copy the whole filing cabinet."

"Hey, c'mon," Lonnie said. "Get a move on. Just get the actives for now. We'll come back for the rest if we have to."

I turned to him, suddenly queasy. "Jesus, Lonnie, we're not supposed to be seeing this stuff. Maybe I didn't think this through too well."

He scowled. "Hell, Harry, there ain't time to think about it now. Let's get started copying the damn things, then you can throw 'em away later if you don't want to read 'em. We got to get moving here, bud. Damn sun's going to be up in a couple hours."

"There's a copy machine out there where all the desks are. You go turn it on. I'll get these files together."

Lonnie reached for the light switch. "Okay, let me kill this before I go—hey, wait a minute. Where's your briefcase?"

I felt a momentary flash of panic. The briefcase? Where had I left the briefcase?

"Oh, wait." I sighed, relieved. "I left it in the men's room."

"Man, you're incredible. Why don't you just go leave your business card on the front desk. I'll get it for you."

"No, wait," I said, stepping in front of him just as he hit the light switch and the blackness crashed down on us. "I got to use it again, anyway."

Back when I was still a reporter, I once interviewed an inmate out at the Walls, the century-old Tennessee state penitentiary that's now been closed by order of the Feds. The fellow I interviewed was suing the state in federal court for locking him up under the old class-X felony statutes, a since-remedied quirk in Tennessee law that could theoretically, under the right circumstances, get you thrown in jail for the rest of your life for spitting on the sidewalk. The conversation drifted around to crime, to how crime is portrayed on television and in the movies. The inmate, known to his fellow residents at the Walls as Wild Bill, said he always got a kick out of how the media portrayed gunfights.

"They always have two guys calmly shootin' away at each other, pistols at a hunnert feet, takin' careful aim at each other and pickin' each other off like paper targets."

He broke into a sloppy wet laugh that shook him so hard he had to stop talking for a few moments before he could pull himself back together.

"Hell, I had a dope deal go sour once. Three of us pulled out nine-millimeters and opened up on each other in a friggin' living room," he continued. "We're screaming, yelling, firin' in a hunnert different directions at once, jumping around like a dog shittin' peach pits. Not one of us so much as got nicked. Iz'a damnedest thing you ever saw. We emp-tied our clips, stared at each other for a second, then jumped out the windows and took off in three different directions at once.

"Yeah." He laughed. "After that, all I wanted to do was go home and sleep. That's the way it is after a gunfight, man—all you want to do is sleep. I went home and crashed for eighteen hours."

Which was exactly what I wanted to do right now, but there wasn't any way I could pull that off. By the time we put Elmore's office back together, turned off the Xerox machine, and managed to sneak out the back without getting nailed, the first glow of sunrise in the east was just beginning to burn like an ember off the horizon. We drove back to East Nashville, to Lonnie's junkyard, to where an alert and nervous Shadow had been waiting up all night for our return.

With a minimum of small talk I cranked up the Ford, which we'd parked hidden from view behind the trailer, and got out of there as quickly as possible. The briefcase sat on the seat beside me, full of papers that I hoped would be as revealing as they were dangerous. Someone had killed for what was written in those pages. Someone had died for what was written in those pages. Just sitting next to them made me sick to my stomach.

The Ford's scratchy radio wailed some heartrending country tune as I topped the hill at Douglas Avenue on Gallatin Road and continued past the old fire station. Then, on impulse, I pulled into the parking lot of the Krispy Kreme, a twenty-four-hour doughnut place at the corner of Gallatin Road and Greenwood.

The Krispy Kreme was Nashville's answer to a Port Authority coffee shop; a small, harshly lit place that drew—especially in the middle of the night—the truly weird of East Nashville. Doughnuts and coffee, that's all you could get, and you sat at a Formica counter under the harsh red neon glare of a sign that blinked HOT DOUGHNUTS NOW relentlessly into the dark blue of the night.

As I pulled the parking brake I realized how hungry I was, and how much I hoped a couple of cups of coffee would help me overcome this decimating urge to fall asleep at the wheel. Decompression sickness, maybe. The nerves could only stand being wound tight so much before they snapped; perhaps committing one's first really major crime a few months short of one's fortieth birthday was too much of a stretch.

What to do with the briefcase? The locks on the Ford were pretty substantial, and I could keep an eye on the car from inside. I didn't feel safe holding on to the briefcase; I felt even less safe with it far away. One fear overcame another, and I walked inside carrying the locked case under my right arm.

I crossed to the end of the rectangular room with its U-shaped counter and sat at a stool facing the street outside, my back to the wall. A tired young black woman, maybe twenty-five years old, tops, strolled over. The smell of frying doughnuts, coffee, and the thick aroma of chocolate filled the air. I felt numb, shell-shocked, exhausted. Now that morning was nearly here, I realized I'd had no sleep since night before last. Fragile, vulnerable, liable to crack at the slightest jarring.

"What you want, bro'?" she asked.

"Coffee, two glazed, a chocolate iced, please."

"What size coffee?"

I gave her a tired smile that was almost returned. "The biggest you got."

"I got that," she rattled, turning her back to me and heading for the coffee machine.

There were only three other ragged-looking denizens besides me. Of the four of us, all men, I was the youngest by at least two decades. The man to my right, at the end of the counter, had to be at least eighty, his wizened, unshaven face pockmarked and sunken. He bent down almost to the level of the counter and sipped a cup of coffee without picking it up, then sat back up into a curve and sucked on an unfiltered cigarette. Across from me a man in perhaps his early sixties shook with palsy as he struggled to get his cup to his lips. To his left, a couple of healthier-looking retirees in golf caps and orange University of Tennessee warm-up jackets were having their morning coffee.

The waitress set the steaming cup down in front of me, with the doughnuts on a sheet of wax paper beside it. I reached down and slid the briefcase between my legs, then squeezed it with my calves, the pressure firm and comforting. I was still dressed in only the light T-shirt and realized for the first time, now that I'd come down off the adrenaline rush, that it had turned chilly overnight. Goose bumps erupted up and down my arms; I took a long, careful sip of the coffee, then rubbed my arms briskly.

"Getting cold out," the eighty-year-old muttered.

"Yeah," I said back cautiously, not wanting to be rude, but also not wanting a conversation. I wondered if I'd be where he was someday, alone, old, dying by inches, hanging around an all-night doughnut joint because I couldn't sleep and didn't have anyone to keep me company, anyone that cared. I felt assaulted by fatigue and stress, and very much alone.

Jesus, I thought, shake that off. Quick. You've got too much to do.

I picked up the briefcase and set it on the counter next to me, then dialed the combination on the locks and raised the lid, careful to keep it turned away from anyone else. A stack of photocopies an inch thick lay scattered loose inside. I grabbed the stack and jogged it into a neat pile, despite the fact that I had nothing to keep it neat once it went back into the case.

Twenty-two patients, twenty-two screwed-up lives, messed-up heads, twisted hearts. All of them looking for solace. And instead of helping them, Will Elmore laughed at them and made cocktail conversation cannon fodder of their pain. The more I thought about it, the more I realized I could have wanted to kill the SOB myself if I'd known.

I perused the photocopies of scrawled notes. Elmore's handwriting, like any doctor's, resembled chicken scratching more than any form of human communication. But I could see that it was going to be decipherable. The only thing I really feared was that I wouldn't understand what I was reading. Just flipping through the first few pages, I could already see words I'd never encountered: dysthymia, dyspareunia, paraphilia, frotteurism.

Why can't these people speak English? I thought irritably. And what in hell is histrionic personality disorder?

I sipped my coffee and flipped through the pages until the words started to run together in an endless stream of black-and-gray toner smudges. I was too tired to make sense of this, but too aware of the pressure of time not to try.

I looked up from the pile just as a Metro police cruiser pulled into the parking lot. Oh hell, I thought, you should have expected something like this. Doughnuts draw cops like garbage draws flies.

An overweight uniform eased out of the squad car and waddled toward the front door. My gut tightened; I looked back at the stack of papers, nonchalantly picked them up and laid them down inside the case. The metal-and-plate-glass door opened. The cop walked in and stepped up to the counter. He sat down, ordered a large coffee and four glazed, and was just beginning to munch down as I carefully closed the lid of the briefcase and set it back on the floor next to my left leg.

"Getting cold out," the old man down from me said.

"Yeah, rain's coming, too," the officer commented. I looked over at the old man, who was struggling to get another cigarette lit. I smiled at him, thanked him mentally for being so outgoing, then stood up and walked around the corner and toward the door. As I passed behind the officer on his stool, he sipped loudly on the steaming coffee, then belched.

Outside, it was clear that what had been one of the most beautiful autumns in memory was sliding headlong into the dreariness of winter. The brilliant oranges and golds of the oak and maple leaves was fast changing into the paleness of the dead. A gentle yet numbing drizzle had begun falling, and the cold was seeping into my bones a layer at a time, headed toward the core faster than I wanted to admit. I didn't want to let go of the heat of the summer and the warmth of the fall, but as always in the cycle of the seasons, I was slowly coming to grips with the fact that I had no choice. I opened the door of the Ford and tossed the briefcase inside with a thump. I crawled in and fished the keys out of my pocket.

It was only as I tried to slip the key into the ignition that I realized my hands were trembling like crazy. Either from the cold or from fear, and I wasn't sure which, I had a case of the shakes that wasn't going away anytime soon.

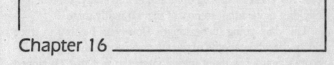

Chapter 16

A shower and shave, another pot of coffee, and I felt almost human, albeit a very brittle and breakable human. I'd gone ahead and rattled around my apartment even though it was barely six-thirty, confident that Mrs. Hawkins was either up and about herself or still asleep in bed without her hearing aids. It was only when I got out of the shower and was standing in the kitchen with a towel wrapped around me that I realized I'd been wrong on both counts; the door downstairs squealed and a furtive-looking Mr. Harriman sneaked out the back and down the driveway.

Mrs. Hawkins had been in bed all right, but she wasn't sleeping. I wondered what would happen when Mrs. Harriman returned from visiting her sister, or wherever it was she was supposed to be.

By seven-fifteen, I was in my office, the earliest ever and well before anyone else on the floor. The silence was both unusual and welcome. Even the downtown traffic had been as thin as I'd ever seen it, and I got a parking space on the first level of the garage. Some of my energy had returned, and even with my eyes burning from lack of sleep, I felt about as well as I could have hoped.

I locked the door to my office, hung my jacket on the wooden coat tree, and spread the photocopies across my already crowded desk. I separated the sheets into individual patient files and stapled them all together. Twenty-two separate files, the shortest being barely three pages, the longest maybe a dozen. I recognized sixteen names, the rest were strangers. Of the names I recognized, I'd either casually met or had a passing friendship with eight. This did nothing to ease my sense of having done something slimy, something I couldn't quite admit to myself that I'd really done.

This was going to be tough. How was I going to trace down the whereabouts of twenty-two people the night of Elmore's murder without giving away the fact that I'd ripped off his office and seen their files? I couldn't even let on that I knew they were his patients; even that much was supposed to be confidential.

On the other hand, the high-visibility people would be the easiest. Friday night was a big night for parties. Everybody wanted to be sure he made the weekend society section and got listed in the local bitchy gossipmonger's column. The rich and powerful in Nashville, probably like everyplace else, reveled in being recognized for their good works. It seemed there was always some kind of high-visibility charity doo-dah going on around here. That, combined with the fact that even though Greater Nashville's got a million people in it but is still a small town, ought to make it easy to trace down the bigwigs and fatcats. But the private citizens, the names I didn't recognize, the ones who sought help from Elmore for the kind of everyday stresses we all live with, that was a different story. How to trace the whereabouts of, for instance, Rocky Ludlum or Melinda Groves—to grab names off a couple of the files—that was going to be a problem.

I did the only thing I could do given the circumstances; I arranged the files in the order of most prominent to least prominent. Somehow I knew I could probably scratch people like the mayor from the suspect list. If Mayor Terrence Durrell wanted somebody killed, he wouldn't do it himself. Somebody else would do the dirty work, and it'd probably be covered up so well it would take somebody with greater resources than mine to unearth it. Then again, he had a lot to lose. Durrell had only been in one term, was almost sure to run for reelection. A story like this could sink it for him. Imagine, a right-wing politico having a steamy, sordid affair with the local head of the ACLU. The tabloids would go nuts.

And let's not even mention Reverend Madison's predilection for young boys.

I thumbed through the pages, trying to make sense of the cryptic notes. The first page of each file was a form containing spaces for name, birthdate, address, marital status, insurance-policy numbers (of course), spouse's name, birthdate, Social Security numbers, all the information that society has become so insane about categorizing. In a box on each form, there was a two-line section for *Primary Dx* and *Secondary Dx*. In each file Elmore had filled in three-digit numbers, followed by a decimal point and two other numbers. I didn't know what the numbers meant, but assumed it was some kind of Dewey decimal system for crazies.

Tough slogging, any way I looked at it. The notes were jumbled and full of unrecognizable expressions, terms, all of them surely intended to be a mystery for the layman. What little I could decipher about the individual patient files was worded in such a way as to sound odd and intimidating. Patients weren't merely down or depressed, I gathered; they were *presented* with depression, anxiety, fatigue.

But other notes were completely comprehensible—and devastating to the patient if they ever got out. I picked up the stapled stack of papers that was Harvey Watts's file. Watts owned a chain of discount stores that catered largely to the poor and disadvantaged. He was a big contributor to charitable causes, and the annual celebrity gala sponsored by the Watts Foundation, Le Grand Bal d'Hiver, had raised millions for crippled and burned children over the past twenty years. It was bad enough, as mentioned in the Elmore letter, that Harvey Watts had a penchant for tying blondes up. But as

Watts had told Dr. Elmore, with as much certainty of confidentiality as if he'd been in confession, he'd also been skimming the take for nearly that long as well. Especially for the
past decade or so, with all the competition from Wal-Mart
and the other national discount chains, Watts had been forced
to subsidize his lifestyle and his image to the tune of a million
or so a year from the generous gifts of people who thought
they were helping out.

I found myself revolted at this ripping off of wounded children. To his credit, Watts was troubled and guilt-ridden by
his actions. In fact, over the past few years, with the onset
of real aging, his depression had become virtually unman-
ageable. He had been hospitalized twice, had been pre-
scribed a host of antidepressant medications, drank heavily,
abused his wife, ignored his grown children, and was generally on a downward spiral of self-destruction.

And yet he continued onward. Projecting ahead a few
years, it was easy to see that only catastrophe lay ahead for
Harvey Watts. Villainy like this is always discovered eventually, and when it is, I calculated, Watts's only recourse
would be to fall on his sword. And Elmore, I remembered
from the letter, had found this all amusing.

Could he kill William Elmore to protect his secret? I wondered. A man who would steal from mangled children, I
concluded, could do anything.

I set the papers down in front of me, my eyes burning, my
forehead tight as a steel band. I rubbed my hands up and
down my face as if to erase the tension, then stood up and
stretched. More caffeine, I thought. I need more caffeine.

In my right-hand bottom desk drawer, my glass jar of instant coffee was empty. But a few boxes of herbal tea lay
chaotically inside as well; I found a box of Morning Thunder, which had, as the box noted, plenty of what I was looking for.

I dug around in another desk drawer and found my stinger,

the metal coil with the plastic hook handle that hung over the side of a cup and produced boiling water. I took my coffee cup down the hall to the men's room, washed it out, and brought fresh water back to my office. I plugged in the stinger, dropped it in, and waited while it did its work.

Outside, the morning clouds had dissipated, the rain had stopped, and the day had turned into a bright, cheery burst of yellow-and-white light. My watch read 9:30, and I was surprised to discover that I'd been reading through the Elmore files for almost two hours.

After a couple of minutes I heard the bubbling of hot water behind me. I unplugged the stinger, draped it over the windowsill so it could cool while hanging in midair, then plopped in the brownish tea bag. Instantly a nutty smell filled my nostrils and the dark water promised a jolt of chemical alertness.

I sat back down as the tea steeped awhile longer. I pulled out a file from near the bottom of the stack and was reading something about dissociative microamnesia when I heard the sound of footsteps coming up the stairs outside my office. In the back of my mind I listened as the footsteps seemed to shuffle wearily up the flight of stairs. Only two of the four offices on my floor were occupied; my office and Ray and Slim's. I knew their footsteps, and the ones stopping briefly at the top of the steps didn't belong to either one of them.

I listened, alert without the tea now, as the footsteps turned down the hall in my direction.

I jogged the files into a neat stack, then panicked for a second as my tired mind tried to figure out what to do with them. The footsteps grew louder. Think, damn it, I cried inside my muddled head. Then, without thought or intent, I opened the bottom right-hand drawer and threw the stack in on top of my boxes of tea.

The footsteps stopped, paused, then a knuckle rapped on my thin hollow-core office door.

I slammed the drawer closed and shot up out of my chair. It wasn't Lanie; I'd have recognized the clicking of her heels. But who?

Only one way to find out, I figured. I crossed my tiny office and opened the door, then prayed that my face didn't give me away.

"Hello, Denton," Lieutenant Howard Spellman of the Metro Homicide Squad said.

"Lieutenant," I said, with as much calm as I could muster. "C'mon in."

I held the door open as he stepped through. Spellman was a Nashville street cop coming up on a quarter of a century chasing down everything from drunk drivers to serial killers. His straw hair was thinning, his suit worn, his shoulders slightly stooped, his face bearing the faint scars of acne. I'd dealt with him a few times in the past, mostly as a reporter, but once a few months ago in my still-new career as a private investigator. We had, I figured, decided to hold each other in uneasy and begrudging respect.

He looked around my office, his eyes shifting quickly as his neck moved slowly on his broad shoulders.

"Cozy," he commented.

"It's not much, but it's home. Have a seat."

He settled down into the visitor's chair across from my desk. I sat down in my chair and tried not to think about the ticking paper time bomb in the drawer beside my right knee.

"So what brings you to my humble digs today?" I asked, probably more jovially than I should have. I've never been a very good liar, despite my best efforts. Especially when it came to my own skin. I could pull off a skip-trace scam with the best, but that was just acting. This was different.

"This is an unofficial visit," he said, his Tennessee accent still layered beneath the degree he'd earned at the John Jay College of Criminal Justice in New York.

"Always glad for a social call from Metro's finest."

"This ain't exactly a social call either, Denton. I know you've been retained by your ex-wife on the Elmore murder."

"Guilty as charged," I said. "Only that's not entirely accurate, technically."

"What is accurate, then?" he asked. "Technically."

He reached into the side pocket of his suit coat and extracted a pack of Camel Lights. "You mind?" he asked.

Of course I minded. I hate cigarette smoke.

"Go ahead," I offered.

He lit the cigarette as I shifted in my chair. "Technically," I said, "I've been retained by the attorney for the Elmore estate. The estate's just as interested in getting to the bottom of this as the police are. And, by the way, just as much as Elaine Herrington."

He glanced up at me, his eyebrows jerking upward on his forehead. "So that explains Marvelous Marvin Shapiro's court action to seal Elmore's records."

"It explains nothing of the sort," I said, feeling a bit more sure of myself. "Mr. Shapiro sought that injunction because those records are private and confidential."

"They're also evidence in a murder case," Spellman said sternly. "We'll get those records."

"That's up to the court."

"I wonder what the court's going to think about its order being violated," Spellman said, his voice softening as he glared at me.

My calmness level went into a tailspin. Jesus, I thought, how did he know? How did he find out this quickly?

"I'm sorry," I said. "You lost me there."

"Elmore's office was burglarized last night."

Oh, hell, here it comes. I've been wadded up, tossed in the crapper, flushed down the pipes.

"Since when does the Metro Homicide Squad concern itself with office burglaries?" I hoped Spellman would mis-

take my nervousness for my more customary smartassed-
ness.

"Oh, nothing was taken. No theft, no vandalism. But the
staff came in this morning and noticed the blinds in Elmore's
office were closed, after they'd been left open the night before."

I shook my head slowly, trying in vain to fight off the
feeling that shock was setting in and threatening to cripple
whatever chances I had to get out of this. "Cleaning crew,"
I speculated.

Spellman shook his head. "That's what they thought at
first. Then they noticed the counter on the copying machine
didn't agree with the log. Elmore was apparently a real stickler for keeping track of his office expenses. That's when they
called us. We went over this morning, checked out the filing
cabinet."

He scooted forward in the chair, placed his elbows on his
knees. "The court seal had been carefully removed then put
back. We checked out the counter on the copy machine and
put two and two together. We can do that, you know. We're
cops. Somebody copied Elmore's files."

I stared empty-eyed at the man across the desk from me.
One of the things that keeps a man going sometimes is when
he just gives himself up for dead. I wondered what a jail cell
would feel like and found myself, of all things, suddenly
missing Marsha.

"Why are you telling me all this?" I asked.

He smiled meanly at me. "Why do you think I'm telling
you all this?"

I sat up straighter in my chair and tried to stiffen my spine.
"You got something to say, Lieutenant, then say it. You got
a search warrant, start searching. You got an arrest warrant,
start arresting."

He leaned back in the chair, slouched down, and stared at

me until I thought my head would explode. ''You look like you didn't get much sleep last night.''

''My sleeping habits are my own business, Lieutenant.''

''Don't get defensive. Like I said, this is an unofficial visit.''

''It doesn't feel like one, and frankly it doesn't sound like one.''

''Where were you last night?''

I thought for a second. I wasn't going to lie to him. I knew I couldn't pull that off, and if I did, it would only make things worse later. But I sure as hell wasn't going to tell him the truth either. At least not yet.

''I'm being retained by an attorney who is representing both the estate of William Elmore and the interests of Dr. Elmore's fiancée. I'm afraid, sir, that if you've got any more questions even remotely connected to the death of Dr. Elmore, you'll have to refer them to Mr. Shapiro.''

I stood up. ''It's been pleasant seeing you, Lieutenant Spellman. Let's do this again real soon.''

Spellman didn't move. He looked up at me, his heavy eyelids hanging like pouches over a dull pair of eyes. ''You telling me Shapiro told you to break in and copy the files? That's the way it went down, Harry, maybe I can help you. Some shyster lawyer's not worth losing your license, taking a fall for.''

My cheeks burned and I hoped I wasn't turning too red too quick. ''You're on the wrong trail, cowboy,'' I said. ''And I'm afraid I can't help you back to the right one.''

''Yeah, well, maybe,'' he said, standing up slowly. ''And maybe not. I don't much like you, Denton. But I've never known you to be this big a sleazeball. Hope I'm right.''

He turned and without saying another word, opened my office door and walked out, leaving it hanging open behind him. I crossed in front of my desk, looked out into the hallway, and watched him disappear down the flight of steps. I shut my office door and felt my knees turn to water.

So Spellman hadn't known me to be that big a sleazeball. Standing there shaking, I finally figured out that he just didn't know me very well.

Chapter 17

Something told me I'd really screwed up this time. Bending the rules was one thing; blowing hell out of them was something entirely different.

Spellman's greatly appreciated absence gave me the chance to pull myself back together, although even that description was pushing it. I sat staring, sipping on the lukewarm tea, my thoughts a scramble of unfocused bursts of meaningless energy. But the eye-opener was that I couldn't undo what had been done, and mistake or not, I was going to have to make the best of it.

Other thoughts kept creeping in, though. Unpleasant, destructive thoughts. My father, for instance. A straight shooter all his life, a decorated genuine war hero, a successful businessman who brought himself up through grit and intelligence and determination, who worked forty-three years for the same company before retiring to Hawaii. Forty-four years married to the same woman. A truly self-made man. I was none of that, except, I supposed, the intelligence part (and I'd begun to doubt that recently). But for all my good schooling and brains, where was I now? A marriage that hadn't lasted a tenth as long as his, a series of unsettling career switches that had led, ultimately, to a one-room office in a roach-infested building, and now, of course, crime.

I slugged down the last of the herbal tea like a sorry imitation of Sam Spade slugging down bourbon. C'mon, I thought, stop beating on yourself. There's too much to do. Spellman knew I had the files; he just couldn't prove it. But it was a pretty good bet he wasn't going to quit trying.

I had time, but not much of it. There was a damn good police detective out there trying to nail my hide, an arsonist and a murderer who was, so far, getting away with it, and a not-so-bad ex-wife who was depending on me to bail her out of a nasty jam.

For a guy who was as busted as a bad gambler the day after payday, I sure had a hell of a lot to do.

I buried myself so deeply in the files, in the work, that when I came back to reality, it was only because the sun had gone down and I was having to strain to read. I stood up, stretched, and turned on the overhead light in my office. Outside, the dusk had settled in over the tops of the office buildings, the sky a brilliant soft palette of hazy oranges and blues. I stood there in awe of the colors, trying to forget the fact that the pretty colors were there only because the air was so bloody polluted.

I turned back to my desk, which was now a jigsaw puzzle of notes. It was a mess, albeit a mess that almost made sense to me. As best as I could figure, here's how it played out:

The six people mentioned in the Elmore letter came first. I assumed that all of Elmore's current patients, and God knew how many off the inactive list, got copies of the letter. For all I knew, everyone on the JCPenney Christmas-catalogue mailing list got the blasted thing. But of Elmore's twenty-two current patients, these six, I figured, would be the most horrified, infuriated, pissed off. Whatever. Maybe that was a bad assumption; after all, the damage had been done to them. It was the other sixteen who had the most to fear. But checking out six was easier than checking out six-teen.

That meant the following people led the list: the Reverend

Jewell P. Madison of the Old Hickory Evangelical Church of Christ; Roy Padgett, head of the chamber of commerce; Nancy Weeks Johnson, head of the City Arts Commission; Harvey Watts, my scum-sucking, charity-skimming rodeo rider; Margaret Rutledge, chairperson of the local branch of the ACLU; and last but not least, the mayor himself, Terrence Durrell.

Of those left over, ten were rather more minor celebrities and players of lesser power. I'd heard of them all, knew most of them by passing acquaintance from my reporting days. Any one of them could be the killer; I'd learned long ago and by hard lesson never to eliminate anyone based on what they were or who they appeared to be. It made no difference if the meanest street-junkie-gang-leader killed you or a sweet, suburban housewife; you were just as dead.

The final six left over I would, for the time being, not worry about. They were private citizens, screwed-up private citizens to be sure, but with no more reason to be exposed by Elmore than by the *National Enquirer*. Thomas Sturges, Rocky Ludlum, Pierce Huntley, Melinda Groves, Angel Slaughter, and Bruce Miller were anonymous and, as far as I was concerned, could stay that way.

The next step was figuring out how to trace the steps last Friday night of the group I called the Top Six, the night that someone bashed in Will Elmore's head and incinerated his house with such fury. And all I had to do was figure it out before the killer struck again, or I got nabbed for burglary and contempt of court, or Lanie was arrested for murder, or the sky fell in on top of us.

It was completely dark now, the autumn days getting shorter one by one, especially since we'd gone off daylight savings time. It was only a little after five, and yet felt more like bedtime. Given as little sleep as I'd had lately, bedtime was awfully appealing.

And yet I wasn't sleepy, certainly not sleepy enough to go

home and try. The thought of another microwaved dinner and an evening spent with work, television, or a trashy novel certainly held no great thrill. It was after business hours over at the morgue, but it was a good bet Marsha'd still be there. I dialed the morgue's switchboard number and waited through ten rings before someone picked up. The voice that answered belonged to one of the attendants.

"Simpkins Center," he said.

"Dr. Helms, please."

"Hold on, I'll see if she's still here."

I settled down in the chair and studied my notes while I waited. Outside my window, a horn blared and an engine raced, the impatient irritation of a tired worker too eager for home to deal civilly with rush hour. Soon the downtown streets would be a ghost town, with only the furtive, silent shapes of the homeless and the depraved flickering from shadow to shadow.

"Yes?" Marsha's voice was heavy with fatigue, but no less sweet.

"Hi, love."

A soft hum came across the line. "Hmmm, how are you?"

"Weary. Burned out. Long couple of days."

"Same here."

"You there for the duration?"

Another sound escaped her lips, this time a kind of sigh, and I imagined her pulling off her glasses and rubbing her eyes tiredly. "Paperwork," she said. "Always paperwork. Not too much more tonight, though. Maybe another half hour."

"We still on for dinner?"

There was a moment's hesitation before she spoke. "Sure, let's do it. I don't feel much like cooking."

"How does Caesar's sound?"

"We haven't been there in a while."

"Should I meet you there or stop and pick you up?"

"I'm dying to go home and get into a pair of jeans. Maybe even take a shower. Why don't I meet you there, say around eight?"

I wished she could see through the phone the smile she brought to my face. "Great. Eight o'clock."

We hung up after another few moments of small talk, something neither of us was particularly good at. To her enduring credit, Marsha was the only woman I'd ever met with whom I could sit for hours in silence. An old movie on television, a bottle of wine, the two of us stretched out from opposite ends of the couch with a couple of paperbacks—that was my idea of complete bliss.

My God, I thought, the woman's domesticated me. . . .

I grabbed my coat off the hat rack and started home to my own shower and change of clothes, when the stack of papers on my desk practically jumped up and yelled at me. What to do with them? Leave them? They were evidence, and damning evidence at that. To carry them with me might invite discovery in a routine traffic pullover. It was not a bad bet that Spellman would have me tailed. On the other hand, he could have someone standing downstairs right now just waiting for me to leave so he could rifle the office, search warrant or no.

Either way I was taking a dreadful chance. But maybe there was another way.

I stacked the files neatly, inserting identifying yellow Post-It notes between each one so I wouldn't have to reorganize them. Then I stashed them in my briefcase and locked it. Balancing myself carefully on top of my desk, I pushed aside one of the dingy gray acoustic ceiling tiles and exposed the maze of metal, pipes, and wires in the crawl space above. A minicloud of dust sprayed down on me and I fought the urge to sneeze. I stood on tiptoe and slid the briefcase into the crawl space, balancing it carefully between two sections of the steel framework.

Another few seconds and the ceiling tile was back in place.
I hopped down, brushed the dust off the surface of my desk,
and examined the ceiling.

"Voilà," I said out loud. At least they'd have to look damn
hard to find it.

I pulled up my sleeve and checked my watch: 5:25. Plenty
of time to go home, catch the local news, take a long leisurely
shower, then meet Marsha for dinner. I made sure the desk
and windows were locked, then locked the office door behind
me as I headed out.

The traffic on Seventh Avenue had thinned somewhat, although the streets were still choked with commuters slogging
their way to the interstate highway. As further evidence of
brain fag, I went all the way to the top level of the parking
garage before remembering that I'd come in early enough
that morning to get a spot on the ground floor. No wonder,
I thought irritably, as I made my way back down the ramp;
I haven't slept since night before last. As a rule, without
seven or eight hours, I'm not worth the powder it would take
to blow me to hell. I wondered if I'd make it to the restaurant
only to fall facefirst into my marinara.

One of the virtues of living in East Nashville is you don't
have to fight the freeways to get home. As I crossed the river
at the courthouse headed toward Main Street, I saw the Interstate spread out left to right in front of me, jam-packed
with headlights that were barely creeping forward.

I got held up at the light in front of the demolished ruins
of the old Genesco shoe factory, but once past that, I pulled
into Mrs. Hawkins's driveway in less than ten minutes. The
air had turned cold again, but unlike this morning it was a
dry cold that was more invigorating than penetrating. Piles
of dried leaves crunched underfoot as I crossed the backyard
and started up the black metal stairway to my apartment.
Through the sheer curtains that covered Mrs. Hawkins's back

windows, I could see her standing alone at the sink washing vegetables for her dinner.

Who could blame her for sneaking Mr. Harriman in for the night? I liked living alone, but I wondered how another thirty years of it would suit me. The day might come when I'd be sneaking out of some little old lady's bedroom at dawn.

My apartment was dark, musty, as if there'd been little in the way of human occupancy lately, which was largely true. I flicked on the kitchen lights, cracked a window for some fresh air, then went into the bedroom and stared at my unslept-in bed. Weariness swept over me in waves, and I started to slide onto the bed for just a couple of minutes. I resisted; five minutes in bed could easily stretch into two days, and it meant more to see Marsha than to find rest.

I pulled off my jacket and lowered the shades, then stripped to my underwear and sat down in my easy chair. My apartment only consisted of two rooms, not counting the bathroom, but the one room off the kitchen was big enough for my bed, a chest of drawers, with room left over for a small desk, a table, and my favorite chair. It was a comfortable place, all the room I needed right now, and I couldn't recall when I'd felt more at home. It was a long stretch from the condo Lanie and I shared, which could have easily been a magazine cover story, but never quite felt like home.

I found the remote control under a dirty T-shirt and flicked on the local NBC affiliate. Tom Brokaw was just finishing up the national news, and I allowed my eyes to close just long enough to endure the commercials before the local news began.

I was gone in about ten seconds, sleep rolling over me like a juggernaut. I was helpless before it, but there was a skill I'd picked up years ago in my early days as a reporter. Young reporters always got stuck with the lousiest hours, and I often found myself pulling the graveyard shift on the city desk, usually doing not much more than monitoring the police radio or covering the phones. One of the tricks of the trade was to learn to drop off to sleep on a half second's notice, but remain just awake enough that if you heard anything important, you were right back to the world before anyone knew the difference. Once learned, it was a skill you never forgot; even now, the phone can jolt me out of a coma and I sound like I've been awake for hours.

That was the way it was as the lead-in music for the local news began. Somewhere in the blackness behind my eyelids, there was enough consciousness to recognize the music, and then the anchorwoman's perky voice as it led off with the day's events.

"Good evening, I'm Margot Chambers, and here's our lead story tonight. In a story broken just minutes ago a Channel Four News special investigative team has learned that slain psychologist Dr. William Elmore routinely divulged his patients' secrets, often joked about their problems to others, and, in fact, may have even had sex with a number of them."

Something began burbling around on the edge of my consciousness as, slowly, the words sank in.

"These shocking revelations follow disclosures that police now consider Elaine Herrington . . ."

Whirling faster now.

". . . Dr. Elmore's fiancée and a former patient of his, a prime suspect in his murder."

Faster now.

"Channel Four investigative reporter Stuart Jones has more on this late-breaking story. Stuart . . ."

Faster.

"Thank you, Margot. Channel Four," a male voice began, "has learned of the existence of a letter . . ."

My eyes shot open like a pair of explosive hatches, and I found myself on my knees in front of the television, my face inches from that of the reporter.

". . . which has been mailed to an unknown number of

Dr. Elmore's current and former patients. In this letter, written by an unknown person, a detailed account of Dr. Elmore's indiscretions and his unethical and perhaps even illegal breaches of client confidentiality is graphically described. Channel Four has obtained a copy of this letter from an undisclosed source. As you can see . . .''

"My God!" I shouted as Stuart Jones held a copy up to the camera. *"They've got the fucking letter!"*

''. . . the names have been blacked out, but chemical tests performed by an independent laboratory were able to discern them.''

Back to Stuart's face now. ''And what we discover is that Dr. Elmore had as clients some of the most prominent of Nashville's citizens, and that—according to the letter—it was not at all unusual for Dr. Elmore to joke about the problems of his patients and to discuss them publicly at parties. It would seem that this highly inappropriate behavior was known by many of Dr. Elmore's colleagues, and that it was common knowledge among the Nashville psychiatric community that Dr. Elmore was behaving in this manner.''

''Oh, no,'' I muttered, my head sinking into my hands. ''You idiots.''

''Surprisingly,'' the reporter continued, ''when confronted with the existence of the letter this afternoon, Nashville homicide investigators admitted they knew nothing of it.''

My head jerked back up again just in time to see an obviously pissed-off Howard Spellman confronting the camera.

''No, we had no knowledge of the letter. We would like to know where you obtained this copy of it, but obviously your source is protected. I will say we appreciate your coming forward, because we do consider the letter a key piece of evidence in this murder case, certainly as pertains to the question of motive.''

''Ironically,'' Stuart Jones's voice-over began as the videotape of Spellman continued without sound, "the woman police now say is their prime suspect in the case, Elmore's fiancée and former patient Elaine Herrington, was not mentioned in the letter. Ms. Herrington, an unemployed advertising executive, has been unavailable for comment.

"Channel Four also sought comment regarding how this would affect the injunction sought by the estate of Dr. Elmore to prevent disclosure of his patients' names. However, both the district attorney's office and attorneys for the estate refused to comment on current litigation. Back to you, Margot."

The young anchorwoman smiled as if she were serving up coffee in a Big Boy restaurant and hoping for a big tip.

"In the interest of protecting the parties involved, Channel Four has chosen not to divulge the names of Dr. Elmore's clients mentioned in the letter."

Well, thanks for that, I thought, and then began counting backward in my head: ten, nine, eight, seven, six, five, four—

The phone bell went off like a land mine. That would be Lanie, and what do you want to bet she's ready to comment now?

Chapter 18 _____

She was out of control. I'd never heard her go off like that, although God knows she had sufficient reason. Even when things were completely falling apart for us, when it was clear the marriage was all over but the taps playing, Lanie had kept it together. But not now.

"Ruined . . ." she sobbed. "Jail."

"C'mon, Lanie," I said as soothingly as possible, although deep in my heart I felt she was probably right. "It's not the end of the world. Not over yet."

This initiated a new eruption of sobbing intermixed with screams loud enough to force the phone away from my ear.

"They haven't come for you yet," I said. "They're just blowing hot air. If the police felt like they had a case against you, you'd already be in custody. And now they're going to start looking at all the other patients."

"Nooo," she wailed, "they're going to put me in jail forever."

She was borderline blubbering now, and I wasn't sure what, if anything, I could do to help.

I stayed on the line with her for over an hour and finally got her calmed down enough to let go of me. So much for my long, hot shower. I barely had time for a quick run under the water before meeting Marsha.

Who, I wondered, had given that letter to the news media? Who would want to cause that much pain to people who had

155

sought help for the overwhelming problems that had filled their lives? The only answer I could come up with is that it was someone who hated Will Elmore more than he respected his own basic humanity.

Maybe, I thought, that was where the answer lay. Maybe it wasn't one of Elmore's patients who killed him; maybe it was the one who wrote the letter in the first place. Maybe writing the letter hadn't done Elmore enough harm. Maybe Elmore didn't care. Maybe he even laughed at it.

Damn it, too many maybes and not enough certainties.

The sun had gone down for real now, the night sky as black as coal, all stars blotted out by the sulfurous glow of the highway lights. From the west, clouds of disgusting aromas from the rendering plant blew over and mixed in with the car exhaust. I realized I hadn't eaten lunch that day, had, in fact, not eaten anything since the doughnuts and coffee at a dawn that now seemed a year ago.

I pulled onto White Bridge Road and looked down at my watch, straining to read the numbers in the dim light: 8:10. Once again I'd kept Marsha waiting. We'd been dating long enough for me to learn that, unlike many people I'd known over the years, Marsha was a stickler for punctuality. She'd be irritated, but irritated I could handle. Irritation was like trouble; the secret was to know exactly how much you could handle at any one time without going over the edge.

I skipped the usual search for a space in the Lion's Head Village parking lot. I drove instead, straight to the restaurant and pulled the car to a halt in a fire zone just as Marsha was walking out.

"Okay," I said, stepping out of the car and leaning across the roof toward her. "Is this a for real hacked off, or just intense aggravation?"

She stepped toward me on the sidewalk. She wore tight jeans, pressed, with a flannel L. L. Bean shirt under a sexy denim jacket. Her black hair was brushed straight back, un-

tied, falling down over her shoulders. She looked great, and
I was determined to muster every bit of fatigued charm I
could to smooth her ruffled feathers.

"What am I going to do with you?" she asked, exasperated.

I bit my lower lip, gave her my best scolded-puppy-dog
look. "Well, I could give you a few suggestions."

"C'mon." She sighed. "Let's go find a parking space for
this heap."

Then she stepped off the curb, grabbed the door handle,
and slipped into the car. I patted the top of the car and turned
my eyes to the heavens.

"Thank you, Jesus," I mouthed.

It was nearly eleven before we saw that parking lot again.
Two glasses of red wine wouldn't ordinarily do me in, but
lack of sleep, general burnout, and a wonderful dish of pasta
in some kind of cream-wine sauce left me vulnerable.

"Why don't you just come home with me?" Marsha said
as we walked toward her black Porsche with the DED FLKS
vanity plate. "I don't want you driving like this."

"Oh, I'm all right," I drawled, pulling her closer to me
and laying my head in the crook of her neck as we walked.
"You know, I've never been able to do this before."

"Do what?" she asked. Her arm was around my shoulders
and felt great.

"Walk like this," I whispered. "I've never dated anyone
taller than me before. I like it."

She laughed. "You are drunk."

I nuzzled into her neck. "I'm sober enough to lick you,
lady." And I did, right below her left ear, and got a mouthful
of black hair in the process.

She giggled like a schoolgirl and pushed me away, but not
very hard. "Quit that," she scolded. "Or at least wait until
we get home."

I put my arms around her waist and pulled her to me. Beneath the flannel shirt and the jacket, I could feel her heat in the dry autumn night. The parking lot was deserted except for the last few cars left in front of the multiplex cinema. We were exposed, out in public, but utterly alone.

I kissed her, full, slowly, pulling her tighter toward me. Marsha moaned and I eagerly moaned back at her. Then I felt a tickle, right at my belt line, only it was kind of like an electric vibrator. Not exactly what I'd expected to feel, but what the heck, I was willing to go with it.

She pulled away from me. "Oh, wait," she said, her arms fumbling down between us. I thought for a moment she was going for my belt buckle right there in the parking lot. No one had ever done that before, at least not to me. In the swirl of alcohol and fatigue, I wondered if I'd be able to keep up with this woman. Then that damn vibration started again.

"What in the hell is that?" I asked, pulling away from her.

She fiddled with her belt again, straining in the darkness to pull something out from under her jacket. Then she got it loose and held it up, straining to see in the orangeish lights of the parking lot.

"It's my beeper," she said. "I've got one of those silent, vibrating ones."

"Oh, jeez, and here I thought we were about to explore some bizarre way to do it that I'd never heard of."

"Hush," she said, "I'm trying to read this. Oh, hell, it's dispatch. C'mon."

She turned and walked quickly away, all business now. We got to the Porsche; she leaned over the left-front quarter panel and disarmed the car alarm, then opened the driver's door and jumped in. She unlocked the passenger door electronically and I climbed in slowly, savoring the sensation of being in a car that was worth more than the house I was living in now.

While I settled back into the soft leather Marsha dialed a number on the car phone. I leaned toward her, nestled my head in her right shoulder.

"Dr. Helms here. You paged me."

I rolled my head down and nipped her playfully on the shoulder. She jerked and pushed me away with her free hand, then covered the mouthpiece. "Quit that," she hissed.

I snaked my arm around her waist and pulled her toward me.

"Okay, patch me through," she instructed.

She leaned her weight against me, letting me squeeze her softly while she waited. "You're driving me crazy," she whispered. Then back to her doctor voice: "Yeah. Okay. When? Right."

Then she stiffened and sat up straight in the seat. "Have they got it under control?"

That got my attention.

"Okay, on my way."

She switched the car phone off and placed the receiver back in its cradle.

"What is it?" I asked.

She turned to me, her eyes dark and piercing. "Somebody torched the Old Hickory Evangelical Church of Christ about an hour ago. They found the preacher's body in one of the offices in the rear."

I sat up straight, suddenly stone-cold rock-hard sober.

"Madison?" I asked, aghast. "Jewell P. Madison?"

"Yeah. The body's partially burned, but whoever killed him botched the job of burning the evidence this time."

She twisted the key in the ignition and the Porsche fired to life. "It seems," Marsha said in her Dr. Helms voice, "that glass and chrome won't burn as well as wood."

She turned to me. "Buckle up, cowboy. We got some ridin' to do."

Chapter 19

I'd never seen a Porsche redlined before. Marsha took the long curve of the ramp off the freeway toward the Ellington Parkway at about sixty-five in second gear, tires squealing, the low humping car hugging the concrete like some kind of burrowing animal. Once on the parkway, she really lit a fire under it and we were on Old Hickory Boulevard in about five minutes, through the interchange at Gallatin Road, then over to Lakewood in less than five more. She'd broken every speed limit and driving regulation in the book, but she'd done it like an ace fighter pilot, with skill and style. Most importantly, she'd gotten away with it.

She downshifted as we approached the flashing blue lights that blocked the road in front of the church. Beyond the squad car, a half-dozen lime-green pumpers of the Metro Nashville Fire Department lined the curb in front of the crystalline church. Down in the parking lot, beside the church on the far corner, a hook-and-ladder had extended itself high above the roof, and a single fire fighter on top was spraying down the shingles. Other bursts of blue light rhythmically flashed against the kaleidoscope of white, yellow, and red. Just outside the perimeter set up by the fire fighters, the television news vans had already set up their cameras and their microwave towers, along with the haphazardly parked cars of the investigators and the detectives. This would be the leadoff story on every newscast in town tomorrow.

A uniformed officer approached the window as Marsha lowered it.

"Sorry, ma'am, this road's been—"

Marsha flipped open a leather ID case. "Dr. Helms from the ME's office."

"Oh, sorry, ma'am," the young officer said. "Just go on through."

Marsha rolled the window up and eased past the roadblock. "That's *Doctor* Ma'am to you, bud," she said tiredly.

We pulled into the church parking lot, then she took a hard right and went to the farthest corner of the lot, which was empty and dark. She turned to me, her face barely visible against the glow of the dashboard lights.

"I think it's better if you stay here," she said quietly.

"Okay," I said.

"It's not that I'm weird about our seeing each other or anything."

"Hey, you don't have to explain."

"I just, well—I want to keep my private life and my professional life separate."

Her hand rested on the gearshift knob. I laid mine on top of hers and squeezed. "Don't worry about it. I'll be fine. And I agree with you. It's better if nobody knows I'm here."

She smiled, leaned over, and kissed me. "I won't be long. The investigators have been on the scene for a while. They'll be nearly done. I just have to make the pronouncement, do a preliminary examination."

"Great," I said. "Don't worry. I'll be fine."

She reached behind the seat and pulled out a small bag, then leaned over and brushed her lips across my cheek.

I watched her in the dim light as she headed toward the circus of activity surrounding the church. From the outside, the damage appeared to be minimal, most of it probably the smoke-and-water type. Certainly it was nothing like Will

Elmore's house; no great exploding conflagration, no structural collapsing into ashes and rubbish.

Funny thing, I thought, sitting there in the car alone, the Reverend Jewell P. Madison would have been near the top, if not the top, of my private suspect list. There's not a bigger fall from grace than that of a man of the cloth caught with his knickers down. Just ask Jimmy Swaggart or Jim Bakker. Jewell Madison's motivation was inescapable; if the reverend's sexual peculiarities ever became known, it would be more than disgrace. It would be catastrophe, the ruination of a lifetime's efforts.

People have killed for a lot less.

Maybe it was the fact that I didn't like the man that made me distrust and suspect him. I've got little patience with fundamentalist zealots, especially ones with their own satellite network. Something about a rich man going through the eye of a needle, I think . . .

One thing was for sure; I'd have to start looking in a different direction now, unless the Reverend Jewell P. Madison took it upon himself to set fire to his own church and then do himself in.

It was past midnight now and I was having a hard time staying awake. Marsha had been inside the church for over half an hour. I lowered the seat back into a semireclining position, closed my eyes, and drifted off in about ten seconds. My eyes wandered open just as Marsha was stepping out of the light and into the shadows surrounding the car. I groaned and stretched as she climbed in beside me.

"How'd it go?" I asked. She reached into her jeans pocket for the keys, then started the car, its low idling rumble secure and comforting.

She was silent for a moment, her face set. I'd never seen her on the job before, and realized that there was something inside her that she simply had to turn off in order to do what she had to do.

"I've seen worse," Marsha said finally as she put the car in gear and eased out of the parking lot.

I raised the seat back up and tried to shake myself awake. "They have the ID right? Was it Madison?"

"Yeah, it was him."

"I don't mean to butt in, but was he . . . was he murdered?"

She turned to me as we maneuvered our way through the roadblock and down the side street toward Old Hickory Boulevard.

"Yes," she said. "Probably head trauma, result of a blunt instrument"—she brought her hand up to the back of my head and rubbed a place just above and behind my left ear— "right about here."

I had a quick sinking sensation in the pit of my stomach.

"Burns didn't kill him. I know that. I'll have to run his blood gases, see how much smoke was in his lungs. Don't know for sure, though. That's just a preliminary. I'll perform the autopsy tomorrow morning. Which reminds me . . ."

Marsha picked up the car phone and held it up, watching the dial carefully as she kept one eye on the road. She punched in a set of numbers, then held the phone to her ear.

"Charlie? Marsha. Listen, we've got one on the way. EMTs are bringing him in. Yeah, homicide. Slide him in the cooler and start the paperwork. I'll be in around five to do the PM. We'll get some calls from the media on this one. . . . Yeah, that's right, no comment. Okay. Yeah, see you in the A.M."

She hung up the phone as we slowed for the traffic light at Gallatin Road. "How long had he been dead?" I asked.

"Few hours at most. Little hard to tell—the heat from the fire affects how the rigor sets in."

"Really? I didn't know that."

"Listen, Harry," she said, her voice nearly gone with weariness. "I'm going to have to pass on the rest of the night.

I've got to get some sleep. I'm the only ME in the shop tomorrow. I've already got an autopsy scheduled for eight, the rest of the day's booked, and the only way I'll get Madison processed is to work him in early.''

Work him in early, I thought. Sounds like a car-repair shop.

''No problem. You mind dropping me off at my car?''

''We'll be there in a few.''

A few minutes later we pulled into the nearly deserted parking lot of the mall we'd left just an hour and a half before. I leaned over, kissed her softly, quickly, knowing that we both needed, more than anything else, to get home and find some sleep.

''Good night, love,'' she murmured.

''Be careful going home.''

''Always,'' she said. ''You too.''

As she pulled away, the throaty purr of the engine rising and falling in time with the shifting of the gears, I realized I was supremely hacked off that Will Elmore's murderer was now interfering with my love life.

It was eleven o'clock the next morning before I came to again. Just over nine hours' sleep, and it only felt like a short nap. I woke up with that thick, sleep-fogged feel to my brain and my tongue; my dreams had been restless, uneasy, filled with images that left me unsettled even though I couldn't remember them all.

So many things in life, I thought as I lay there struggling for consciousness, were like dreams: hidden secrets, dark corners, frightening and threatening places that were often invisible and formless, but there as surely as a mugger behind a tree or in a dark alley.

I made a pot of coffee and realized that with the discovery of the Elmore letter and the murder of Jewell Madison, the fire had been turned all the way up under the pressure cooker. A quick call to Marvin Shapiro confirmed that.

"Yeah," he said nervously, his voice strained and tight. "I spoke with the DA's office this morning. They're going back into court to ask for an immediate hearing on the search warrant for the files."

"What does this mean in terms of Lanie?" I asked.

"I spoke with her this morning," he said. "She's calm, but barely. She wanted to go ahead and release the files, but as executor of the estate, I can't go along with that even if it would mean a lessening of suspicion on her."

"You can't? Why not?"

"There's a little problem here, Harry, called malpractice. The law is a little unclear on this. Not too many shrinks get murdered where it looks like one of their patients did it."

"But why malpractice?"

"There's a pretty good chance that Elmore's estate is going to be sued for malpractice as a result of the letter. His clients are going to figure Elmore was breaching confidentiality and sue the stew out of the estate. On top of that, I'm not even sure if Elmore's malpractice insurance covers him after death. It almost surely does, but you know how insurance companies are. If there's any way they can weasel out of covering the claims, they'll do it."

I struggled against the fog to try to see the situation clearly, but that was impossible. "Let me see if I can't get this straight," I said. "We've got a bunch of pissed-off people out there, one of whom may be a murderer, who are quite likely going to bring a class malpractice action against Elmore's estate and the corporation for breach of confidentiality, while at the same time the threat of them being exposed is likely to bring an even bigger lawsuit? Right? The cops are after us, Elmore's patients are after us, and there's somebody out there still setting fires and whacking people up side the head."

"Yeah, that's about it. But I've got one ace up my sleeve."

"Which is?"

"I've gone out on the limb and called a few of the people mentioned in the letter."

"You've what?" I shouted.

"And told them privately that they need to have their attorneys file John Doe amicus curiae briefs on behalf of the patients and their confidentiality concerns. We get enough lawyers in that courtroom screaming that their clients are going to be permanently and irreparably damaged if those files are obtained by the police, then that might swing some weight with Judge Dore. We can argue that once the police get the files, they're on their way to becoming public record after the case is solved."

I calmed down and thought for a moment. "You think it'll work?"

"No, not really. But it may buy us enough time to get Lanie off the hook."

Time, then, that I was wasting standing around in my boxer shorts drinking coffee with half the day gone.

I showered and shaved, got dressed, then hammered the Ford to life and scooted downtown as quickly as possible. There was much work to be done.

Ray and Slim were down the hall with their office door open, strumming guitars in some kind of catchy melody. I walked quietly down to my end of the hall, knowing that I didn't have time to get caught up in any extended conversation. I locked the door behind me, then climbed up on top of my desk.

This time not quite as much dust sprinkled down on me as I slid the acoustic ceiling tile out of the way and retrieved Elmore's files. I slipped the tile back into place and brushed off the front of my shirt.

I carefully spread the files out in front of me, organizing the stack and placing each patient in his or her own place in the schematic. That took fifteen or twenty minutes, and when I finished, I stood back and admired my handiwork.

Okay, what do I do now?

I sat down and stared for a while. Then when I was finished with that, I stared awhile longer.

This was no good. There had to be a better way. I couldn't really approach any of Elmore's clients; I'm not supposed to know who Elmore's clients are. If I go tracking down his clients, then I'll betray myself as well. On the other hand, these files in and of themselves, while certainly enlightening, weren't doing me much good. If only I could open up one of them and find that one of Elmore's patients had been diagnosed a homicidal maniac arsonist who'd threatened to kill his therapist . . .

But that would be too easy, right? And if it was easy, everybody'd be doing it.

There was one way, though. I picked up the phone and dialed Marvelous Marvin Shapiro's number again.

"Yes, what is it this time?" he asked irritably after the secretary put me through. "I'm really busy today, Harry."

"Then stop fussing at me so I can stop wasting your time."

Another irritated sigh. "What is it?"

"I know I can't see Elmore's patient files. They're under court seal—"

"Only the police seem to think someone violated that seal," he interrupted.

"Who'd do anything that stupid?" I asked. "Besides, it doesn't matter. I don't need the files. But as your agent, in your employ, wouldn't it be all right for me to know who the patients are? That way I could represent to them that you, as executor of the estate, are trying to establish that none of Elmore's patients could have had anything to do with his death. That way the court can order the seal to remain. They'd cooperate then, wouldn't they?"

There was silence over the line for perhaps ten long seconds. "Well, I suppose so. As long as we can maintain confidentiality. Which means, Harry, that you don't tell anyone—got that, bud?—anyone—what any of those names are."

"Right," I agreed immediately. "Complete confidentiality and integrity. Keep in mind, Marv, this is my livelihood, what little there is of it, and I've got a reputation to protect as well."

"I've always believed self-interest was the best motivator," he said.

"Good basis to do business on."

"Right, so let's get going."

Another moment's silence, then another sigh, this time one of resignation. "Okay, you win. I'll make a call and arrange it. You'll need to speak to Mimi Webster over at Elmore's office. She's his private secretary and office manager. She can get you the names. But nothing else, you understand?"

"Gotcha," I said. "Just the names. Complete discretion."

"You're not to ask anything about why they were even seeing Elmore. That's out of bounds."

"Right. Anything else?"

"One other thing," he said. "The police get wind of this, you tell them nothing. This is all privileged. They take you in, call me straightaway. Got it?"

"Check, boss. All taken care of."

"Boss." He sighed one last time. "Why do I get the feeling that's a concept you've never quite grasped?"

Oh, I thought, if he only knew . . .

We hung up and I put my head down in my hands and tried to squeeze some of the tension out of my forehead. I thought of all the lies I'd just told Marvin, who was a nice guy and deserved better. But he's an officer of the court and I'm his employee, not his client; if he learns of a crime, he has to report it. No gray area here.

How, I wondered, did I get to be such a liar, not to mention burglar and thief?

Well, as Scarlett O'Hara said, I can't think about that today. I'll think about that tomorrow.

Chapter 20

Something cold went through me as I pulled into the parking lot of Will Elmore's building. I'd always wondered how bad guys felt returning to the scene of the crime; now I knew. I almost drove around back and went in by the rear entrance out of habit.

I fought the urge, though, and soon stepped out of the polished brass elevator onto the carpeted hallway leading to the offices of Psychology Associates. The afternoon sun faced the building now, shining hard and bright through all the tinted glass. It felt hot, stuffy, or maybe it was just my conscience getting to me.

I stepped through the door and up to the receptionist's desk. "Hi, I'd like to see Mimi Webster, please."

"May I give her your name, please?" the middle-aged woman asked, staring at me suspiciously, as if she'd seen me before. Which, of course, she had. Fortunately for me, and every other criminal in the world, people are generally too out of it to remember every face they happen to pass by during their busy days.

"Harry Denton," I answered amiably. "Mr. Shapiro said he'd call and let her know I was coming."

"All right, let me ring her. Just have a seat, please."

I was two articles into a worn, year-old copy of *People* by the time Mimi came out for me. I heard the door open to my right as I sat on the visitor's couch. I looked up as a stern-faced young woman, all business from head to toe, stood a step into the doorway glaring at me.

"Mr. Denton?"

"Yes," I said, glancing back down at an article on Bonnie Raitt. No wonder I wasn't paying attention . . .

It came to me after a moment that she was waiting for me to do something, like maybe get up and follow her into the office.

"Hi, I'm Harry Denton," I said as I approached her. "Did Mr. Shapiro get in touch with you?"

"Yes, follow me."

I did just that, stepping behind her through the door into the crowded pool of computer terminals and busy data-entry drones. "Looks kinda hectic around here," I commented, trying to make small talk as she led me through the maze of desks and filing cabinets. She didn't know I was already familiar with the path to Elmore's office, and it would be prudent of me to keep it that way.

"We're always busy," she said brusquely. "Of course, we were thrown for a couple of days after Dr. Elmore's death.

"But," she added, unlocking his office door and holding the door open for me, "life goes on."

Mimi Webster seemed exceptionally young to have such a cold regard of death, or maybe it's only the young who can be so callous toward it. She also seemed too young to be in charge; she couldn't be a day over twenty-five, and if she weren't so obviously anal, she'd be quite attractive. Light brown hair down to her shoulders with traces of red, pale skin, deep hazel eyes, thin, probably an aerobics buff and a diet watcher. There was a stiffness to her, though, a coldness that gave her an edge I didn't care to rub up against.

Besides that, however, I also got the distinct feeling she was hunkered down, somehow protecting herself. And I thought of Elmore's reputation as a ladies' man, and of the letter that was written to betray him.

"Nice office," I commented. As if I hadn't seen it before.

She shut the door behind us and flicked on the overhead. "Dr. Elmore appreciated quality," she said. "In fact, he tolerated *only* the best—in his surroundings and from his people."

I turned, looked her over from the far side of the room. "How long had you worked for him?"

She crossed her arms and stood there a moment, as if trying to decide if she cared to answer that question.

"Lighten up," I said as she stared at me. "It's not like I was asking your shoe size or anything."

I started to say bra size, but I had a feeling she wouldn't consider that funny. I wondered if there was much of anything she'd consider funny.

That did seem to crack a little of the veneer. "Three years. I started right out of college in Interviewer Support. Mostly keying in data. I double-majored—computer science and psychology. Intended to work here for a year or so before graduate school."

"But?"

She uncrossed her arms, walked over to Elmore's desk, and sat in his chair. "What can I say? Dr. Elmore recognized talent when he saw it. I've got superb organizational skills, which was an area Dr. Elmore was personally weak in."

"I see." I took a chair across from her. "So you wound up staying."

"More responsibility, a couple of promotions, a sizable increase in salary. He made it worthwhile."

"I'll bet he did."

She stiffened again. "What's that supposed to mean?"

"If you don't mind my saying so, you're awfully young to be so in charge."

Mimi Webster sat up straight in the chair and shuffled a stack of papers in front of her. "Dr. Elmore promoted from within. He recognized effort and ability, regardless of age."

"And that's what made him so good to work for," I said, staring straight into her as hard as I could.

She blushed slightly, a reaction I hadn't exactly expected and didn't know how to interpret. "Dr. Elmore was a good employer," she said softly, a hint of something approaching regret in her voice. "None of us wanted to see anything bad happen to him. There are twenty-two people on staff here, many of whom had passed up other opportunities to stay."

I leaned back in the chair, trying to give the illusion of being relaxed. "I guess you knew about the letter."

"The letter?"

"You catch the news last night? Or the morning papers?"

"Oh, yes, the letter," she said numbly. She ran a hand through her hair carefully, so as to achieve the effect people desire when they're uncomfortable, but not so as to mess it up. "I did hear something about that. Some talk among the other girls."

"Yeah, terrible, isn't it? I wonder if it's got anything to do with that preacher fellow getting killed?"

I figured she was too young to be that cool. I was right.

She blanched, her voice caught in her throat. "Yes, that was terrible."

She shuffled the papers again, then straightened the stack, pulled the top page off, and handed it across the desk toward me.

"Names, addresses, phone numbers," she said, attempting without much success to patch the veneer. Her eyes wouldn't meet mine. I let her hand remain there, stuck in midair, the paper standing stiffly out.

"The police are going to figure the motivation for Elmore's murder was somewhere in that letter."

Her hand shook, just a bit, but the movement traveled through the paper and caused it to vibrate sharply.

"It'd be too bad if the police were to make the wrong assumptions about the person who wrote the letter."

"What assumptions?" Her voice shook. She let the paper fall to the desk and removed her hand.

"Such as the person who wrote the letter wanted to see Elmore murdered. Or"—I hesitated—"maybe even did it themselves."

She sucked in a quick gasp of air.

"Of course," I continued, "that'd be quite a jump to make. Certainly to prove. But the police are persistent."

Mimi Webster appeared to be struggling for control. I reached across and picked up the piece of paper, a motion that caused her to scoot back in the chair as if I were going to haul off and slap her.

Spellman, I thought, wouldn't take long to crack her.

"Then again, it'd be my guess that whoever wrote that letter probably had some pretty good reasons for wanting to see Elmore disgraced. After all, he wasn't exactly Albert Schweitzer. But wanting him murdered? No, I doubt it. My guess is that it was just a misguided gesture that got out of hand.

"Wouldn't you agree?" I asked, almost as an after-thought.

She raised her head to me, her eyes filmed over in tears. I had this urge to put my arm around her, to tell her it was going to be okay. She was just a kid, and the reality was that Elmore probably bedded her, then tried to buy her off with a promotion in lieu of any real kind of commitment. For all I knew, she loved him. Women sometimes love stinkers. Then I remembered my own life and realized men sometimes do, too.

"I'm sure," she said, "that whoever sent the letter certainly didn't want anything like this to happen."

"Yeah, you're right. I almost wish I could talk to the person who sent that letter. Know what I'd tell them?"

She shook her head. "What?"

I pulled out one of my business cards and wrote down a

name and number on the back. "I'd advise them to call this number and speak to this man. He's a good lawyer. He listens to people. A real human being. Tell him Harry said to call. Then I'd lay it all out and let him handle it. He can probably have a word with the cops, set it up so he goes in on the interview. I'd tell whoever wrote that letter to tell the truth, lay it all out piece by piece. Then you know what I'd do?"

"What?" She seemed to shrink in the chair.

"I'd forget it, chalk it up to a hard knock. Take a long, hot bath, maybe a glass or two of wine, and get a good night's sleep. Then I'd get up the next morning and start all over. What's done is done and can't be changed. That's what I'd tell them to do."

I slid the card across the desk and left it there halfway between us. She made no move toward it. I stood up, folded the single sheet of paper, and stuck it inside my jacket pocket.

"But then again, it's all imaginary, ain't it . . . ?"

"What?"

"Since I can't talk to the person who sent the letter, I mean."

"Oh, yeah."

"Thanks a lot for all your help, Ms. Webster."

She removed her focus from some imaginary place in front of her and looked back up at me. "Oh, sure, and please, it's Mimi."

"Okay, pal. Call me Harry."

I opened the door and walked through it. I was halfway across the room when I heard her voice behind me.

"Excuse me, Harry?"

She was leaning against the doorjamb, her face much softer now than the first time I saw it.

"Yeah?"

"Thanks. I mean it."

Damn, I thought, take the edge off her and she really is quite a looker.

I smiled. ''No charge.''

I'd have tipped my hat to her, only I don't wear one. I walked back to my car feeling like I'd just made one small step toward restoring my karma.

Chapter 21

Sometimes in life you know things, but you don't *know* things. I had no reason whatsoever to think that Mimi Webster hadn't killed Will Elmore. She was pretty, young, intelligent, hardworking; none of these disqualified her from being a murderer. The Almighty's book was no doubt full of pretty, young, intelligent women who'd been dumped by older men and sought the final, ultimate revenge.

But sometimes you just had to go with your guts, and my guts told me that Mimi Webster didn't burn him. Her rough veneer was just that: veneer. And beneath the veneer her core was soft Georgia pine, not ax-handle-hard Tennessee ash. And, I'd discovered, the facade simply cracked too easily.

One mystery, though, was solved. Mimi Webster had written the Elmore letter, had in her fury and her hatred for the man who betrayed her decided that if she couldn't destroy him physically, she'd take a shot at ruining him professionally. It might have worked, too, if someone who hated him even more hadn't gotten to him first.

There was one other piece of this part of the puzzle I wanted to solve, and for that I'd need a telephone. As I pulled to a stop before the traffic light at West End Avenue and Twenty-first, I glanced to my left where some middle-aged, blonde real-estate-agent type had a car phone mated to her ear as she sat there with her Mercedes idling.

Damn it, I thought to myself. Why am I so damned broke?

Just then, I envied her that car phone, and a car that would idle steadily at a stoplight without requiring the driver to gingerly tap and release the accelerator pedal in just the right rhythm to avoid stalling.

The light changed and the Mercedes shot away. I put the Escort in gear and felt the clutch slip as the driver behind me jerked forward impatiently. I signaled a right turn and circled into the pizza-joint parking lot on the corner.

Inside, I ordered a large Coke to get change for the pay phone, then huddled against the corner with the receiver to my ear.

"Hello," Lanie said.

"Hi," I said. "How are you?"

"Well, I was wondering if you were going to call again. Thought maybe you'd left town."

This time I figured she was seriously ticked, although trying hard to hide it. I pretended I bought her teasing as just teasing.

"Not a chance. Life's too exciting here. Have you talked to Marvin today?"

"Not since he called this morning. I don't know, Harry, at this point I'm just numb. I keep expecting the police to show up at my door and tell me they found my fingerprints in that church somewhere."

"Is there any chance they'll do that?" I asked.

She sighed. "Oh, Christ, Harry, get real. The only time I ever saw the man was at Will's funeral."

"I don't think you've got too much to worry about, Lanie. As the police get further and further into this mess, I don't think you'll continue to be much of a focus to them."

"I'm glad to hear you feel that way. Marvin's not so sure. He says I need to get a criminal lawyer, and that if my predicament gets much blacker, I'll have to. Only problem is—"

"I know, you can't pay one."

"Justice doesn't come cheap."

"Lanie, tell me," I said. "I met Elmore's office manager today. Got some information from her that Marvin authorized. We're going to try a slightly different tack in all this. Level with me. What's your read on Mimi Webster?"

The very next word out of Lanie's mouth, I thought, would let me know.

"Snippy," she said, her own voice tightening to quite a degree of snippiness. "I thought she was obnoxious. A know-it-all. She was the Peter Principle in action."

"Why did Will keep her on?" I asked.

"It always mystified me. Maybe she *had* something on him."

It was a measure of how shell-shocked Lanie was that she wasn't even hearing her own words. If she had, she would have figured out the source of the Elmore letter as fast as I did. But I'd solved that part of the puzzle; Lanie didn't know about Mimi's writing the letter. If she had, she wouldn't have been able to hide it. That, at least, meant Lanie had been straight with me on that account.

"One thing, though," Lanie said. "After this is all over and I'm in charge of that office, you can bet there's going to be some housecleaning."

I'll take that bet, I thought. Sure winner.

The West End rush hour had begun early that day, and to worsen matters, the sky had clouded over and a cold, slow drizzle had begun falling. I bumped along in first and second gear all the way down to the I-40 entrance ramp, then crossed over the freeway. Slowly I made my way from traffic light to traffic light all the way to Second Avenue, a revitalized area known among locals as the District, then made a left and was lucky enough to turn just as a pickup truck loaded with what looked like Christmas trees pulled out of a slot.

Christmas trees, I yelled inside my head. *Hell's bells, it's not even Halloween yet!*

I banished that grim thought and grabbed the parking space before somebody decided to shoot me for it. I stepped out into what had grown from a drizzle to a steady, gloomy autumn rain and pounded quickly up the sidewalk the better part of a block and ducked into the Fugazi Gallery. I ran my fingers through my hair, pushing it straight back and squeezing out as much water as possible. I wished I'd brought an overcoat, but truth is, I hate to wear the damn things. I hate umbrellas, raincoats, and galoshes as well. I'd have made a lousy British private detective; Aruba for the winter, I think, is more my style.

An exhibit of local artists filled the first floor of the gallery. A huge Polly Cook tile painting filled one wall, the broken, jagged edges of the tile running throughout the portrait of a just-married couple in ceramic blues and grays like a nightmare filtered through a cracked mirror. Other artists' work occupied the rest of the walls and floor display stands, but the haunting Munch-like visage of the starkly rendered married couple dominated the room.

I couldn't take my eyes off it.

I heard soft footsteps on the carpet behind me and turned, the rainwater soaking through my suit jacket like icicles now. Chopped black hair, white pancake makeup, black lipstick, black turtleneck, black fingernail polish, black workout tights—hell, black everything stared at me.

"You're soaked," she said.

"Sorry. I'll stay away from the paintings."

"Please do. Can I help you?"

"The City Arts Commission offices still upstairs?"

"Yeah."

"They still open?"

She turned, looked at a clock on the wall, which read in Day-Glo oranges, bloodreds, and neon blues, 4:15. "Fifteen minutes," she said, her voice so hollow I wondered if she wasn't the shell of a piece of art herself.

"Stairs back through here?"

"They were this morning." She turned away and walked off. What is it with young people today, I wondered, that makes them eager to become corpses?

I cut through the back room, refusing to be distracted by anything else, and pushed open a heavy double door leading to a back stairwell. The stairwell revealed in cruel detail the building's former identity as a warehouse. Dust, exposed red brick and plumbing, and the faint smell of mold assaulted the senses. The gentrification and revitalization of the downtown area had only penetrated as far as the facades, with the soul of the city still camouflaged beneath all the hype.

A hand-lettered sign read CITY ARTS COMMISSION, with an arrow pointing up. I took the stairs two at a time.

The City Arts Commission was actually a misnomer; it wasn't really part of the city government, although it had received a small stipend during the previous Mayor's administration. That mayor had been a well-educated and cultured man, he and his wife both prominent patrons of the local arts scene. The man who'd succeeded him, though, our current mayor and Elmore patient Terrence Durrell, probably had fuzzy paintings of dogs playing poker on his living-room wall. This meant the City Arts Commission's stipend had not shown up in this year's budget, which had reduced the nonprofit agency to renting space above a struggling gallery down in the District.

A gray steel door with a wire-reinforced window stood blankly in front of me at the top of the landing. Another hand-lettered sign confirmed I'd come to the right place. I pushed open the door and walked into a stark, depressing office that brought home just how much that Metro government stipend was missed.

The City Arts Commission had fallen far and hard in the

lean years of the early Nineties. Battleship-gray surplus furniture with torn cushions sat around gathering dust. A
scratched metal desk stood mute and unattended. A framed
poster from the commission's exhibit at last year's Summer
Lights Festival hung on the wall crooked and neglected.

I cleared my throat. There was no one in the outer office.
Paper-shuffling sounds, followed by the scrape of metal chair
on linoleum, answered my throat clearing. An elegant
woman, perhaps five-eight, with salt-and-pepper hair and
shiny skin, stood in the doorway. She was attractive in the
way that cultured, older women can be, with a certain porcelain finish to her looks. She wore a gray skirt and matching
jacket, which were set off by stockings and high heels. What
little makeup she wore had been expertly applied and heightened the sense she gave of being from old money. She could
have been a corporate executive steeped in success, except
for the drab surroundings and the general air of decay.

"May I assist you?" Nancy Weeks Johnson asked. I tried
not to let myself be distracted by the description of her contained in the Elmore letter. It was hard to imagine this sophisticated and impressive woman bingeing herself on
laxatives and emetics. It was equally difficult to imagine her
engaging in some of the sexual gymnastics that Will Elmore
apparently found so amusing.

"Ms. Johnson, I'm Harry James Denton. We met several
years ago. I was doing a story on the Arts Commission and
its support of local artists. You had awarded a series of grants,
I believe."

I realized that I was standing there in an off-the-rack suit
that had seen better days. I tried to straighten my wrinkled
lapel and to retighten the knot of my necktie. My clothes
were wet, clammy, dark. My efforts were useless.

"Of course, Mr. Denton, I remember you. From the
newspaper. How can I help you?" She stepped forward and
clasped her hands together in front of her. "Since we've

largely had to cease operations, I can't imagine what interest we might be to your newspaper. Unless you're writing our obituary, of course.''

"No, Ms. Johnson. I'm not with the paper anymore. I'm here on an entirely different matter.''

I reached into my jacket pocket and retrieved my ID as Nancy Weeks Johnson's unspoken question worked its way onto her face. "I'm a private investigator now,'' I explained, holding the license toward her. She reached out and took it from my hand and carefully examined it. "I've been retained by the estate of Dr. William Elmore to try and get a few questions answered. Privately, of course.''

She folded the license case back up and held it out to me. If my mention of Will Elmore had unsettled her, there was no visible evidence of it. Unlike Mimi Webster, this was a veneer that would not crack so easily. I detected hardwood at Nancy Weeks Johnson's core.

"Very well. What can I do for you?'' she asked, her voice steady, unwavering.

"Are we alone?''

"My volunteer secretary left at four.''

I trembled with the cold as the wet clothes began to feel like they were plastered to my skin. The temperature inside was dropping as fast as outside.

"Ms. Johnson, it's raining like hell. I forgot my coat this afternoon and I'm drenched. You don't have a room in here anywhere that's got some heat, have you?''

She studied me for a moment, then decided, I suppose, that I wasn't a serial killer. "In here,'' she instructed, stepping back into her office.

Once through the door, I spotted the small electric space heater glowing red in the corner and shot straight for it. I leaned down, spread my hands out in front for a moment, then stood back up, the backs of my legs warming deliciously.

"Thanks. I appreciate it."

"You're welcome. Just don't catch on fire. Now tell me, Mr. Denton, why you're here."

"I'm here because it's a matter of extreme concern that the patients and former patients of Dr. Elmore be protected. I don't know how much you're aware of what's happened since Dr. Elmore's death, so I can bring you up to speed by saying that the attorney for the estate has sought a court injunction against the police search warrant. The estate wants Elmore's files sealed permanently."

"I'm aware of *all* that," she said. "My own attorney has recommended that we become part of some kind of class action on behalf of Will's patients."

"I'm sure your attorney knows best. My purpose in being here is that I've been retained by the estate to see if I can establish that none of Dr. Elmore's patients could have had anything to do with his death. All considerations of client privilege and patient confidentiality extend to me. Once we're able to give that assurance to the court, we hope to be able to keep those files sealed."

The clicking of expensive heels on linoleum was my answer. Nancy Weeks Johnson crossed to her desk. She sat in her high-backed leather executive's chair that apparently was left over from the days when the commission had money, and swiveled around away from me. I kept my place, standing in front of the space heater—partly out of the need for heat, partly from a sense that she didn't want to talk to me face-to-face.

"You know what you're playing with here, don't you?" Her voice was low, almost threatening.

"Ma'am?" I asked.

"Let's not try and obstruct each other's vision, shall we, Mr. Denton? You've seen the letter, haven't you? You almost have to have."

I hesitated, then decided what the hell. "Yes, ma'am, I've

seen the letter." I don't know why I kept doing that; ordinarily I'm not the most mannered person in the world. Nancy Weeks Johnson just seemed like the kind of woman you always called ma'am, and you always used all three of her names.

"Then you know that I—we—had all the reason in the world to kill Will Elmore. He betrayed us in the cruelest way. We all went to him for help, and he exposed us to people as if we were sideshow freaks."

"Yes, ma'am," I said after a moment. "He did that. It was unconscionable."

"It was more than unconscionable," she said sternly, spinning her chair around and facing me once again. "It was savage. What kind of man could he have been? What kind of twisted, cruel . . ."

I shook my head. Something told me that this woman was not going to forget this, and that Lanie better not start spending her inheritance. Not just yet.

"Will Elmore's clients included some of the most prominent and powerful people in Nashville," she said. "Once word of that letter got out, he was finished. My guess is the state ethics board probably wouldn't have even gotten involved. The risk of publicity was too great. I think that eventually it would have been arranged for Elmore to quietly close his practice and leave the state. Let him go somewhere else and ruin other people's lives."

"Yes, ma'am, that's possible." I offered.

"But that's neither here nor there," she said finally. "The matter before us now is whether or not I killed him. Last Friday night, I was at the symphony until ten-fifteen with a gentleman friend. I won't give you his name. It's none of your business. If the police want it, I'll have to give it to them. But you're not the police. Here is my ticket stub."

She reached over the side of her chair and retrieved an expensive-looking large leather purse. She snapped it open, went immediately to a certain compartment, and retrieved the stub. I stepped over to her desk and took it from her.

Section C, Row J, Seat 11: first level, dead center, ten rows back. No big surprise . . .

"After that, we went to Arthur's in Union Station for a late dinner. You can confirm that if you like. I didn't get home until well after midnight. According to the newspaper and television accounts, I'd have to be a lot more versatile than I am to have driven all the way to that part of town, murdered Will, then set up such a monstrous fire."

"Versatile, yes," I said. "Superman, no."

Her eyes blazed as hot as Elmore's house for a second, then calmed immediately. "That's also not my way," she said. "No matter who did it, the death of Will Elmore has not compensated me for the pain and suffering his actions have caused. As Dr. Elmore's estate will learn . . ."

I handed the stub back to her.

"Furthermore, your questioning me in this manner," she added calmly, "has, in my opinion, been harassment. Which has, of course, only aggravated the preexisting pain and suffering."

Something told me Nancy Weeks Johnson's beloved Arts Commission was soon going to have its funding restored, only not by the Metropolitan government of Nashville, Tennessee.

"I'm sorry you feel that way, Ms. Johnson. I certainly haven't meant it as harassment. As I told you, the estate's sole interest is protecting Dr. Elmore's patients."

"The estate's sole interest," she said sternly, "is protecting itself."

I walked toward the door. Yeah, the estate is only interested in protecting itself, just like you. "Thank you for your time, Ms. Johnson," I said, turning to her one last time before leaving. "Have a nice day."

Which was something I imagined her not having many of.

As I took the staircase back down toward the rain, I couldn't help thinking of what she told me, that she'd gone to Arthur's for dinner Friday night.

Arthur's: that's a lot of money to spend on a meal, only to go home, lock yourself in the bathroom, and stick your finger down the back of your throat.

Then I felt very small for thinking that.

Chapter 22

The rain had stopped, but the temperature had plummeted. I couldn't recall it ever snowing this early in the year, but it sure felt like it was ready to tonight. Rush hour was in full bloom now, the mud-splattered cars lined up all the way from Broadway up the Second Avenue hill to the courthouse. The shock of the cold was abrupt and painful, and the prospect of fighting the traffic about as inviting as electrolysis.

I huddled in close to the brick storefronts to avoid as much of the wind as possible and bundled myself down to Laurell's, the oyster bar down the Avenue from the Fugazi Gallery. I slipped inside, grabbed a table near the window, and sat down alone, staring out into the grayness of the traffic and relieved to be in safe from it.

The warm brick and polished oak of Laurell's was a welcome break. A young blonde, long white apron over her jeans and T-shirt, stepped over, pen and pad poised for action.

"Getting cold out there, isn't it?" she commented cheerfully. I was anything but cheerful, but the warmth of her smile bled off enough of my bitchiness to make me civilized.

"Yeah, and I got drenched earlier. Now I'm freezing."

"Here." She held out her hand. "Let me go hang that jacket up next to the fire for you."

I was as grateful as if she'd just delivered my Publishers Clearing House check. "Thanks, Nurse, and may I please have an Irish coffee and a bowl of gumbo as well?"

I worked my way out of the jacket and handed it to her. "Sure," she said sweetly. "Be up in a minute."

And it was, delivered as advertised. Ordinarily I don't eat soup. Childhood prejudice, I guess. I only got soup when I was sick. I always knew that when my mother started pulling out cans of Campbell's chicken noodle I was as sick as I felt.

This day, though, was perfect for it. And for the first time in days I felt safe and secure and isolated from the world. A regular cup of coffee followed the Irish as I sat there thinking, watching the endless parade of honking cars, the squealing of wet brakes, the occasional zany slide on the soaked pavement.

Midway through the second cup, I walked over to where the waitress had hung up my jacket and took out my pen and a small notebook that's always in my jacket pocket. I sat back down and opened the pad to the next clean page.

Nancy Weeks Johnson, I wrote at the top of the page, then summarized my interview with her. She seemed to me a woman who would quietly and discreetly cut your heart out if she had to, although she would always maintain that edge of civility in her voice as she wielded the knife. She'd had the deep Southern twang bred and educated out of her; hers was more of a Virginia patrician accent than Tennessee native. But in every other respect, she was the classic late-middle-aged former Southern belle, a woman who could in the same breath plan a bridge party for the girls and run a billion-dollar-a-year corporation. I knew from my days at the paper that the demise of the Arts Commission had nothing to do with her management skills. It was more a sign of the times. When people are worried about bankruptcy, and believe me, some of the wealthiest people in Nashville fear precisely that, it's hard to maintain enthusiastic support of the arts.

I scratched off Nancy Weeks Johnson's name from my list. One suspect at a time, I was figuring out who hadn't killed Will Elmore. That would have been more frustrating than anything else, except that I'd lived much of my professional life by what I called the Edison Axiom: it can be just as valuable to know what doesn't work as what does.

I slapped the notebook shut and looked at the clock over the bar. I was surprised to find that I'd been sitting in Laurell's for two hours, oblivious to the growing dinner crowd and the fact that the restaurant could really use my table. It was one of the few remaining vestiges of Southern grace that lingering over coffee in restaurants was sacrosanct, and that no restaurant would demand its table back as long as it was still in use.

Still, though, I'd had enough to eat, and one more Irish coffee would render the evening unusable. So I thanked the waitress for saving my life and health, tipped her far more than I should have, then retrieved my now dry and warm jacket.

The Ford didn't appreciate the cold any more than I did, but it did finally agree to get me back up to Seventh Avenue, where I parked it in the nearly empty garage and scooted across Seventh and into my office building just before the cold drizzle started in again.

The building was empty, even Ray and Slim's usual guitar strumming happy hour already over. It was a night to be locked away warm and cozy, and I wondered why I wasn't as I stood up on my desk and shoved ceiling tiles out of the way once again. I pulled down Elmore's files, then replaced the tiles carefully.

I pulled out Nancy's file and reread it, what I could understand of it, that is. The problem was that Elmore's scribblings were largely indecipherable. Elmore didn't keep extensive session notes; that much was evident from the sparseness of the files. In fact, I thought of the few times Lanie and I had seen him in marital counseling, and I couldn't remember him even having a notepad in hand. Maybe he dictated or made notes after we left, but I never saw any evidence of it. Maybe therapy was like anything else; once you'd done it long enough, you didn't need to take notes. You remembered and used what was relevant and the needless you let slip by.

Take Nancy's notes, for instance. There were a few scratches about her ex-husband, and some notes about what Elmore described as a *family system*, with a drawing of names and connecting lines. From what I could gather, Nancy Weeks Johnson had suffered some form of sexual abuse as a child, that she had serious self-esteem problems, that control was one of her *issues*, and her bulimia had been intermittently serious throughout her adult life. This tortured woman, who appeared so together and in control, was, in fact, caught up in something that had made her life miserable since adolescence.

I found myself intensely curious and intrigued by this catalogue of human misery, and wished that I understood more of what I was reading. As night settled in over downtown I pulled the shades on my office, loosened my tie and my belt, and settled in to study the files once again, searching for some clue as to who might have enough human misery in them to brutally murder another human being.

Hours passed, with the handwritten scribbles finally blurring into an endless line of photocopied ink. Frustrated, I sat up, tossed aside the bipolar bank president's file on which I'd just spent fifteen bewildering minutes, and stood up. I'd been through every file of every prominent active patient Elmore had. I stretched my arms way over my head and bent back as far as I could without falling over.

At the far corner of my desk was a stack of papers that I

hadn't yet studied. I'd made the assumption all along that whoever killed Elmore had to fear public exposure, and that the only patients Elmore would find amusing were people that everyone in his circle knew. What would be the point, I wondered, of going to a party at the Belle Meade Country Club, tossing back a few Stoli martinis, and joking about the sexual habits of some truck driver from Flatrock?

But maybe there was something else. Elmore was into power, prestige, status. If you were a famous executive, politician, or entertainer, you got right in to see him. So why would he have taken on a patient who didn't fit the mold? Why would Dr. William Elmore, for instance, give a good goddamn about a truck driver from Antioch? Let him go to a public mental-health clinic where they charge on a sliding scale.

So who were these people? Who were Thomas Sturges, Rocky Ludlum, Pierce Huntley, Melinda Groves, Angel Slaughter, and Bruce Miller? And why would the shrink-to-the-stars agree to see them?

I picked up the first file off the stack: Thomas Sturges. Thomas, it seemed, was practically one of my neighbors. He lived down in a neighborhood bordering Shelby Park in East Nashville. I'd not spent much time in that area since moving to this side of town, but the park and the surrounding area was mostly gentle rolling hills bordering the Cumberland River and older homes inhabited by blue-collar families that had been around for generations. Mixed in were a few professionals, lots of retired folks, and as the East Nashville Arsonist had been pointing out for the past year, a growing community of gay and lesbian gentrifiers.

Thomas Sturges was twenty-nine-years old, five feet eight inches tall, one hundred and ninety pounds—bit of a chubby, it seemed—and still lived at home with his invalid mother, Virginia. A note on the intake form indicated that he had an IQ of 142 as measured on the Cattell Intelligence Test, yet he apparently had only a high-school education. His father, an old-line cop back in the days when the city and county had separate governments, had been killed when Thomas was eight.

Another observation noted that at the age of fourteen, he had experienced the first of a series of episodes of *psychogenic fugue*, whatever that was, and that at the age of seventeen, he had been briefly hospitalized. Thomas Sturges, it would appear, was a mess.

I turned to the next page of his file, and realized that in the onslaught of paper, I had somehow missed this sheet. On it, someone, presumably Elmore, had drawn a diagram. There was a large circle in the middle, with the initials T.S., and around the center circle a network of other circles, like this:

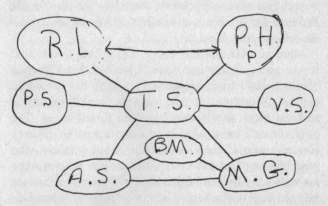

"What the hell?" I whispered. Some circles were bigger than others, some connected by lines to each other, some not. All but the second smallest were connected to the center circle. I went back to the first page and scanned the information in the intake; there was no indication of what the circles might be. Was this Thomas's family? The *V.S.* could be Virginia Sturges, but who was the *P.S.* out to the side? And what were the other circles? Who was *P.H.—P*?

Inside a box on the first page, the typed words *Primary Dx* were followed by a line. On this line someone had handwritten in *300.14*. Below that was a second line, *Secondary Dx*, with a still-blank line in front of it.

It was a mystery locked inside a code, scribbled by dead fingers in a shorthand that they alone knew.

I was stalled, completely stalemated. I picked up another file, this one belonging to Pierce Huntley. Unlike Thomas Sturges's file, the intake on Mr. Huntley's file was only partially filled in. I gathered, though, that what we had here was a thirty-two-year-old male professional, a father with five children, who had been under a lot of stress lately. No address or phone, though. I'd have to track him down. On the line for his *Primary Dx* Elmore had filled in *300.14* as well, with the second line filled in *311.10*.

None of this made any sense, and it didn't seem that it was going to anytime soon. I wished that I knew a doctor I could trust, someone I could go to who would explain all this stuff to me, someone I could rely upon to keep quiet about what I needed to tell them. The only shrink I knew outside of Elmore was Dr. Sidney Hughes, who I interviewed once about a fellow who pled insanity and got away with it when he murdered his wife's family and buried all six of them in a manure pile out behind the barn. Only problem was, when Sidney wasn't doing his private practice, he was serving as consulting psychiatrist for the Metro Police Department. And somehow I didn't think he'd be too understanding of my ripping off a colleague's office.

No, that wasn't the answer. There had to be someone else. If I only knew . . .

Then it hit me. I did know another doctor, some-

one I could trust. Someone who'd never let me down
before. Someone I felt I could call on if I got in trouble.

Marsha.

Chapter 23

The phone rang six times before Marsha's sleepy voice picked up. "Yeah," she muttered.

"Code Blue, Doc, how's it going?"

"Arrghh," she moaned.

"You already asleep?" I glanced at my watch. "It's only eight-thirty. Hell, I'm still at my office."

"What do you want to bet you weren't at your office at five this morning?"

"I'm sorry, lady. Didn't mean to wake you. I didn't realize that was for-real lights out."

"It's not," she grumbled. "I fell asleep watching a movie on cable."

I thought for a moment. Probably better to ring off than keep her up, but I knew I wasn't going to get a wink's sleep tonight until I got some answers. It was the same sort of compulsive bent that made me a good reporter and at the same time kept me in constant trouble.

"I need your help on something. Can I come by?"

"Oh, Harry, couldn't it wait? I was too tired to even eat dinner tonight."

"How about I bring you something?"

"I don't want anything," she complained. "I want sleep."

"Aw, c'mon," I whined in about four syllables.

"Don't activate that Denton charm on me," she warned. "I haven't got the strength for it right now."

"I'll bring over a nice bottle of wine. We'll have a glass, talk for a few minutes, then I'll split and let you get to sleep. Please, it's important."

"Well, if it's important enough for you to say please, then it's probably a matter of life or death."

"Not quite that important."

"But it probably is the only way I'll ever get you off the phone. Right?"

"That," I said, "is probably accurate."

I could have asked my questions over the phone, but the truth was that I wanted to see her and maybe just needed a good excuse for it.

I gathered up the files into one neat pile and laid them down in my briefcase. I locked the case, trying to decide what to do about it. For the time being, I figured it was best not to have it with me. I didn't need the files for Marsha to help me; in fact, it was probably better if she didn't see them.

The streets were slick and glistening, the cold settled in for the night. The air felt heavy, laden with moisture that could easily turn into one of the earliest snows in memory. I pulled my collar up around my neck and clenched my teeth against the cold as the Ford ground its way to life.

At least icy nights drive most of the traffic indoors. The streets were gloriously empty and I managed to hit most of the lights just right. Within twenty-five minutes I was knocking on Marsha's door.

She answered in a bright green jogging suit, her hair pulled back and tied with a scarf. There were dark circles under her eyes and she'd scrubbed all her makeup off, and I felt grateful that she felt okay about leaving it that way.

"How'd you get here so fast?" she asked as I stepped inside. Over in the corner, the fake gas logs were burning deep blue and cherry. The room was cozy.

"On fleet-footed longing for you, my dear."

Marsha turned as she led me down the hall into the kitchen.

"Oh, puh-leeze," she drawled, taking my hand. "Let's go sit in front of the fire."

I let her lead me into the living room, which was sunken a couple of steps down from the rest of the apartment. We settled into the couch next to each other. I reached down and pulled my shoes off. As I sank into the pillows, her softness and warmth next to me, I felt as if I could stay there forever. Let the damn East Nashville Arsonist burn down the whole city; just leave me alone with Marsha right here, with the doors locked and the rest of the world at bay.

"Okay, Sam Spade," she said, "what's so all-fired important?"

"To begin with, I don't want to put you in a bad place," I said. "Not ever."

"And I gather you're afraid this might do that."

"Maybe."

"Okay," she said. "Let's take it a step at a time. I smell a bad place coming on, I'll let you know."

"Those are okay ground rules by me. First of all, I'm in a little deeper with this business of the Elmore murder than I've told you."

"Okay," she said cautiously. "I knew you were working for your wife."

"Ex-wife," I said. "And I'm not working for her. Not technically. And when I say I'm in deeper than I've let you know, I didn't mean personally."

She shook her head slowly. "All right."

I placed my hand on her leg and squeezed her just a bit. She let it stay there.

"Technically I'm working for Marvin Shapiro, the executor for Elmore's estate. The biggest reason for that is that it preserves confidentiality. Marvin says the attorney-client privilege extends to me when I'm working for him. Maybe it does, maybe it doesn't. But that's the way I'm playing it for now."

"Okay, still with you."

"Good." I smiled at her. "I hope you stay that way. But what I mean by attorney-client privilege is that there is some information I can't divulge."

"There are probably things I'm better off not knowing."

"Oh, darling, if you only knew. But my problem here is that I've obtained some info that I think is going to help. I'm not sure how, and I'm not sure why. But there's more at stake here than just William Elmore's murder. My hunch is that Madison's murder is tied in as well."

Her eyes widened a bit.

"The problem," I continued, "is that the information I've got is of a medical nature, and to tell you the truth, I just don't understand it. Why can't you doctors speak English?"

"Because we don't want just anybody in the club," she said, smiling. "You should understand that."

Then her smile disappeared. "What kind of information have you got?"

"Well, on diagnoses, and case notes, for instance—"

"You've seen diagnoses?" she gasped. "And case notes? There's only one way you could've seen those, Harry. I do watch the news, and I do talk to cops. You—"

I held two fingers to her lips. "Shhh," I said. "If you don't say it, you haven't asked me anything. And if you don't ask me anything, I don't have to answer anything. That's a part of this conversation that just didn't happen. Let's keep it that way."

I pulled my hands away from her face. "Okay?" I asked.

Her eyes flicked back and forth nervously. I could see her inserting Tab A into Slot B and finding that the pieces fit together better than she expected.

"Okay," she said. "What information do you need?"

I thought for a moment. "Well, there's a bunch of terms that I don't understand, but I can research them at the library, I guess. What I don't understand is that on what I guess you'd call an intake form, there's always a place that says *Primary Dx* and a number, then *Secondary Dx* and sometimes another number, sometimes not. I figured the *Dx* is doctor shorthand for diagnosis.''

"It is," she said. "You've got a primary diagnosis and sometimes secondary ones."

"But what about the numbers?"

"Those came out of the ICD-9-CM."

"The what?" I asked. "Would you do that again? In English?"

"Yes," she said, exasperated. "Most doctors use diagnostic shorthand codes from the ICD-9-CM, which is the clinical revision of the International Classification of Diseases, ninth revision. But as a clinician, Elmore would probably have just had on hand the DSM-III-R, which is the revised third edition of the *Diagnostic and Statistical Manual of Mental Disorders*. Same code numbers, but just for the head.''

"The Diagnostic and Statistical Manual of Mental Disorders," I repeated slowly. "Boy, have you got a mind. . . . "

"Yes, I have, and thank you for noticing. In those two manuals, virtually every emotional and mental disorder is assigned a code number so that everybody in the field agrees on how they're labeling people. It's also a shorthand for providers and insurance companies.''

"So if I have a DSM number for somebody, I can look up in this manual and see what's wrong with them.''

"Yeah, in a clinical, broad sense. It won't give you the gory details, and as you know, every person is different. But that'll paint a reasonably accurate picture.''

"That explains why the notes are so short," I whispered absentmindedly.

'The what?''

"Oh, nothing, nothing at all. Marsh, have you got a copy of this *DSM-R2D2*, or whatever the hell it is?''

"The *DSM-III-R*." She laughed. "And no, I wouldn't have any use for it. Except maybe to find your number."

"Babe, you've got my number."

She scooted over next to me and put an arm around my shoulders, then pulled me closer. "That's *Doctor* Babe to you," she said.

"Right, Doctor Babe."

"You know, I always had a feeling you're the kind of guy who'd take a few chances if he had to. But I never thought you'd do anything like—"

"Hush," I said. "For all you know, I haven't done anything. And that's the way it's going to stay."

"All the same," she whispered, "it's kind of exciting. In a demented sort of way."

Our faces were about an inch apart. "Well," I said, "you told me you were tired tonight. Maybe I should go."

"Not yet," she said. "You owe me."

"Yeah?"

"Yeah."

"Want to take it out in trade?"

She smiled. Then I felt myself slide toward her as gently and as easily as if we'd been cast from the same mold. Her face filled my view as she kissed me, softly at first, then harder until we were sweetly and tightly mashed together. We kissed for a long time, and I felt this wave sweep over me, and I understood why back in those old black-and-white movies from the Forties, back before they could show naked people heaving away at sweaty sex, filmmakers always used the image of waves crashing over a lonely beach whenever they wanted to tell the audience that two people were about to make love.

So I shut the world out and let the waves crash over us until there was only blackness and the delightful relief and oblivion of sleep.

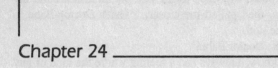

Chapter 24

I felt a shuffle of movement somewhere around me and the soft scrape of shoes on carpet. I told my brain to signal my eye to open, an effort akin to pulling scabs off my eyelids.

The room was dark, except for the soft glow of the bathroom light sneaking in. I heard the shuffling sound again, and a pair of long legs in stockings, high heels, dark skirt passed before my eyes. I rolled over and looked up.

"Hi," I said.

"Oh, didn't mean to wake you," Marsha whispered. "Go back to sleep."

"What time is it?" I asked. No light came in from the windows.

"A quarter to six," she answered.

"In the morning?" I gasped.

She giggled. "Yes, I can see you're not an early riser."

"Hell, we just got to sleep."

She came over and sat next to me on the bed. I brought my arm out from under the comforter and slipped it around her waist. This nest was soft, warm, safe; I wanted her back in it with me.

"Come back to bed."

"I've got a seven o'clock appointment with a dead person," she said.

"So be late. The stiff won't mind."

"But Dr. Henry will."

Dr. Henry was Henry Krohlmeyer, the chief medical examiner for Metropolitan Nashville and Davidson County. He was a forensic genius, Marsha's idol and mentor, and a notorious stickler for punctuality and paperwork. I knew as soon as she brought him into the picture that I was fighting a losing battle.

"Okay," I said, resigned to being up before the sun. "Just give me a minute."

"No," she said, pushing me back down with her right hand. "Back to sleep with you. Doctor's orders."

"But I—"

She brought her left hand up and opened it. In the palm of her hand were two keys.

"It's about time you had a set of these," she said. "The gold one's the dead bolt, the silver one's the doorknob."

I stared at her palm for a second, then looked up at her sleepily. "You sure?"

"There's a clean set of towels and a washcloth in the bathroom for you. I found a spare new toothbrush. It's the blue one in the holder next to mine."

I moved my head down and scraped my stubbly jaw against her silk skirt, then rubbed the small of her back for a moment.

"If you're sure . . ."

"I'm sure. For now, anyway. Listen, I've got to go. Roll over and go back to sleep. Just lock up when you leave."

She bent down and kissed me on the forehead, which was probably the only safe place to kiss me if she didn't want to be grossed out. Even coroners have their limits.

"Okay, Doc," I said, rolling back over as she stood up. Her footsteps on the carpet slipped away from me, and in a moment I heard the shutting of a door and the click of a deadbolt lock.

I reached behind and retrieved the two keys, which were held together by a twist tie like the top of a garbage bag. I snuggled into the pillow and smelled her hair next to me. The keys were hard but warm in my hand.

As I let myself drift back off to sleep, I thought of all the keys I'd had in my life. No one ever gave me keys quite like these.

The main branch of the public library, the Ben West Branch, didn't open until eleven A.M. More budget cutbacks. So I drove by a fast-food place and got a cup of coffee, breakfast, and a newspaper. I sat there lazily reading the paper, trying hard to focus on today's events rather than last night's. It's weird, you know, after a divorce you think you're never going to get involved or committed to anyone else again, and you're both glad and relieved to have come to that conclusion. Then you meet somebody else and you think you're just going to have a good time. You know, a few laughs, a night out, occasional decent sex. Then something happens and you realize that whatever that profound, unexplainable human drive to latch up with somebody else is, you've still got it.

It was frightening. I tried hard not to dwell on it, without much luck. But I had the keys to Marsha's apartment now; it felt like a big step.

Enough of that sort of thing, I finally decided, and finished the newspaper, relieved to find that there had been no other torchings or murders beyond the daily quota of normal street killings. A second cup of coffee and a good stretch and I was ready to deal with reality.

Back at the office, Ray and Slim were pounding away on some song so hard it sounded like they were going to bust a few guitar strings if they weren't careful. Not like their usual stuff at all. I stopped at the top of the stairs for a second, debating left or right, then finally turned right and headed in their direction.

I rapped on their door a couple of times and the music stopped.

"Yeah?" Ray's voice was deeper and more clipped than usual.

I pushed the door open. "What's up, boys?"

Slim sat quietly in the corner, an acoustic guitar resting in his lap, his right leg crossed over his left knee. Ray sat behind the desk, with what he called his work guitar across the tops of his thighs.

"My pucker factor," Ray snapped. "Harry, this ain't exactly the best time in the world to drop by."

"Sorry." I backed away. "Didn't know it was a bad time."

"Don't pay no attention to him," Slim, who normally had few words to say to anybody, apologized. "He's just hacked 'cause we lost the cut on Garth's album."

"Aw, guys, I'm really sorry," I said truthfully. "What happened?"

"We never really had it," Ray explained. "That slimy dog who told us we did turned out to be one of Garth's roadies. A roadie, for chrissakes. Said he got the song to Garth and it was a done deal. Turns out there ain't no such thing as a done deal, least not till the check clears."

"I've always been told it's a brutal business, Ray. I'm sorry."

Ray broke a weak smile. "It's okay, Harry. We'll live. All it cost us was a case of beer. But it looks like we're gonna be neighbors awhile longer."

"I can live with that. See you later, guys."

I shut the door behind me and walked down the hall to my own office. For the moment I was glad the only thing I had to deal with was arson and murder.

There was the usual dearth of messages on my answering machine. I either needed some new customers or an extension on my retainer from Marvin Shapiro. The constant pressure of cash flow was beginning to take its toll on me. I already lived as cheaply as I could, as I ever had, in fact. I wondered where else I could cut back.

I picked up the telephone and got a dial tone; at least the phone company hadn't cut me off yet. I flipped through my Rolodex and found the number for the reference desk at the library, then waited patiently through ten rings before somebody answered.

As I expected, the library had a copy of the *DSM-III-R*, but it was in library reference and couldn't be checked out. I'd have to sit there in the reference section and use it.

Back on top of my desk again, I slid aside the ceiling tiles with the ease and dexterity that practice had given me. The stack of files sat safely undisturbed on the metal framework above the ceiling. I retrieved them and replaced the tile.

I wasn't comfortable carrying them around with me, but there weren't a lot of other options. If Spellman had someone following me and they decided to stop me on the street for a search, I was dead in the water. I hoped I was just being paranoid, although I've always considered a good measure of paranoia healthy in today's world—more a reflection of reality than anything else.

I locked the papers in my briefcase and shut my office door behind me, then headed down the stairs and out the building. The sun was out, a cold, crisp clear autumn day, and I decided to walk the several blocks over to the library rather than hassle with finding another parking space. Office workers on early lunchtime and downtown shoppers filled the sidewalks, while the first few Christmas decorations were beginning to fill the store windows. I felt almost lighthearted and carefree compared with the way things had been since Elmore's death. Already the images of that night, the shattering of glass and the fiery collapse of the grand old mansion, were receding from my memory.

I cut right off Church Street and walked up the hill to the library entrance. Outside, the usual contingent of street peo-

ple loitered on the sidewalk, huddled in out of the wind in
front of the massive gray and glass building.

The woman behind the business reference counter retrieved the *DSM-III-R* and handed it to me. It was a thick,
bright blue, heavy paperback volume. I thought, as I carried
it to the farthest, most hidden table in the corner of that
section of the building, how odd it was that of all creatures,
only humans felt the need to categorize their misery.

I sat with my back to the wall and opened the briefcase,
retrieved the first file, then closed the lid back. I settled back
in the padded wooden chair and opened the manual, hoping
that somewhere near the front the authors would explain how
to use the book in a way that made sense to a barely informed
layman.

I managed to get enough deciphered to start looking things
up. The first file off the stack, lo and behold, was the very
late Reverend Jewell P. Madison's. Let's see, primary diagnosis 301.81, secondary diagnosis 302.20.

I thumbed through the manual and found the index at the
back, then scanned the list of diagnosis codes. 301.81 was
something called *Narcissistic Personality Disorder.* I flipped
back through the book until I got to that section, then read
what seemed to me a textbook description of someone like
Madison:

> "People with this disorder have a grandiose sense of
> self-importance. . . . These people are preoccupied with
> fantasies of unlimited success, power, brilliance, beauty,
> or ideal love. Self-esteem is invariably very fragile. . . .
> This often takes the form of an almost exhibitionistic need
> for constant attention and admiration. . . ."

Yep, I thought, sounds like your garden-variety televan-
gelist to me.

I grinned despite myself. This still had a certain naughty

feel to it, almost as if I looked up my own code number, it would be filed under the section labeled *Voyeur*.

On to Madison's secondary diagnosis: 302.20. Back to the index, scanning down the page, let's see here.

Ah, yes, Pedophilia. So the letter was right; Reverend Madison did have a thing for young boys. I decided to pass on reading all the details of this particular disorder. I knew the essentials.

The next three hours I spent huddled over the files without a break, finally beginning to wonder exactly what all this research was buying me besides an understanding of just how damn crazy the whole world was. The wealthy, the prominent, and the powerful exhibited, by these accounts, a whole bucketful of mental kinks, knots, bumps, bruises, obsessions, compulsions, peccadilloes, weaknesses, imperfections, and emotional blemishes. Dysthymia, panic disorder, bulimia nervosa, fetishisms of every imaginable variety, kleptomania, adjustment disorders, sleep disorders, anxiety disorders, gender identity disorder, organic delusional syndrome: the list went on and on, a dismal catalogue of all the curses inflicted upon humankind because of our ability to think and feel and remember our sufferings.

After a while it got to be downright depressing, and that certain naughty thrill that I'd gotten seeing someone else's dirty secrets wore off very quickly.

By the middle of the afternoon I had worked my way through the sixteen patients whose names I was familiar with, to little effect beyond wishing I could take another shower.

The only ones left were the six ordinary, anonymous clients who were least likely to have anything to lose. Wearily I picked up the first file: Thomas Sturges, Primary Diagnosis 300.14, no secondary diagnosis.

Funny thing, I thought, thumbing through the last of the files. Unlike with his more prestigious clients, Elmore hadn't even bothered to fill in all the information on the intake forms of these last six clients. Only Thomas Sturges's form had an address listed, for instance, and only his had the names of other family members. The rest of the files were just a name, a short description, and a diagnosis. Plus Thomas's file had the strange circles and connecting lines. The rest of the other five files consisted mostly of some drawings, apparently done by the clients. The drawings seemed dark, intense, troubled, and, in the case of Rocky Ludlum's file, violent. Bruce Miller's file was full of infantile, badly rendered drawings, which befitted the age Elmore had listed on his intake: eight.

Weird. Then I noticed every one of the last six had the same primary diagnosis: 300.14. Now a few of his other patients had similar diagnoses as well; dysthymia, for instance, seemed to be a common diagnosis for the women clients. Given that dysthymia was characterized by a kind of low-grade depression and irritability, combined with things like low self-esteem, low energy, and general yukkiness, that made sense.

But what was 300.14? I opened the manual and, feeling like I knew the book well enough by now not to have to bother with the index, thumbed through until I found 300.14. And when I did, something in my chest clutched like a runner's side stitch four miles into a five-mile race.

300.14 was Multiple Personality Disorder.

When I read through the description, the cramp in my side not only didn't go away, it got worse.

"The essential feature of this disorder is the existence within the person of two or more distinct personalities or personality states," the book explained, and later: "At least two of the personalities, at some time and recurrently, take full control of the person's behavior. The transition from one personality to another is usually sudden (within seconds to minutes), but, rarely, may be gradual. The transition is often triggered by psychosocial stress or

idiosyncratically meaningful social or environmental
cues.''

I didn't know what the hell an idiosyncratically meaningful social or environmental cue was, but it sounded serious.

I read the full section, understanding most of some of it,
less of the rest. What was clear, though, is that each of these
people had suffered an emotional or physical trauma early in
childhood that was so severe, so horrible, that the only way
they could survive was to disassociate. It was like having the
lights on, but nobody home. To cope with the terrible events
in their lives and the awful pain, each one of them had created
other people within themselves, people that could handle the
terror and the agony.

How in heavens name had Elmore managed to find six of
them?

I wished he'd kept better notes. This had to be a find of
considerable importance. Real MPD appeared to be rare,
that much I could infer from what I'd read. For Elmore to
have found six of them . . . Holy Christ, what a mother lode
of anguish.

I turned back to Thomas Sturges's file, and the diagram
with the circles and the lines. *T.S.* was in the middle. That
had to be Thomas. *V.S.* was on one side; again, that was
probably his mother. Then there was a *P.H.* and an *R.L.*
across the top, with lines to Thomas in the middle. On the
bottom was an *A.S.* and an *M.G.*, with a tiny *B.M.* between
them, connected only to them and not to Thomas.

Who were these people?

I picked up another file, Rocky Ludlum's, and stared at it.
He was a 300.14 as well. And Angel Slaughter, and Melinda
Groves, and little Bruce Miller. Jeez, you'd think he wouldn't
be old enough to . . .

Something caught in my throat.

Pierce Huntley.

P.H.

Rocky Ludlum.

R.L.

"Oh, my God," I whispered. At the table next to me, a dirty, ragged man with a grease-stained face and a tow sack full of something that smelled awful answered: "Yes, my son?"

I ignored him. Angel Slaughter. A.S. Melinda Groves. M.G. Something cold ran through me.

There weren't six clients. There was only one. Thomas Sturges was six people, and Will Elmore had kept a separate file on each of them.

I leaned back in the chair and rubbed my eyes. This was something I'd never expected. The trail had meandered and drifted and wandered from one place to another, meaningless and unfocused. And then, somehow, I'd taken a step that led someplace different and new. I didn't know what it meant, but I sure as hell intended to stay with it.

I took the six files and spread them out on the table in front of me, no longer concerned that anyone would see them.

Pierce Huntley, primary diagnosis: Multiple Personality Disorder; secondary diagnosis: 311.00. I searched the manual until I found it. 311.00 was Depressive Disorder Not Otherwise Specified, which from the description sounded like real bummed out but doesn't fit anywhere else, we don't know what to do with you, and it usually accompanies some other bad stuff.

Pierce Huntley, the thirty-two-year-old father of five. What do you want to bet his five children all lived inside Thomas Sturges's body, and that Pierce was the father Thomas never had?

Melinda Groves, sixteen, primary diagnosis: Multiple Personality Disorder; secondary diagnosis 312.00. Let's see, that makes her a Conduct Disorder, Solitary Aggressive Type. This meant, I gathered from the text, that she was a bad seed from the get-go. She could steal, lie, and be physically violent if the mood struck her. And, as a scrawled note in her file indicated, she also engaged in what Elmore euphemistically referred to as *inappropriate sexual behavior.*

Angel Slaughter, twenty-two, primary diagnosis: Multiple Personality Disorder; secondary diagnosis: 302.79/302.73, a two-parter. I flipped through the pages. Poor Angel was afflicted with a combination of Sexual Aversion Disorder and Inhibited Female Orgasm. Another of Elmore's notes indicated that Angel was suicidal as well. What do you want to bet she and Melinda don't get along very well?

Bruce Miller, the eight-year-old boy. His was easy. Secondary diagnosis: 309.89, Post Traumatic Stress Disorder. Bruce was the tiny little boy-child inside Thomas Sturges who never got past whatever awful series of events fragmented him all to hell and back in the first place.

That's four, with Thomas being the fifth file. Only one left, Rocky Ludlum, who had a double secondary diagnosis as well. I searched the manual until I found 312.34, and that cramp in my side went off again.

312.34 was something the shrinks called Intermittent Explosive Disorder, and it meant what it sounded like. According to the *DSM-III-R*, Rocky Ludlum could experience "discrete episodes of loss of control of aggressive impulses resulting in serious assaultive acts or destruction of property."

I wasn't too sure, but I took that to mean Rocky Ludlum would beat the shit out of you in a New York minute.

In my concentration, I'd momentarily forgotten where I was. I stopped for a second and stared off at the people crowded around the library tables. School had let out and most of them looked about high-school age.

I wondered what we were doing to our children and had a feeling we were producing whole new crops of Thomas Sturgeses every day.

The file lay in front of me, only one code left to look up. Rocky Ludlum had a second secondary diagnosis written on the margin in a different color ink. A later addition, it was 312.33, which seemed remarkably close to the other one. It was, in fact, on the next page. And as I turned the page and saw the bold subheading, my heart jumped into my throat, locked itself up solid, and it was all I could do to keep from crying out.

312.33.

Pyromania.

Chapter 25

Now I knew. I knew who the East Nashville Arsonist was; had his name, his address, everything but a picture of him. And I knew who killed Will Elmore, and I knew why. Will Elmore, who wouldn't ordinarily have given a rusty freak about some blue-collar yo-yo from East Nashville, jumped on this like he was Madame Curie and Thomas Sturges glowed in the dark. Why wouldn't he? I'll bet there's not one psychotherapist in a thousand that ever sees an MPD this clearly defined in an entire lifetime's practice.

I knew all right. Finally I knew.

I've never been so scared.

For one thing, Thomas Sturges was an unpredictable and violent man, clearly homophobic and prone to explosive fits of temper. He could burn and he could kill. If he could murder Will Elmore, and almost certainly Jewell Madison, then he'd ice me without breaking a sweat.

And I couldn't tell anyone. If I went to the police, I was certain to be arrested for B&E, burglary, contempt of court, and any other damn thing Howard Spellman could think of to throw on. At the very least I was going to lose my license, and at the very most I was going to be enjoying an extended vacation on Brushy Mountain with the likes of James Earl Ray.

My sense of paranoia suddenly bloomed into overwhelming, and it seemed like everyone in the library reference room was staring at me. I quickly stacked all my illegal files back into a single pile and locked them away in the briefcase.

"Thank you," I whispered to the reference librarian as I placed the *DSM-III-R* on her desk and got out of there as quickly as possible.

The three blocks back to my office seemed to take forever. I flinched every time a coat sleeve brushed mine or an oblivious passerby happened to get too close to me. It was late afternoon, cooling off and getting dark fast. I scooted across Seventh Avenue and into my building, my heart racing like someone was gaining on me.

At the top of the stairs, I could hear brighter music coming from Ray and Slim's office, but decided the last thing I wanted was to make small talk with anyone. I fumbled nervously with the keys to my office and finally got the door unlocked.

I was cold, almost shaking, and decided a cup of hot tea might warm me up and give me something to do all at once. I washed my cup and refilled it down the hall, then plugged in my stinger and dropped it in the water. While I waited for the water to boil, I pulled out Thomas Sturges's file again.

I struggled with the scrawl on the first page after Thomas's intake form and managed to make part of it out: "Subject denies report of extreme physical and emotional abuse by mother, although an interview with his social worker indicates abuse was chronic, extreme, and long-term. Social worker also said neighbors reported that when subject was early adolescent, thirteen–fourteen, he became heavily involved with a local church, and that the pastor of the church later resigned and left the state after being accused of molesting several children. Subject denies molestation by the preacher, but social worker believes it happened."

Jesus, I thought, this poor guy has enough emotional baggage to sink the *Queen Mary*.

My water boiled, so I dropped in a tea bag and unplugged the stinger, then hung it carefully over the side of the desk to let it cool. I sipped the tea slowly, letting it warm me up from the inside out, as the night-lights of the city slowly grew in intensity outside my window.

Where was he?

I looked again on the intake form for his address. I didn't know the area well, but my sense as a relative newcomer to East Nashville was that it was a marginally dangerous part of town; dark and foreboding at night, a few dope deals going down here and there, an occasional rape, a murder every now and then.

I picked up the phone on impulse and dialed his number. Three rings later a female little old lady voice answered.

"Hello," I replied calmly, a film of sweat erupting on my palms. "May I speak to Thomas?"

"He's not home yet. He doesn't get off until eight tonight."

Before she could ask who's calling, I said, "Thank you, I'll call back," and I hung up quickly.

A little over three hours before he got home. That almost had to be his mother, Virginia. Okay, I thought, I'll go talk to Virginia. See where she's at. I was playing this out blindly, all by myself. I couldn't go to the police, and there was nobody else to fall back on.

I planted the briefcase back in the ceiling and locked the office up. The drive down Church Street, then across to and around the courthouse took forever. I'd hit rush hour right at its peak. I joined the long parade heading over the river and managed to keep the Ford from overheating until I could go right on South Fifth Street, and then down past the old, closed Metro workhouse. Beyond that, a road ran parallel to the river and snaked through an area of warehouses, factories, and industrial plants, eventually winding its way around to the back entrance of Shelby Park.

A park ranger had set up a radar trap at the entrance to the twenty-mile-an-hour-speed-limit park, but I'd slowed down enough to get by him. This part of the park was almost deserted, but at the far end the lights on the ballfields indicated something was going on.

I turned up the hill before I got that far, though, and went back out onto a street of older houses that faced the river from the top of a long sloping field of grass. The homes were tiny, jammed in together with barely a shoulder's width between them, all seemingly shuttered against the night's chill and the heavy darkness.

I drove slowly down the street until I came to the Sturges house. I pulled onto the shoulder, stopped the car under the massive cover of a century-old maple, and doused the headlights. The neighborhood was deadly quiet, the only streetlight the one on the corner three houses down.

I tightened my tie and ran my fingers through my hair, pushing it back and hoping I looked reasonably professional. I wanted to talk to Virginia Sturges, not scare her to death, and it was my guess that it wouldn't take much to get people in this neighborhood to pull out the old trusty Smith & Wesson if you even looked like you might cause them problems.

I climbed the flight of cracked, buckled concrete steps up the incline of the front yard to the decaying wooden steps of a high front porch. Cautiously I made my way up through the darkness to the porch and knocked on the front door.

The porch light next to me flashed on. Through a pulled curtain, I saw the dim outline of a body slowly making its way toward the front door.

"Yes," a voice inside called.

"Mrs. Sturges," I said firmly, "I'm sorry to be dropping by so late, but I was hoping I could have a word with you about your son, Thomas."

I reached inside my jacket pocket and retrieved my ID case. There was a clattering as Mrs. Sturges fiddled with the lock and cracked the front door just a bit. A security chain kept it from opening any wider.

I held my license up, hoping she could make out the official-looking piece of paper and my gold badge pinned in the case next to it.

"Mrs. Sturges, I'm Harry Denton. I'm an investigator hired by the estate of Dr. William Elmore to look into certain circumstances regarding his death. It's come to my attention that your son Thomas was a patient of the doctor's, and the estate has asked me to contact the families of all of Dr. Elmore's patients."

A wrinkled face and a dark eye with a garish purple circle under it stared out at me.

"Tommy's not home right now," she said.

"I understand that, ma'am, but may I speak with you?"

Her voice deepened, became almost guttural. "What's he done?"

I tried to soften my own voice, make it warmer, more relaxed. "I don't know that he's done anything," I said. "We're only trying to make sure that all of Dr. Elmore's patients have their rights as patients protected. May I come in, please?"

The eye flicked from my license to my face. "Okay, I guess so. Hold on."

The door closed and I heard the rattle of a chain being unlatched. Then the door opened wider and I pulled aside the wooden screen door and stepped in. Mrs. Sturges was behind the door, as if protecting herself, and pushed it to after I stepped in.

She was a thin, bony woman, her shoulders bent with the ravages of osteoporosis. A black cane was held in her left hand, her hands wizened, drawn, and covered in liver spots. A circular network of lines surrounded her mouth, almost as if she'd spent her life with a tense, stern pucker on her face.

"Thank you, Mrs. Sturges."

"Go in there," she instructed.

She motioned with her cane toward a doorway on the far

side of the living room. Flickering light from a television set jumped around the doorjamb. I stood aside to let her go first, but I guess she preferred not to turn her back on me. We walked through the dark living room, me in front, and into what was a small, cramped den.

She motioned me to sit on a wooden chair in the corner, then set herself down on a faded velour couch in front of the muted television. The room was stale, as if it hadn't been aired out in months, and the heat was turned up uncomfortably high. The remains of a half-eaten frozen dinner lay coagulating on a TV tray pushed to one side of the room.

"What's he done now?" she demanded. Her body was going, but there was a hardness to her voice that was still intact. It was a hardness that seemed to me based in meanness, though, rather than strength.

"Like I said, Mrs. Sturges, I don't know that he's done anything. Have you been watching the news, though? The news about Dr. Elmore's murder?"

"I've seen it."

"Then you know the police want to see the confidential patient files of all of Dr. Elmore's patients. Needless to say, the estate feels those files should be kept secret."

She stared at me, her cloudy eyes narrowing as the blues and grays of the television light crackled across her face. She said nothing, so after a moment I went on.

"I've been hired by the estate of Dr. Elmore to do some checking into Dr. Elmore's patients' whereabouts the night of the murder. If we can make the claim to the court that none of Dr. Elmore's patients could have possibly had anything to do with his death, then perhaps we can keep these files locked up where they belong."

She sniffed and wrapped her hand tighter around the handle of the cane. "I knew it was a bad idea to go to that doctor. They're all wicked, all evil. I tried to talk to Tommy, but he never listens to me. He's bad, too. He said he needed to talk to somebody. He should've talked to me. I'm his mother. If he's got a problem, he should talk to me."

What could I say to that? "Yes, ma'am, I understand—"

"I brought him into this world," she interrupted, "and he's been a curse on me ever since. He tried to leave once, you know. Said he wanted to live by himself. I put a stop to that, fast. He disappeared once, you know. When he was just a boy. He was only twelve. Gone for two weeks. The police found him at a trailer park in Mississippi. He gave them the wrong name, said he couldn't remember how he got there. The liar . . . He'll burn for what he put me through. The ungrateful liar."

She almost spat the words out. No way was I even going to attempt to juggle the dynamics of this one.

"Well, ma'am, I certainly don't have any information on why Thomas was seeing Dr. Elmore. That's none of my business. I'm only interested in being able to tell the police that all of Dr. Elmore's patients were accounted for the night of Dr. Elmore's death and therefore the confidential patient files are none of their business."

"You mean you want to know everybody's alibi?"

"Well, I didn't exactly want to use that word. No one's under suspicion here. I'd like to keep it that way."

"What'd you say your name was?"

I took out one of my cards and handed it to her. "Harry James Denton, ma'am."

She studied the card. "It was Friday night. Tommy had to work until nine. I heard him come in around nine-thirty. I was already in bed. But I heard him in here watching television. Then I fell asleep. The next morning I looked in on him and he was asleep."

That wasn't an alibi, at least not for the time when Elmore was murdered. I decided, though, not to tell Virginia Sturges that.

"Then we don't have anything to worry about, do we?" I

asked as friendly as I could, then again, almost on impulse: "Just out of curiosity, ma'am, would you mind if I took a quick look inside Tommy's room?"

Her hawk eyes narrowed again. "Why would you want to see inside Tommy's room?"

"Well, I just thought it might help me understand a little more about him."

"Don't touch anything," she ordered after a moment's thought. "Tommy doesn't like to have his things touched. By strangers, I mean."

The tone of her voice was chilling, as if even in her hardness and her bravado, there was a part of something inside Virginia Sturges that feared her son as much as I did.

I wondered if she knew. Somehow I thought not. She was a twisted, mean old lady, and if she knew her son had done anything like what I suspected he'd done, she'd probably be the first one to turn him in, and with great delight.

"It's at the end of the hall," she said, indicating the door behind the couch that was the other way out of the small den.

I stood up and walked through the doorway, through a tiny kitchen with an ancient porcelain sink and an old Westinghouse refrigerator in the corner that looked like it needed a jump start. Past the kitchen, the darkened hallway continued down past a narrow bathroom, then stopped with a bedroom off to either side.

Neither bedroom, hers or Tommy's, had a door.

What must it be like to be nearly thirty years old and still sleeping across the hall from your mother, and not even be able to shut her out?

I drove that one quickly out of my mind and quietly entered Thomas Sturges's bedroom. Inside, a child's twin bed sat low to the floor, a plaid bedspread neatly covering it. Shelves nailed into the wall above the bed were covered in comic books and model airplanes. On the walls, heavy-metal rock posters depicted women in various stages of harness, adorned with spiked dog collars, and surrounded by guitar-wielding studs, dry-ice smoke wafting up between their legs. An enormous stereo system with a pair of massive head-phones connected filled a small table next to the bed. Across from the bed, so it would be the first thing he saw every morning upon waking, a life-size poster of a tattooed, bare-chested Ozzy Osbourne covered the entire closet door. Ozzy was standing, fists out and clenched, as fire erupted every-where around him.

And on another shelf nailed to the wall, chemistry books. A whole row of chemistry books. Chemistry, it seemed, was one of Thomas's great passions.

The hair on the back of my neck stood up. The bedroom was that of a fourteen-year-old psycho, although I'm aware that may be redundant.

I'd achieved my goal of getting a better sense of who Tommy Sturges was, so I flicked the light off. Down the hall, Mrs. Sturges sat staring at the silent television as if in a trance. I cleared my throat so as not to startle her.

"Thanks for your time, Mrs. Sturges," I said. "I've found out everything I needed to know. I believe we'll be able to protect Dr. Elmore's clients very well now."

"God," she mumbled softly, staring off into space like she was barely aware of my presence. "God protects us. What man has done, God can undo. *Mizzam sistus, homam sistus, mizzam sistus.* Mercy on us, Lord. Have mercy on us. . . ."

"One last question, Mrs. Sturges."

The old lady kept staring at the dancing light coming from the television.

"Mrs. Sturges?"

She shook her head slightly, as if entering the approach path to this planet. "Yes?"

"Where does Thomas—Tommy—work?"

Her eyes darkened and I knew she was back in the room with me. "The supermarket. He works at the supermarket."

"Which one, ma'am?"

"The Inglewood Kroger. He's been a cashier there for years."

"Okay. Thanks again for your time, ma'am," I said. "Please don't get up. I'll just show myself out."

She mumbled something else, but by that point I was halfway through the living room and reaching for the front door.

The cold outside was nothing compared with the cold that swept through me in the aftermath of Thomas Sturges's house. I stepped over to the car quickly, my senses alert and on guard to any noise around me. I locked the car door as soon as I was in and ground the starter until the engine caught.

I'd just put the Ford in gear when it hit me.

The Kroger, the Inglewood Kroger. Tommy S . . . The one who was so rude to the gay men.

"My God," I said out loud. "I know him."

Chapter 26

The next thing I remember was driving under the railroad bridge on the back side of Shelby Park and turning left on Riverside Drive. Fog had settled in over the Cumberland River floodplain and the houses near the river became enshrouded by silver.

Almost subconsciously I found myself driving toward the supermarket where Thomas Sturges, as his nameplate indicated, had been PROUDLY SERVING YOU FOR 10 YEARS. If what his mother told me was true, he still had an hour or so left of his shift. I could call Spellman, have him and a couple of uniforms meet me there. My guess is it'd take at least that many to hold Tommy down once he was caught.

But that little problem remained. If I called Lieutenant Spellman, I had to tell him how I'd discovered what I knew. And that meant trouble for yours truly. A little trouble I didn't mind; I could handle a little trouble, had been doing it most of my life. But this was serious.

If I thought Tommy was any threat to anyone, I'd do it. I couldn't sit on what I knew if it meant somebody else got hurt. As far as I could figure, though, Tommy had done what he had to do, and until the urge to burn out another gay gentrifier took him over—which by his past record would take some time—he would be laying low. His core personality would take over, either that or Pierce Huntley, the father

224

and protector, would go to work and take care of his mother and live out his days.

I knew, though, that it was a gamble. The demons would still be there. Sooner or later they'd fight their way to the surface. I had to stop him before they got there.

I had ten dollars that was burning a hole in my pocket, so I decided to stop at Mrs. Lee's and get a plate of Szechuan chicken rather than go home and scrape something out of the refrigerator. The day had been a long one, from the languid moment when I had awakened to the sight of Marsha's stockinged legs passing in front of my bleary eyes to that moment when I drove past the Inglewood Kroger and decided to pass on seeing Thomas Sturges. I was tired and needed time to think. A steady downpour had begun as I rounded the curve at Riverside Drive and I learned for the first time that the Ford had developed a roof leak. A steady drip fell on my left knee from the door seal as I drove.

I pulled into Mrs. Lee's and jumped in before the rain had nailed me too badly. Three of the tables were occupied; the other six were being cleaned by Mary Lee.

"Hi, Mary," I said, delighted as always to see her. Mary Lee brought out something new and unsullied in people, and right now I could use a dose of anything that wasn't twisted and ruined.

"Harry," she called brightly. "Where've you been?"

She walked over in her T-shirt and tight jeans, damp dishcloth in hand, and threw her arms around my neck. I hugged her back, but primly and properly, and smiled over her shoulder at Mrs. Lee as she came out of the kitchen.

"Weah outta chicken!" Mrs. Lee called the second she saw me.

"Doesn't matter," I called across the restaurant as Mary and I disengaged. "I promised this time I'd try something else."

I walked up the counter, Mary by my side smiling.

"Get back to woke," Mrs. Lee chided her daughter.

"Oh, Mama, they're all clean."

"Then go help yoah fadah," she ordered.

Mary smiled and tossed her dishcloth on the counter, then walked behind the cash register. "She's such a bear," Mary called lightly as she disappeared through the door.

"You a bad infruence on her," Mrs. Lee said. I couldn't tell if she was teasing or not.

"C'mon, Mrs. Lee, she's a great girl and you know it. If I could be guaranteed kids like her, I'd have a dozen of them."

Mrs. Lee leaned over and smiled. "You couldn't handle it. Take my word. Now what you want?"

"You pick for me."

She thought for a second. "I tink you like a Kung Pao beef."

"Go for it."

She was right. About five minutes later I bit into this spicy, sweet, wonderful concoction of beef and vegetables that completely took my mind off the cold and the rain and the crazies. I hung around until nine o'clock, until Mrs. Lee and her husband were locking up and heading for home in time for Mary to do her homework. We said goodbye in the parking lot, and I realized how much they had come to mean to me. My life had been altered so drastically over the past year of change, and while I missed some of the trappings that came with a high-visibility, high-stress career, I had to admit my new life gave me a freedom to enjoy people that I'd never had before. I'd always been in a hurry before, often without ever figuring out why. Life was different now.

Now the only thing I had to worry about was murder.

I chose to put that out of my mind for the time being and drove home. The message light on the answering machine was blinking, so I punched the button as I removed my tie.

"Hi, love," Marsha's voice said. "Are you as exhausted as I am? What a day. I'm thinking about you. If it's before ten, give me a call. Otherwise see you tomorrow."

I looked at my watch: nine-twenty. I punched her number up and settled back in bed.

"Hi," I said when she answered.

"Hello there." She sounded sleepy.

"Long day, huh?"

"Like having the whole family over for Thanksgiving."

"Sounds bad."

"Know what?" she asked.

"What?"

"I miss you."

I settled deeper into the pillow, finally relaxing. "I wish I could tell you everything that happened today."

"What? You can't?"

I thought for a second. "You're going to know sooner or later, anyway. But I really can't say anything now."

"You're teasing me. But I can wait if I have to. Patience is a virtue of mine."

"Wish I could say the same. But I'm learning. Gets a little easier as you get older. You know, though, one of the things I've learned over the past couple of weeks is that there are some things in life that you just can't get over. Sometimes all you can learn to do is live with pain."

She was silent for a moment. "You're right. We're all so concerned with stopping pain and disease and injury like there's some way to protect ourselves a hundred percent from it. And there's not."

"If you're alive, at some point you're going to suffer."

"Tell me about it. Harry, I autopsied an eight-month-old boy this afternoon who weighed not quite ten pounds. It was a real contest between whether he was actually beaten to death or was just allowed to starve."

"Jesus . . ." I muttered.

"Parents are two young kids, both under twenty. Both high-school dropouts. The father's working at a fast-food joint, the mother's staying home, smoking a little hootch, getting mellow. The guy comes home at night, they go have a few drinks, smoke a little more hootch, bring home strangers for little parties in the back bedroom. Father says he couldn't get the kid to stop screaming the other night. All he was trying to do was quiet the kid down. Well, he got him to be quiet, all right. Permanently."

"Well, darlin', like John Prine sang, it's a big old goofy world," I said. "You ever think you need to get into another line of work?"

She sighed into the phone. "Every day. Only problem is, I love the work. What gets me down is there's so much of it these days."

I nestled the phone between my head and the pillow. "I got a great idea, Doctor Babe. Why don't we take a vacation, just the two of us? Get through the holidays together, then get a cheap flight to the Caribbean or something. Say in January. Lay on a beach for ten days. What do you think?"

"I don't know if I can do ten days. But something like that sure sounds good."

"Let's work on it."

"Right now, dearie, I think I'm going to turn this light out and see if I can't sleep through the night without dreaming about dead babies."

There was a lump in my throat at the thought of her autopsying and dreaming about dead babies.

"Yeah, you do that," I said. "Sleep well. I'll call you tomorrow."

"Bye," and then she hung up. I held the phone to my ear for a few seconds longer, then put it back on the set. Something about this woman was getting deep in me.

I jumped in the shower and got my pilot light lit again by standing under a scalding spray. I dried off and threw on my heavy bathrobe, then searched through my kitchen cabinets until I found a pouch of instant hot chocolate. I mixed the powder with water, then nuked it about two minutes.

I lay in bed sipping the hot chocolate until the local news came on. I think I made it partway through the weather, but was sound asleep by the time the sports guy started his rap. I don't remember how long I dozed off, but I woke up long after Jay Leno's monologue and reached for the remote control, then flicked the light off next to me. The room sank to black, and I faded right along with it.

I was floating in a black cloud when I heard the noise. Couldn't figure out what it was at first, as always, but then some nonverbal cognizance recognized it as the telephone. I fought to bring myself to consciousness and got my arm to move toward the phone. I picked up the handset and held it to my ear.

"Yeah," I muttered. My mouth was fuzzy and foul with the taste of the hot chocolate. One should never go straight to sleep after warm milk.

"Harry?" a voice demanded. I opened my eyes. The room was illuminated only by the golden glow of the streetlights filtering through my curtains and the red glow of the digital numbers by my bed: 4:45. In the morning, no less . . .

"Yeah, this is Harry."

"Well, Harry, boy, you better get right on down here."

"Who is this?"

"Who is this? Hell, boy, it's Ray. Ray Forbus."

"Who?" I asked. I didn't know any Ray Forbus.

"Damn it, boy, this is Ray. Down at the office. Slim and Ray, you know?"

"Oh, I'm sorry, Ray. Didn't recognize your last name. What's up?"

"What's up?" he yelled. "I tell you what's up. Your office. Up in flames, boy. You better git your ass on down here."

Chapter 27 _____

Shock does funny things to you. Thought processes that are normally sharp and focused become dull, blunted. I didn't remember much between the time I hung up the phone with Ray and suddenly finding myself on the James Robertson Parkway in front of the courthouse.

The rain poured down; the temperature was dropping and the streets were getting slick. The heater on the Ford had gone south for the winter.

So much for my nice warm bed.

I made a left, then a quick right to get on Charlotte Avenue and hauled butt up the hill between the state capitol and Legislative Plaza. I made another left, then ran a red light and slid into a parking space in front of my office building. There was only one fire truck left, a pumper with flashing lights, droning engine, noise everywhere. Two police cruisers and a fire-department chief's car were double-parked as well, which pretty well blocked Seventh Avenue from Church Street on.

Just over the top of the building, the first glow of dawn began lighting up the sky. I muttered a long series of vulgarities under my breath as I ran across the street, between the cars, and up the stairs to my office. I was drenched, freezing, miserable, still not fully awake and aware of what was happening.

I bolted upstairs, dodging two fire fighters in their massive brown canvas suits and helmets as they hauled a thick, rop-ing, snakelike fire hose down the stairs. I stopped at the landing. Ray and Slim were standing in the hall quietly talk-ing to a uniformed officer who was filling out a report on the fire. Behind them, a fire captain was talking to another fire fighter. Standing next to them was Mr. Morris, the building manager. Morris was a cranky old cuss, balding, black hair slicked back like something out of the Forties, with a per-petual green cigar between his lips.

"There he is," Morris shouted, pointing at me like I was a purse snatcher.

"Jesus," I muttered, taking the last step. "What hap-pened here?"

"What happened?" Morris shouted again. "You almost burned the whole building down. That's what happened!"

"Me? How could I? I was home in bed asleep!"

"Hold on, Mr. Morris," the fire chief said. He walked over to me, stuck out his hand. I shook it numbly. I felt defensive, thoroughly shaken up. He seemed a kindly man, thin, older.

"I'm Harry Denton," I said. "What happened?"

"I'm Assistant Chief West. Step through here with me, Mr. Denton."

It was then that I noticed there was water everywhere, and the acrid smell of smoke. Black tongues licked up the wall around my door, as if an urban graffiti artist had been locked on the landing with a half-dozen cans of spray paint. Only it wasn't paint.

I stared dumbly, then followed the older man as we stepped over another leaking fire hose, through a series of puddles, and into what was left of my one-room office. As we stepped through the door I noticed my office door had been hacked away by fire axes. The hollow-core panels lay splintered to either side of the doorway.

Through the dim glow provided by the hallway lights outside, I stared at the mess. It was as if someone set off a black paint bomb inside the room. My chair and desk were still standing, still recognizable, but they had been charred beyond ever being usable again. The top of my desk had burned clear through, leaving a ragged hole through which I could see the floor.

The ripped and broken remains of burned ceiling tiles were strewn all over the place. Apparently the fire fighters had ripped the ceiling down to make sure the fire hadn't spread through the crawl space above. The walls were stained and streaked as well, and there was a terrible, sickening, overwhelming stench inside. I fought back gagging.

"Aw, man, look at this," I muttered.

"We were lucky," Chief West said, flicking on a flashlight and shining it around the room. "If those two outside hadn't come in early and smelled the smoke, well, I don't want to think about it. Old building like this, no sprinklers. Could have been a real tragedy."

I walked over the soaking linoleum and the charred remains of my rug to my single filing cabinet. I pulled open the drawers; the papers inside were singed, but looked readable. Over in the corner I spotted my briefcase, intact and lying in a pile of debris. I left it where it had fallen, hoping no one else would notice.

"How did it happen?" I asked.

"Carelessness," the chief said. "Your carelessness, Mr. Denton."

"*My* carelessness," I asked, aghast. "How could I—"

He reached over the side of my desk, in a pile of seared and blistered junk in the space between the desk and the wall, and picked up a chunk of molten metal, plastic, and wire. "This, Mr. Denton," he said, shining the flashlight on it.

"What is it?" I asked, staring.

"Looks to me like an immersion coil."

My jaw dropped. "The stinger?"

"When the fire fighters chopped the door down, this was in the middle of your desk, on top of a stack of papers. It was still plugged in."

The chief shook his head. "Very negligent, Mr. Denton. Personally I think these contraptions should be outlawed."

I stared at his hand, dumbfounded. How could I have done anything so stupid, so goddamned careless?

Then it hit me. I hadn't.

Thomas.

My heart banged in my chest like a terrified child who'd been locked in a closet. "Chief," I said. "I didn't do that."

He looked at me, disbelieving. "Now there's no point in that, Mr. Denton. We all make mistakes. It's not like there are going to be any charges or anything. The insurance company will take care of things."

"But I'm telling you, Chief, I didn't do it. Look. . . ." I stepped past him back out into the hall, the reek of the charred wood more than I could stand.

"I want you out of here!" Morris yelled when he caught sight of me again. "You're a menace!"

I'd had enough. Just plain damn enough.

"Quiet!" I yelled, thrusting my right index finger in his direction like a dagger. "Not another word!"

I turned back to the chief, who'd followed me back out into the hall and was now staring at me like I'd gone stark staring bonkers. Along with everyone else in the hall.

"Listen carefully, all of you," I said, lowering my voice to a level that sounded even more threatening than a yell. "I left this office by about three this afternoon. If I'd left that heater coil plugged in, it wouldn't have taken until the middle of the night to start a fire."

Ray put his right arm out and pressed his palm flat against the wall, leaning toward me like he was expecting a barroom brawl any second. "You mean you think somebody else did this?" he drawled. "C'mon, Harry, you can do better'n that."

"Ray, damn it, I didn't do it. I've been careless before, but I haven't burned down a building in I don't know when."

Chief West turned around, looked back into my office. "Well, I don't know. . . ."

I pushed past him, over to the splintered doorjamb, and squatted down in front of it. "Chief, when your men bust into a burning room, they ain't exactly delicate about it, are they? They get in fast, right?"

"Yeah, they have to."

"Let me borrow that flashlight, please, sir."

He handed it to me. I slid the switch forward and got down close. On the smudged brass strike plate, a series of deep scratches ran parallel to the floor. The soft metal was bent in the middle as well, like someone had used it as a fulcrum for a heavy lever.

"Look."

Chief West bent down. I shone the flashlight on the strike plate and held my finger next to the scratches.

"Well, what do you know?" he said.

"Yeah." I moved over to the pile of scrap that used to be my office door. I started to grab the doorknob, then stopped. I grabbed it by a chunk of splintered wood instead and held it up.

"See, on the plunger. Scratches just like on the plate."

Chief West flicked his eyes from the lock to my face. "Somebody jimmied it."

"What is it?" Morris demanded, coming up behind the chief.

"Somebody broke into my office," I said. "They jimmied the lock, and not very delicately either. I didn't set this fire, Chief. It was arson."

"Arson," Morris said, his voice softer now.

Chief West put his hands on his hips. "Damn, son, I believe you're right. I think we better get the police officer back up here. There's no presence of accelerant or anything. Don't need to get one of our investigators here. Pretty straightforward."

I echoed his sentiments. "I believe you're right."

"You know anybody who'd want to do this to you?" Ray asked.

I stared at him. At that moment I'd never needed anything more in my life than to sit down and tell somebody else what was going on. I knew now just how stalking victims felt, and it was the worst feeling I'd ever had.

"No," I lied, again. "Haven't a clue."

It was five-thirty in the morning before I got out of there. Morris agreed, reluctantly, to let me stay in the building for now. "But no more trouble from you," he warned. I couldn't figure out what the hell he was talking about, since before now I'd never been any trouble at all.

I was too far gone to be mad at him. I gathered up a few papers and the briefcase with the bootlegged Elmore files and left the office as soon as the officer finished taking down my statement. I figured the police would not only never catch who started the fire, they probably wouldn't put that much effort into it. In the grand scheme, it was no big deal.

But in *my* scheme, it was a very big deal. What it meant was that Thomas Sturges, for whatever reason, took my questioning of his mother to be a threat. I didn't understand it, but then again I didn't figure I was exactly dealing with a rational person here. Maybe escalating the rage from arson to murder had put the other five personalities who weren't explosive pyromaniacs on guard.

The stakes had risen, that much was for sure.

Outside, I scanned the street in front of my building before leaving. It was so cold even the usual street people were out of sight. Something had frozen on the Ford, and the starter

ground away helplessly without ever catching. There was no
traffic on Seventh Avenue, so I turned on the ignition, let off
the parking brake, and began coasting down the hill. When
I got up to about twenty, I popped the clutch and the car fired
up. I drove all the way down to Broadway, made a left, cut
down to the Riverfront, then back up the hill to the courthouse and the bridge to East Nashville. The convoluted nav-
igation gave me the chance to see if I was being tailed. As
far as I could tell, that wasn't happening.

Right now I needed sleep and warmth and a safe place to
hide. I couldn't go to Marsha's; if Tommy were following
me, that would put her in the soup, too. My only option was
Lonnie's. All I had to do was pack, give Lonnie another hour
or so to wake up, then escape to safety behind his chain-link
fence. If Thomas Sturges wanted me, he could deal with
Shadow.

I pulled the car up right next to Mrs. Hawkins's storage
shed and doused the lights. She had a battery charger and
electricity in the shed. If I needed to boost the car off, I'd be
close enough to reach it.

I tiptoed up the stairs, not wanting to make any more noise
than I had to. My apartment was toasty, dark, felt almost
safe. I set the briefcase down in the kitchen, made sure the
house was locked securely, then went into my bedroom/liv-
ing room and plopped down on the bed still dressed. I closed
my eyes for a moment, then fought to raise them before I
was completely under. I had to pack, get out. No time for
sleep, no matter how badly it was needed.

I sat on the edge of the bed. It was then that I noticed the
blinking light on the answering machine. I hit the playback
button.

"Hello, you have one message," the electronic voice
chirped. Then another voice came on the tape, one that sent
a frozen jolt down the back of my spine.

"This is Pierce," the voice said. It was high, tense,

strained. "You know, don't you? That's why you came by here and talked to Virginia today. You can't come here anymore. It upsets Thomas when you talk to his mother like that. When you upset Thomas, I'm the one that has to put him back together. When I can, that is. Sometimes I can't. Then we have to get Rocky. But he's very bad, and sometimes I can't even control him. So don't do that again. Understand?"

The message ended and I doubled over on the edge of the bed, my ears ringing, my head swimming. Jesus, how did I get in this mess.

"Five-thirty-five," the computer voice chirped, letting me know when Pierce, or whoever, called. I reached for the erase button out of habit, then stopped and punched the save button instead.

"I will save your message," the answering machine said.

"Thanks," I answered. "You do that."

Lonnie had told me before that I ought to keep a pistol around the house, just for safety's sake, but I'd always resisted. I don't know enough about guns to keep from getting hurt by one, and I'd covered too many stories where some heartbroken parent who kept a piece around the house for protection came home to discover his four-year-old had shot his three-year-old sibling to death while playing cowboys and Indians.

I hate the goddamn things; but right now I wish I had one.

I walked into the kitchen and stared out my backdoor. Snow was falling, the flakes just visible in the corona of light cast by the small, bare light bulb over the entrance to Mrs. Hawkins's garage. Everything was deathly, winter quiet. I wedged one of my kitchen chairs up against the doorknob, turned out all the lights, then carried a butcher knife into the bedroom with me and laid it on the nightstand next to the answering machine.

I opened drawers and started tossing clothes onto the bed.

Strange, I found myself wishing Marsha were here. Funny how fatigue and danger in just the right combination can result in arousal, like the stories I've read of men under fire in foxholes suddenly finding themselves, as they used to say during the war, in the mood.

I sat down in my chair for just a moment and, despite myself, drifted off. I slept fitfully maybe an hour, maybe longer, then came to and started packing again. I was struggling with a broken snap on a suitcase when the phone rang. I all but bounced off the ceiling, instantly alert, out of the starting blocks like the gun just went off.

"Yeah," I said into the phone. My bedroom was flooded with light. The clock read 8:19.

"Oh, good," Mrs. Hawkins said. "I was afraid I'd wake you up."

"No, Mrs. Hawkins, I've been up for hours. What can I do for you?"

"Mr. Harriman said he'd shovel the walks for me if I'll let him borrow my shovel for his own driveway. Only you've got your car parked so close to the storage shed, he can't get the door open."

"Oh, okay. I'll be right down."

"Thank you, Harry. I'll tell him to be outside."

I hung up the phone and dug my car keys out of my pants pocket. Then, out of curiosity, I walked over to my bedroom window and pulled back the curtains.

Outside, the world was blanketed in quiet white, the earliest snowfall in memory. There was no traffic and everything was beautifully, crystalline silent and achingly cold. I touched the glass; the slightest coat of icy condensation had formed on the inside. Suddenly I was taken back to boyhood, to that quiet thrill that came from seeing the first snow, and the delight of having a day out of school. Even the ugly ruins of Will Elmore's house were covered in hushed white calm.

All the terrible events of the night before, of the past days, disappeared.

I stepped into a pair of worn moccasins, walked through the room into the kitchen, then unwedged the chair from under the doorknob. I felt almost silly being so paranoid. Maybe the fire in my office really didn't happen; maybe it was an accident. Maybe the message on the answering machine was just someone's idea of a cruel joke. Maybe none of this was really happening.

I pulled the door open and stepped out onto the landing. The snow wasn't deep yet, barely an inch or so at most, but enough that it scraped over my shoes and onto my socks.

Mr. Harriman stood below, a stocking cap on his head, wrapped in a thick brown jacket and plaid scarf.

"Morning, Mr. Harriman," I called.

He turned and looked up at me. "Hello, Harry."

"Beautiful, isn't it?"

"Sure is. Can't remember having one this early. Weatherman says it won't stick long."

"I don't care," I said. "I may even take the day off and enjoy it."

What the hell, I thought, I don't have much of an office to go to anymore.

"Sorry about the car. I couldn't get the garage door open far enough to get in. Tell you what," I said, suddenly feeling the chill. "I think I'm going to need a coat. I'll be right down."

"Don't bother with that," he said. "Just toss me the keys."

"Sure you don't mind?"

"Not at all."

"I just hope you can get the darn thing started," I said, tossing them into the air in a lazy arc.

He held out his hand and caught them expertly. "I'll leave them in the ignition."

"Great," I called. "I'm going back in and put some coffee on."

As I stepped back into the kitchen I heard the rusty, frozen hinges of the Ford squeal in protest as he pulled the door open. A couple of seconds later there was a strange sound, a kind of a muffled thump, like the pilot light of a gas furnace igniting the main burner. I turned and looked out the window.

A split second later the blast of air and scorching light rattled the windows like a hurricane. A heartbeat later the windows shattered as the roar of a terrible explosion sent me to the floor.

I crawled across the broken glass on the linoleum and got up on my elbows to look above the aluminum kick panel on the kitchen storm door.

Outside, a perfect sphere of bright orange and red consumed the end of the driveway and the front of the storage shed. The glass panes of the shed were gone and the doors themselves concaved inward.

My seven-year-old Ford with 106,000 miles on the odometer had burned its last drop of oil and, along with it, poor Mr. Harriman.

Chapter 28 _____

"I ca-ca-ca-can't stop, sh-sh-shaking," I chattered. "I'm so-so-sorry. . . ."

Lieutenant Spellman squatted down on his heels in front of me. I was bent over, sitting in a kitchen chair, shivering uncontrollably. Spellman reached out, put a hand on my shoulder. I jumped at his touch and he jerked away.

"I'm sorry," he said sympathetically.

I nodded my head, unable to speak. I was beyond cold, beyond terror. My guts had turned to jelly; muscles quivered like I'd been plugged into a wall socket.

God, Mr. Harriman . . .

"Have you got someplace to go?" Spellman asked. "Someone to stay with?"

I tried to sit up straight. When I did, I caught a glimpse of the burned shell of the Escort, what was left of Mr. Harriman still in it. A crowd of firemen with hoses and foam extinguishers were still gathered round the smoldering metal, the thick smell of burning rubber, gasoline, and burned flesh still hanging in the air like a pall.

"Harry, you gotta talk to me," a voice said. I looked up. The voice was Spellman's. We were in my kitchen alone. No one else was there.

All I could remember was the roar that deafened me for a moment, then the crackling of fire and things popping somewhere.

And Mrs. Hawkins's screams. Dreadful wailing . . .

The screaming of the fire engine from the Holly Street Station.

Cuts. Cuts on my arm from broken glass.

"Harry, talk to me."

"Oh-kuh-kuh-kuh-kay," I stuttered. "What—"

My knee. I'd fallen, running down the stairway in the snow. My knee hurt.

"Harry, you're in shock." His voice was soothing, steady.

My hands. I held them up in front of my face. They were red, a few small blisters on the palms, a couple on my fingers.

Had I tried to pull him out?

I couldn't remember.

The steps clattered as someone came up. My gut clenched again. Threatened . . .

"Lieutenant," a uniformed office said, "firemen say the car's cold. The coroner's on the way to—"

Coroner. I looked up at the two of them, the shivering halting momentarily.

"—sign the DC. Then the EMTs'll take him on. We got a statement from the old lady downstairs, once she stopped screaming. Seems she's about as deaf as a signpost. Didn't know what happened until her kitchen windows imploded."

"All right," Spellman said. "You finish canvassing the neighborhood, okay?"

"Sure, Lieutenant. Looks like whoever set the device did it real early. Not much chance anybody saw anything."

"Yeah, I know. Send one of the EMTs up here. This one's shocky. Cuts, burns. He may need transporting."

No, I thought. Not the EMT. Marsha.

Thoughts becoming more coherent now. Almost complete sentences running through my brain. I should've expected something like this. He'd been teasing with the fire at the office; this was serious. He meant to kill me. Damn near succeeded. I should have gotten out quicker, but I fell asleep, drifted off. Couldn't help it. Should've run, left town . . .

I'd had trouble before, been threatened. Even a tangle or two back there.

Nothing like this.

Some feeling was coming back into my hands. Not good feeling, either. I'd jumped toward the fire, a panicked, vain effort to pull Mr. Harriman out, but never gotten close enough to actually touch the car. If I had, I'd have left most of my hands on the door handles.

I hit something hot, though. Can't remember what it was. I have this image of my hands in snow. Probably why it isn't any worse.

No matter now. Mr. Harriman was beyond help.

A man in an orange jacket came in with a black case. He knelt down in front of me, Spellman standing behind him, leaning against my kitchen sink. The air coming in through the broken windows had always been cold, but I was just now beginning to feel it.

"How ya' feel, buddy?" the man in orange asked. He seemed bright, friendly. "Looks like you've had better days."

"Yeah," I said blankly.

He pulled out a penlight, shone it into my eyes. It hurt; I squinted.

"Let me take a look at those hands." I held my palms out toward him.

"Hmmm, not too bad. Could've been a lot worse. Your landlady said she found you on your knees with your paws in the snow."

I shook my head. "I guess so."

He pulled out a blood-pressure cuff and wrapped it around my arm, then pumped it up. "How's the knee feel?" he asked.

"Okay, just skinned."

He had a stethoscope on my arm, listening. In a few seconds he unwrapped the cuff.

"Can you hear me okay?" he asked. I nodded.

"How many fingers am I holding up?" He held up four fingers.

"Four," I answered.

"What's your middle name?"

"James," I said. "Harry James Denton."

"What's your phone number."

I reeled off seven numbers. Spellman turned and looked at the kitchen wall phone and shook his head.

"Where are you?"

"Nashville, Tennessee."

"Blood pressure's okay, no sign of concussion, superficial burns, a couple of scrapes," the man said to Spellman. "I'll transport him if he wants, but I think he's okay. Except for having the bejeesus scared out of him."

"No," I said. "No hospital."

I was feeling, little by little, solid again.

"Take you anywhere, Harry?" Spellman asked.

"No thanks, Lieutenant."

The EMT packed up his case. "You don't want to go to General, I got to get you to sign a release. That okay?"

"Yeah," I said. "I'll sign it."

"I'll have it right up." Then he walked out the kitchen door and carefully down my slick steps.

Spellman knelt down in front of me. "Listen up, Harry. It's lecture time," he said quietly, but firmly. "Your ass has had enough smoke blown up it for one day, so I'm not going to blow any more. This is real simple. You need to tell me what's going on before you really get hurt. Whoever killed Elmore is after you now. We both know it. If I have to lean on you, goddamn it, I will."

"Let me get myself back together. I'll come down to your office later. We'll talk," I said.

He stood back up. "All right, fair enough. In the meantime I'm going to have East Sector assign an extra car to this neighborhood for the next few days. The investigators will be here another couple of hours. As far as your car and the damage to the house goes, hell, I guess the only thing you can do is call your insurance agent."

I shook my head again. There were footsteps coming up the metal stairway outside. I looked up just as Marsha stepped into the kitchen wrapped in a down coat, carrying a medical kit.

"Hi, Lieutenant," she said calmly, looking at me as if she didn't know me.

"Oh, hi, Doc," he said. "Sorry to get you out in this weather."

"No problem," she said seriously. "I examined the victim, made the pronouncement, signed the DC. The EMTs are downstairs removing the body."

I flinched. Glad I wasn't down there to watch that one. "EMT says this gentleman's a little shocky. Thought as long as I was here . . ."

"Sure, Doc," Spellman said. "The uniform downstairs finished making out his report?"

"I don't know," she said. "Go ask him. I'll be down in a minute."

Spellman walked to the storm door, pushed it open, and turned. "Remember what I said, Harry."

"Yeah, Lieutenant, I will."

I heard his heavy footsteps stomping down the stairs. Marsha set her bag down on the kitchen table and stood at the window watching him. I sat staring at her back, still not sure she was really here. When Spellman hit the last step at the bottom, she turned to me.

Her face, this time, was bright red and her eyes were watery. Her voice shook and her breath seemed to come in short, ragged gasps.

"You son of a *bitch*," she snapped, one harsh word at a time. "How *dare* you put yourself in this position!"

I'd never felt such cold fury. She dropped down in front of me and grabbed my shoulders, her nails digging painfully in.

"There is someone out there trying to *kill* you, damn it. Do you grok this, Harry? Is this in your vocabulary? Can anybody reach you?"

I grabbed her hands and pulled them off my shoulders. The effort sent icy shocks of pain through my hands.

"Stop," I said. "Don't you know how well I understand? That's an innocent man in that car downstairs. He didn't do anything to anybody, except die in my place."

"Oh, God," she gasped, a single tear rolling down her left cheek. Somehow, though, she felt solid, her composure shaken but intact. "Harry, I guess, I—I didn't know how much all this meant to me."

I wrapped my arms around her, pulling her toward me, the thick down coat a foamy padding between us. "I didn't either," I whispered.

She pulled away, stared straight into my eyes. "I don't want anything to happen to you."

I smiled despite myself, for the first time since I got knocked off my feet some two hours ago. "Hell, Doctor Babe, I don't either."

"You've got to tell me what's going on."

"I can't," I said. "If I do, then you're in it. I can't handle that. But Spellman, he's right. I'm going to talk to him. Doesn't matter what else happens. This has got to stop. But I've got to take care of a couple of things first. See a lawyer, for one thing. I think I'm in trouble."

"C'mon," she said. "Get your clothes on. We'll go right now."

I stood up. She started to grab my hands, then saw my palms. "Oh, God, Harry. That looks like it hurts."

"It's not so bad. Reminds me I'm still alive."

She stood up, opened her bag, pulled out a can of some kind of spray. "Open up." I held my palms out front as she sprayed them. It felt cool, soothing.

"How long does this stuff take to dry?"

"Couple minutes," she said.

"I'm freezing. How'm I going to finish packing? I've got to get out of these wet clothes. . . ."

She wiped a streak of tears off her face with the bulky down sleeve. "Guess I'll have to do it for you."

"What if somebody—"

"Nobody'll see."

"Okay," I said.

"Then we go to Spellman's office. First thing."

I turned to head for my bedroom, then stopped. My thoughts seemed to be coming clearer now. And I discovered, to my surprise, that I was mad as hell.

Royally pissed off.

"No," I said, something in my voice catching her attention immediately. "Not first thing. I've got somewhere else I want to go first."

Chapter 29

"No," I insisted. "I won't have it."

"But you won't even tell me where you're going," Marsha sighed, exasperated once again.

"Just drop me off here, on this corner. Then get lost."

I looked over at her. I'd hurt her, without meaning to, but hurt just the same.

"I didn't mean it that way," I apologized. "It's just that for all I know, he could be watching us now. If he knows who you are in my life, then that puts you at risk. If he's following us, and he thinks you're just giving me a lift somewhere, then you're off the hook."

She coasted down Gallatin Road toward the parking lot of the old Inglewood Theatre. The marquee was blanketed in frost and snow, and unlike the slushy, muddy pavement of the street, its parking lot was still layered in glittering white.

"I don't even know who you're talking about. But if he's following you now, and you're alone on the street, aren't you at even greater risk?"

"I won't be for long," I said as she pulled off the road into the parking lot. "My friend lives very close to here."

"Harry, I—"

"Do it, love. Because I asked you to. Because I wouldn't have unless it was important. No other reason."

She stared over the top of the steering wheel, the Porsche idling rock steady and sweet. Her face went blank a moment, and she seemed not to be here anymore. Then she turned to me.

"I don't want to have to deal with you on a professional level."

That one took a few seconds, then I laughed. "What a grim thought."

"Harry, this is serious."

"I know that." I put my hand gingerly on the door lever. "I'll call you later, okay?"

"Yeah," she said, resigned. I pulled the car door open and stepped out into the melting snow.

"Be careful," she warned.

"Don't worry," I said, shutting the door. I saw her slender arm grab the gearshift and slide it forward. Then she was gone, the deep-throated growl of the Porsche gradually fading away as she disappeared under the railroad bridge.

I was alone in a parking lot off a five-lane road, across from the supermarket where the man who tried to kill me was probably ringing up groceries and chatting with customers. That seemed funny to me, in the way that people who are on the edge often find disaster whimsical.

Beneath the funny, though, was the raging. I wanted to walk across the street, drag the man by the scruff of the neck out into the middle of Gallatin Road, and stomp him to stew meat right in front of the whole world. Losing control like that, though, wasn't going to do anything but get me hung out to dry. Without proof of what I knew, it wouldn't even get him off the street.

I struggled to remember that.

I started walking, the melting snow crunching under my feet as I trod on in the cold. Behind the movie house, a side street curved around to a junkyard surrounded by an eight-foot chain-link fence. I'd driven it dozens of times, but this was the first time I'd ever walked. It seemed different; everything seemed different, as if my near miss with catastrophe had heightened my senses. I smelled the crisp, biting air in ways I'd never experienced. The brilliance of the penetrating sun off the dazzling snow blinded me. I thought again, almost without control, of Mr. Harriman and how he'd never see a day like this one again.

Sadness and rage propelled me on.

Lonnie's junkyard came into view. As I approached on foot it seemed to resemble more of what it probably was: an urban fortress. The chain-link fence seemed impenetrable. I noticed more clearly the security camera attached to the wooden light pole in the center of the compound that scanned the area. My footsteps mushed through the snow, up the slight rise in the pavement to the gate in the fence that was never locked.

It didn't need to be.

I rattled the gate and whistled. From behind the pale green, washed-out trailer that was Lonnie's office and sometimes home, the silent hulk that was Shadow, part German shepherd, part timber wolf, came suspiciously into view.

"Shadow," I called.

She stopped, sniffing the air, staring at me. Seconds later she connected the scent and the voice with the man, and bounded over to the gate, tail slapping side to side like the brushes in a car wash.

"Hey, girl," I said. I always waited until I was sure she recognized me; one gets used to being in one piece. I unlatched the gate and stepped in.

I ran my fingers through her ears. Her fur was warm. Lonnie, I knew, heated her doghouse. He took good care of the old girl, and she did the same for him.

"Where's Daddy?"

She barked, tongue spraying me as she drooled from side to side.

"Shadow, no chicken this time." It was the first time in a

while that I'd been to Lonnie's without stopping off at Mrs. Lee's first.

"Where's Daddy?" I asked again, then walked over the littered junkyard to the trailer.

I rapped on the door with my gloved knuckles, surprised that it didn't hurt any more than it did. I was suddenly ravenously hungry. No wonder, I thought. It'd been nearly fifteen hours since dinner.

There was a shuffling from inside, the sound of a chair on rollers being pushed across a floor, then steps. Lonnie opened the door in a pair of greasy jeans and a thick sweatshirt. He looked at me and knew immediately something was wrong.

"Where's your car?" he asked, looking beyond me to the street.

"Lonnie," I said. "I need your help."

An hour later I was snarfing down a Wendy's single with cheese as we pulled into Mrs. Hawkins's driveway in Lonnie's tow truck. Across the street a television news camera was taking footage of the house. A Metro squad car was parked in front, the lone officer staying warm in his car, keeping the news hounds at bay and off the property. I dipped my head a little as we pulled into the driveway, avoiding the camera. It was only after I got a glimpse of the blackened metal skeleton of the Ford that the taste of cooked meat went sour in my throat.

"Whoa," Lonnie muttered at the sight of the car. "Check it out." The investigators had finished their on-scene, had taken their photographs, collected their samples, made their notes.

"Yeah."

"You want to get that out of here first or patch up the windows?"

"Let's do the windows first. This neighborhood, somebody's liable to break in before we get back."

We spent the next hour trying to ignore the scorched car while we nailed plywood panels over the broken windows. A neighbor came by, said Mrs. Hawkins had telephoned and was going to stay with her sister out in Hendersonville a few days. Here was her insurance agent's name; would I mind giving him a call and securing the house?

I told her to call Mrs. Hawkins and let her know it was all taken care of, and that I hoped she was all right.

Mr. and Mrs. Harriman, she told me, had filed for divorce two weeks earlier and Mrs. Harriman had gone to live with her mother up north. She'd been notified of his death and was taking a plane back tonight to claim the body and make the arrangements.

God damn Thomas Sturges, I thought. If I didn't do it first.

I went inside, made a few calls to appropriate insurance agents, gave them police-report numbers and investigators' names, all the bureaucratic crap that has to be taken care of when calamity strikes.

There was nothing left to do now but haul off the Ford.

"You sure this is okay?" I asked. "Won't the cops want it as evidence?"

"Where they going to put a whole burned car? They took pictures, samples. The rest of it's junk."

Lonnie rolled the truck back out into the street, then backed in winch first. He raised the back end of the car off the ground, then we put a dolly under each burned tire on the front.

I avoided with all my strength looking inside the car.

We towed the car over to Lonnie's junkyard and dropped it at the farthest corner of the lot, behind a pile of automotive corpses that hid it from view. I never wanted to see the damned thing again. Then we went inside, Shadow with us, and locked the door of the trailer.

"So what are you going to do?" he asked. By now, the

afternoon sun had settled down over the railroad tracks on the horizon, the faint orange of twilight fading to the gray of dusk. It had been the longest day of my life.

"I don't know."

"You going to go see Spellman?" Lonnie walked over to the refrigerator, pulled out a beer, and pointed it in my direction.

I shook my head. What little wits I had left I needed to keep.

"I don't know. I want him, Lonnie. I want the little SOB."

Lonnie shook his head. "Pretty wired dude, man. You get too close, you're liable to get burned, literally."

"If I go to Spellman, he'll haul Sturges in. But he'll bust me. Almost a sure bet."

"Bust us."

"No, not us. Your name'll never come into it."

"I was with you."

"You don't need that kind of heat."

"Okay," he said after a moment. "Play it any way you want to. Only going to Spellman's not going to get you Sturges. You still ain't got proof."

I leaned back in the chair, ran my sore hand over Shadow's head, between her ears, over the soft, thick fur. "Yeah, I know. I've got to figure out a way to nail the bastard myself. Even if I go down with him . . ."

"You could stay here, get a decent night's sleep," he suggested. "Deal with it tomorrow."

"Maybe that'd be the best thing."

Lonnie looked at his watch. "You'd be safe here. Afternoon paper's going to have the story about your car, about Harriman. Sturges is going to know he missed you."

"You got an extra set of wheels I can have for a few days?" I realized that in my numbness, the dumb shock of the explosion, I'd left my briefcase in the apartment. That was the last place it needed to be. "I've got a couple of things to take care of. I'll be back here later."

"Sure," Lonnie said, reaching behind him to a pegboard on the wall next to the fridge. Six key rings hung in random order. He pulled off a set and tossed them across the room to me.

"Take the black Jimmy," he said. "It's got a car phone. Use it."

"Thanks, pal. I owe you one, big time." I was relieved he'd loaned me the largest pickup on the lot. Something about having all that metal around me felt like protection, although God knows it didn't help Mr. Harriman much.

I rubbed my hand over my eyes, the stinging in my palms reduced to a slow throb by now. Exhaustion was catching up with me again.

"You look like hell, man," he said.

"Flattery will get you everywhere."

"There's something else I want you to take with you."

"What?" I asked as he walked into one of the trailer's back bedrooms. I heard him fumbling with what sounded like a key in a lock and the tinny metallic sound of a cheap filing cabinet being opened.

I was too tired to follow, so I sat there dazed until he returned. In his hand he held shiny metal. I'd expected that.

"Lonnie, I—"

"Quiet. Take it and shut up."

"I don't know anything about guns."

"It's about time you learned," he said. "That guy's already killed what—two, three people? And that's only the ones we know about."

He was right. I didn't want to admit it, though. But like I said, I hate guns. Anybody who'd ever seen a gunshot wound close up would.

"If I had my druthers, I'd give you the Sig Sauer or the

Glock, but since you're a novice, I figure we better keep it simple." He handed the gun butt first to me.

"The safety on?"

Lonnie grinned. "It's a revolver, Elliott Ness, it ain't got a safety. Just point and shoot. Bad guy go bye-bye."

"Oh." If I'd had the energy, I'd have been embarrassed.

He handed it to me. "Not too heavy," I said. "Pretty small, actually."

"Fits in a coat pocket that way. It's a Smith and Wesson Model 38 Bodyguard Airweight. Five shots, two-inch barrel. It's no cannon, but it'll put you down. You gotta wait till he gets close, though. Real close. Don't try to nail the guy from two rooms away. Ain't like the freaking movies. And if you use it, make sure you get him in front coming at you. Self-defense that way."

"I don't like this, Lonnie."

"Get used to it, dude. It's a whole new world out there." He handed me a box of .38 rounds. "I'd give you the speed loader, only you probably ain't going to have time to practice it enough. Besides, you don't nail him with the first five, he's probably going to fry your ass anyway."

"That's a comfort," I said.

He shrugged his shoulders. "You want hearts and flowers, I'll give you the 1-800 number."

He showed me how to pop the cylinder and reload the pistol. I slipped it into my pocket. It felt heavier there than it did in my hand.

"This thing registered to you?"

Lonnie smiled. "Get serious. It's clean, though. Untraceable, but clean."

I stood up and walked over to the door, stopping midway to run my hand over Shadow's head one last time. "I owe you, pal," I said.

"Yeah," he drawled. "Just make sure you're around for paybacks, okay."

The GMC pickup felt big enough to haul off what was left of the Ford and still leave room for a good-size bag of groceries. I opened the chain-link gate, coasted the pickup out into the street, then got back out in the sleet and shut the gate behind me. I put the truck in gear and felt the engine roar just in front of me as the back tires spun on the ice, connected, then shot forward.

I parked one street over from Mrs. Hawkins's house, away from any streetlights. I sat for a few minutes, saw no one, then got out and ducked through a neighbor's backyard. If he was watching the house, I didn't want him to see what I was driving. I never make the same mistake twice if I can avoid it.

Everything was dark back at the house. I unlocked Mrs. Hawkins's backdoor, went in, made sure everything was battened down, and turned on all her houselights. Outside, the outline of the burned Ford on the driveway was barely visible in the deepening twilight.

Upstairs, my apartment was still freezing, the plywood over the windows barely keeping out the draft. I locked the door, turned on the kitchen lights, then went into the bedroom and turned on both of those lights as well. I kept the jacket on, my hand brushing almost subconsciously against the pocket to make sure the pistol was still there.

That was another thing I was furious about; I'd never had to carry a weapon to feel safe before. Somehow it sullied the world.

I packed a quick bag and called Marsha's house.

"Just come over here and spend the night," she said. "Please. I'll feel better if you're here."

"Not yet," I said. "Not till this is over."

"Where are you going?"

I hesitated. "I shouldn't tell you. I'll be safe, though. For a couple of days, anyway. By then, we'll both be safe. For good."

"Be careful, okay? Make sure you're not followed."

"I will. Get some rest, love. I'll call you in the morning."

I'd barely hung up the phone when it rang again. She must have forgotten to tell me she loved me, right?

"Yes, darling," I said, jerking the phone to my ear.

"So it's *yes, darling*, is it?" the voice said.

It was like somebody sucker-punched me in the gut. "Who is this?" I said.

It was a question that didn't need asking.

Chapter 30

"This is Pierce. Remember me?"

Something in my gut gave me a whole new insight into the concept of peristaltic motion. "What do you want?" I snapped.

"Don't be like that." The voice was smooth, older, like on the answering machine.

"Screw you. You blow my freaking car up, kill my neighbor, try to kill me, and I'm supposed to be *nice* to you."

"You don't understand, that wasn't me. It was Rocky. He's been a bad boy lately, almost out of control. It's getting really tough. In fact, that's why I called you."

I fingered the pistol in my pocket, wished I could fire it through the phone line and blow his brains out. "What have I got to do with Rocky?"

"It's not Rocky. It's Tommy. Tommy can't handle this anymore. He knows that what Rocky is doing is wrong. There's been too much blood, too much killing. Tommy wants it to stop."

"There's an easy answer, Pierce. Have him go downtown, turn himself in."

"Oh, there are no easy answers anywhere, Harry. Believe me, I know. Tommy can't stop Rocky. Only I can. I'm the Protector. I can do it. I'm going to stop Rocky, and you're going to help me."

This is crazy, I thought. I'm sitting here talking to a guy

who's talking about himself in the third, fourth, and fifth person.

"Okay, Pierce." I sighed. "How am I going to help you?"

"Tommy wants to turn himself in, but he's afraid. He's most afraid for Brucie. And Angel and Melinda . . . they're completely panicked. All they do is yell. It's a terrible job to get them to shut up. No quiet time anywhere.

"Nowhere at all . . ." His voice trailed off.

"Pierce, how am I going to help?"

A beat, then: "Tommy says he'll go with you to the police. But only you. He wants you to come here and get him. Take him to the police."

I sat on the edge of the bed, my senses heightened, my heart beating like fury, every hair on my body bristling. "What?"

"He'll give himself up. But only to you."

"Why me?"

"Tommy feels bad about what Rocky did to you. He thought this might make things up to you, in some small way. And there's Brucie. Brucie's terribly afraid of policemen. They do bad things to him."

I tried to remember Thomas's file. Yeah, his father had been a cop. And policemen do bad things to him.

"So Tommy wants me to make sure the cops don't hurt Brucie?"

"Yes. Can you do that?" His voice sounded almost plaintive, pleading.

I thought for a moment. If I said no, my chances of bringing him in were gone. But if I said yes, who knows what this demented creep was up to.

"How do I know you're not setting a trap?" I asked.

"How suspicious of you!"

"Well, excuse me, but given the circumstances."

"How about this? Tommy's sitting here next to his mother

right now. Tommy wouldn't do anything to endanger Virginia, now, would he? Just come over here and pick him up.''

My heart let loose with another 9.5-on-the-Richter-scale
thump; he was a few blocks away from me, at Virginia's
house. Down by Shelby Park and the river.

"Okay," I said, almost on impulse. "When?"

"Right now," Tommy—make that Pierce—said. "Only
thing is, Tommy sees a single police car, he's booking out of
here. Fast. And Rocky is going to be really angry. I can't
promise to keep him under wraps much longer. That's why
we need to settle this once and for all. Agreed?''

"Yeah," I said. "Agreed."

Pierce hung up the phone, leaving me alone and freezing
inside my solitary bedroom. Jesus, I thought, I'm out of my
mind. But if I call Spellman, Tommy'll be out of there like
a jackrabbit. This way I've got a chance of getting him off
the streets. And that, I figured, was priority one. I wasn't
even worried about my own legal problems anymore; seeing
Mr. Harriman burn up like that in the Ford had rendered the
prospect of going to jail almost irrelevant. I locked the house
and scampered down the stairway to the Jimmy.

Okay, so maybe this is just a guy thing. Macho craziness
from hell. "What the heck," I said as I climbed into the cab,
"I can handle this jerk. He needs six personalities just to get
through the day. Only takes me a couple . . .''

Shelby Park at night is the wildlife equivalent of a dark
alley. Packs of dogs scatter across the golf course; rats scour
the riverbank looking for food. And on the bluffs overlooking
the river, white frame houses perch silent and dim over the
unlit streets.

I parked the black pickup truck two houses down from
Virginia Sturges's and killed the engine. In the right pocket
of my down jacket, the pistol lay cold and heavy. In my left,
the box of shells sat waiting.

I glanced at my watch. It had taken me barely five minutes to get over here. He was expecting me. Suddenly all the resolve and the brittleness drained out of me. I couldn't make my legs move. The cops, I thought, I've got to call the cops.

No, another voice said. You call the cops, you blow it.

"Oh, hell," I said out loud. My mouth was dry; my palms sweaty. "C'mon, man. Do it."

Get it over with.

I zipped my jacket and opened the door, slipped out, then closed it quietly. I gambled that the cold weather had driven most of the car thieves inside and left the truck door unlocked in case I needed a quick reentry.

What struck me most was the penetrating silence. Something about it cut clear through to my core. The only sound came from the river; the chugging of a tugboat pushing a barge upriver against the current. Standing still was the only thing worse than moving. I walked quickly up the street and climbed the sidewalk to Mrs. Sturges's front porch.

The front door was cracked open and it was dark inside. I pulled open the screen door and rapped on the wooden doorjamb a couple of times.

"Mrs. Sturges?" I called. Nothing. A moment later: "Tommy?"

I stood there a moment, the silence deepening into thunder. A floorboard creaked painfully. I reached inside my jacket pocket and pulled out the revolver. The muscles in my hand and arm had gone watery on me; I only hoped I could do whatever it was I was going to have to do.

I pushed the door open and stepped in.

The living room was dark, empty, the vaguest, fuzzy outlines of the furniture in the room barely visible. From the doorway into the den at the end of the living room, I could see light so faint it almost looked like candlelight.

I held the gun out in front of me in the two-handed stance I'd seen used by police. I wished that I'd had the chance to go by a firing range and pump off a few just to see what it felt like.

Damn it, where was he?

"Pierce, where you at, man?" I asked in a conversational tone. Silence.

I walked toward the doorway into the den. I stopped in front of it, pausing for just a second, then peeked in. Virginia Sturges lay stretched out on the sofa, her hands folded on her abdomen in the traditional pose, illuminated by candlelight from a half-dozen candles in the room. Ugly, garish purple bruises encircled her throat.

"Holy shit," I muttered. There was no need to even check her pulse. No gentle rise came from her ancient chest, no rhythmic breathing, no stirring of sleep. She had caused her son pain for the last time.

Get out of here, fast. I backed up two steps, heard something behind me, thought, Oh, hell . . . and whipped around, ducking low as I did.

Too late. There was a whooshing sound from above my left ear. Something exploded against the side of my head and the glow of the candles sparkled, danced before my eyes like the sugarplum fairies. It was a sharp thrust of cold, stabbed in the head by ice, numb, stunned, then falling. . . .

Falling.

Against something cold, hard, my cheek jammed painfully, throbbing. There was a lump behind my left ear so big I didn't need to touch it to feel how big it was.

I tried to move, couldn't. Hands behind me. Where was I? Christ, I hurt all over. I breathed in deeply through my nose; something sharp, pungent. I opened my eyes. Candles everywhere, it seemed. I looked up. The old lady on the couch still lay there, unmoving, above me.

I was on my side on a cold wooden floor, my hands pulled behind me, my legs tied together at the ankle. Slowly my brain was working again. What was that smell? Acrid, oily, like my father used to smell when I was a kid and he was tuning up the Chrysler in the garage, and I would—

Oh, my God. Gasoline. Faint whiffs of it.

I fought panic, stuffed it back into its hole, tried to beat it to death. In my mind I saw Mr. Harriman again in the Ford, and stuffed that back down into the black hole as well. My wrists hurt like hell. That was good; it meant I could still feel them.

I rolled onto my side, off my arms, then pulled myself up on my haunches like doing crunches at the gym. What was I tied with?

Duct tape. Silver air-conditioning duct tape. Too strong. Can't break it.

Wait, duct tape. I remembered the last time I'd used duct tape, to repair a leaking radiator hose on a car Lonnie and I'd repossessed. The stuff was incredibly resilient, tough, sticky, but the way you got it off the roll was to start one little tear, one little break in the weave. Then it ripped cleanly, in a straight, even tear, clean across the roll.

If I could just . . .

Footsteps, down the hall. I relaxed, let myself roll over on my back, half closed my eyes.

Thomas Sturges walked in, a claw hammer in his right hand, a five-gallon gasoline can in his left awkwardly pulling him off center. He walked over, then kicked me roughly on the soles of my feet. I rolled and moaned, doing the best imitation of half consciousness I could muster.

Through the net of my eyelashes, I could see him smile. It was a mean smile, more of a leer. Then he walked past me, into the living room. There was a thump as he dropped the can; the floorboards of the old house shook. I rolled over and caught a partial glimpse of him as he raised the claw hammer, then brought it down, hard, against the wall.

He punched a hole in the plaster, then used the claw end of the hammer to yank several larger chunks loose. He picked up the can and poured into the hole, behind the wall, between the decades-old studs.

My God, I thought, he really means to do it right this time.

I scooted over as quietly as I could toward the couch. My wrists were immobile, locked together. I twisted, fought, but that only made it worse. My hands scraped across the hardwood floors. A mortar burst of pain went off as a splinter the size of a telephone pole sliced through skin like paper.

It was all I could do to keep from crying out.

Something wet ran down between my fingers. In the other room, Thomas moved down a few feet, then punched another hole in the wall. I heard the glugging of liquid being poured.

I twisted again, terror building within me, but a terror that fought side by side with a growing fury. I knew I was going to die someday, but I'd be damned if I'd die trussed up on a floor like a pig, then roasted like one on top of it.

The hand slipped in its own blood. My fingers probed the length of the jagged splinter; it felt about four inches long and still firmly attached to the floor. Frustrated, I tried to squeeze the rip in my hand to stop the blood, but it was no use.

Wait, the splinter. Jagged, tearing, ripping; that was the splinter. My hand still bled onto it, still hurt like blazes.

I ran my finger carefully along the edge. It was a nasty one. My head jerked up at the sound of more hammering from the living room, more brittle breaking of plaster. He was moving along every few feet, dousing the house down to its innards.

I couldn't see what I was doing, but I wedged a finger under the splinter and pulled up. The hard, angular sliver of wood came up slowly, painfully, like the blade of a rusty knife. I got the end of it up a couple of inches off the floor, then backed back over it and slipped my wrist under it.

I tried to feel the edge of the tape, but I was working blind.

The tape scraped against the splinter and pulled it back some more, then slipped out.

I cursed under my breath, then set up to try it again. This time I felt resistance as the edge of the duct tape got caught in a notch in the splinter. I shifted to get some leverage, then pushed as hard as I could straight down.

I felt the tape rip, just a bit, but a good start. In the living room, I heard Thomas Sturges moving down along the front wall of the house. Another couple of holes and he'd be ready to start the fireworks. I didn't have much time.

None too subtly this time I sat up on my butt, jammed my wrists over the pointed end of the splinter, then pushed with all my might. The tiny rip widened, then split further. I got enough room to bring up a couple of fingers of each hand, grab each side of the rip, and pull like the devil.

The tape gave way and my hands separated with a ripping sound I prayed Thomas wouldn't hear. I reached down to my ankles, pulling at the tape that held them together.

Too late again. Thomas walked out of the living room on the other side from where he'd entered, on his way down the hall. I stuffed my bloodied hands behind me and lay back down on top of them.

He walked in just as I got back down.

"Oh, so you're awake now." His voice was steady, in control. Not like a lunatic at all. Still Pierce, I think.

"My head hurts," I mumbled.

"I know. If you hadn't ducked, I'd have got you good enough that you wouldn't be feeling anything right now. My apologies."

"Pierce?"

"Of course. Who'd you think it'd be?"

"I thought Rocky was the firebug and the head basher."

He took a step toward me, his face darkening. "Rocky started it. He hates the sodomites, the wicked. Moving in and souring our cleanliness, soiling our community with licentiousness, their lustful passions. Polluting the innocent, the children. It's against God's way.''

"But Rocky was just having a good time, wasn't he?" I was starting to understand. "Just looking for a few thrills."

"Until it got out of hand," Pierce said. "Until the evil one, that doctor, began threatening to expose him. He wanted to lock them all up, in one of those hospitals. I let that happen to them once. I couldn't allow it again. I had to step in, take control."

"I thought the fire at Elmore's lacked a certain . . . spontaneity."

Pierce smiled. "I take that as a compliment."

"What about the preacher, the Reverend Madison?"

"Tommy got the letter," Pierce said. "The one that talked about all those terrible things those clients of Elmore's were doing, the way he was making fun of them. You know, Tommy went for help once, to a preacher. Before Rocky killed the sergeant."

"The sergeant?" I interrupted.

"Yes." Pierce smiled. "The sergeant. The sergeant used to whip Tommy all the time, until Rocky took care of him. But before Rocky did that, Tommy went and told the preacher. And the preacher told Tommy he was a bad boy and that the only way he could atone for his sins was to let the preacher, the man of God, have him. So Tommy did, only he didn't know that having him meant taking him like one of the sodomites. That preacher moved away before Rocky could take care of him, but Madison? Well, Madison didn't get away quick enough."

Bile filled the back of my throat and I felt suddenly, overwhelmingly, nauseated. Tommy had killed both his parents, Elmore, Madison, Mr. Harriman, God knows who else. And now it was my turn.

"What about Virginia?" I asked, motioning my head toward the couch.

"Oh, her," Pierce said casually. "I got tired of listening to her. Bitch got what she deserved."

"And now me," I said quietly.

"You're the last one," he said. "You've got to go, too."

He squatted down in front of me, grinned meanly. "Sorry about that."

Below me, there was a thump, followed by crackling sounds coming up through the heating vent in the floor behind my head.

"What was that?" I said, fear a riptide in my voice.

"Just a little something I rigged up downstairs. A candle, some fusing, a little straw. Then it all catches fast. You'll see. It won't take long. You won't hurt. Not much. Take deep breaths. All be over before you know it."

"Wait," I said.

"Oh, I can't. It's time for me to go. By the way, thanks for the truck and the pistol. Every little bit helps."

"Where are you going?"

"Far away, where they can't find me."

"You're not thinking right, Pierce. They'll find you."

"No, they won't," he said. "They'll figure Virginia and her son, Tommy, were murdered by burglars, and the house set afire to cover it up."

Panic danced up and down my spine like electricity. "Wait, Pierce, let me ask one thing," I said. "Just one thing before you go."

He squatted back down in front of me. Smoke began drifting up through the vents, and I imagined I felt the first glow of heat through the floor. The crackling and snapping from the basement grew louder.

"What?" Pierce asked, grinning. "Is this like a dying request?"

"Sort of. I just want one thing. This has all been to protect Brucie, right? All of it, to take care of him."

Pierce's face darkened at my mention of Thomas Sturges's

frightened, terrorized little boy. "What about it?" he demanded.

"If I'm going to die to protect Brucie, at least let me say goodbye to him."

He seemed momentarily stunned. "What?"

"Please, Pierce. Let me say goodbye to Brucie."

From the end of the hallway I thought I saw faint orange. The smoke was thickening, beginning to choke me. Time—my time—was nearly gone.

"No, no one can—"

"Please," I begged. "Brucie . . ."

Pierce's face softened a bit, and his eyes seemed to haze over. "Well, I guess that's—"

In the dim candlelight his face underwent the most remarkable change. His jaw muscles slackened and his mouth hung open just a crack. A line of drool ran down his chin and his eyes went blank, then filled with tears. His shoulders slumped and he seemed to relax within himself, and slowly the tense, burdened adult face of Pierce Huntley, the Protector, became that of Brucie Miller, the Scared Little Boy.

"Brucie?" I asked.

His voice had changed as well, becoming higher, less strong, that of a child, a pitiful, scared, scarred child.

"Yeah?"

I gritted my teeth as hard as I could, threw all my weight forward, and hit him with my balled-up right fist, square in the nose. So hard I felt the jarring all the way up my arm, through my elbow, into my shoulder.

He fell back deadweight, his nose exploding in a burst of red. Stunned, he fought for breath, and then a cry like that of a child who'd just fallen off the swings and had the wind knocked out erupted from his child's lungs.

I jerked forward, up onto my knees, my ankles still bound, and fell on top of him. He squalled in pain and terror and panic. I hit him again, solid, in the side of the face. I was on top of him, swinging madly, my teeth clenched, every muscle in my body rock hard in panic and rage.

He brought his arms up to protect himself, then tried to huddle into a ball. Only I was too on top of him.

There was a tremendous boom as the vapors in the wall caught. The plaster in the living room blew inward, bright orange surrounding us, heat, choking fumes, and smoke, all the oxygen being sucked out fast. Glass shattered in another room as a window exploded.

Below me, the face of Brucie Miller switched off instantly and the face of a monster stared back at me. With a terrible howl and strength that suddenly became superhuman, Rocky Ludlum threw me off him like a pillow. I slammed against the sofa, the corpse of Virginia Sturges rolling off behind me and bouncing to the floor with a heavy thud.

He screamed again in a madman's fury and jumped on top of me, his hands around my throat, his eyes blazing. His fists were like two massive vises, shutting off my wind, my blood. I pushed against his chest. He let go with his right hand, then cocked back, made a fist, and smashed it into the side of my head.

Everything went blurry and sparkly, pretty colors and ghostly sounds. Music, perhaps. I wasn't sure.

He hit me again, only this time I dodged enough to miss most of the impact. With only one hand around my throat, I could breathe a little bit now. He was sweating with effort, yelling guttural, banshee sounds, his lips pulled back over his teeth like a mad dog.

I hung on. It was all I could do.

Another *whump* came from the hallway and the stairway to the basement exploded. Flames burst down the hallway and into the den. Rocky's face turned to the left, his eyes searching the hallway first in panic, then terror as the flash erupted and came toward us.

He screamed again, turning back to me and letting go of

my neck. He swung his fists wildly, flailing away at me. I ducked my chin into my chest, tried to cover up with my forearms as he mauled me. Then he stood up, wailing, and tried to push me away from him.

I hung on like a leech.

He jerked up, dragging me behind him, and ran from the den into the living room. Pouring the accelerant down between the studs had worked better than he expected. The four walls of the living room were a solid blanket of flame, noise, conflagration.

He screamed in terror and rage. I shut my eyes, blindly holding on to him. He swung his arms, trying to knock me off. I locked my arms around his waist from behind, my taped ankles towed behind us uselessly. He turned around, faced me, and pounded on my head. Then he stopped, looked around for a second, swiveled in alarm, and ran for the door, his legs kicking me, my deadweight a burden he couldn't shake.

He yanked open the front door and the blast of air rushing in simultaneously knocked us over and caused the living room to literally explode. We were in an inferno. I felt conscious thought slipping away from me, my muscles going.

Rocky Ludlum kicked at me again. This time my grip slipped. He bent over, hit me in the face one more time, then turned.

I let go of his waist, but before he could break away, I reached up, wrapped my arms around his neck, found a bare fold of skin on the nape, and sunk my teeth in him as far as they would go.

He screamed louder and sharper than ever, then jumped to his feet with me hanging on to him like a pit bull. He darted out the door, stumbled, then we both rolled down the hard concrete steps. He shrieked like a wounded animal caught in a trap, howling in helplessness and frenzy as we slopped around in the frozen slush and snow on the lawn.

He fought. I hung on, the taste of raw meat, blood, sweat in my mouth. All conscious, verbal thought left me, and I blindly clamped onto him as he assailed me, pounding away like a crazed maniac. He was crying now in pain and frustration, half words and lunatic bursts of vile obscenity spewing uncontrollably out of his mouth.

That's the way the firemen from the Holly Street Station found us when they pulled up in front of the house.

Epilogue

Somehow they managed to find a quiet corner of the General Hospital Emergency Room and shove me into it. Good thing, too. I was weary beyond expression, sore, and frustrated as hell at having already told my story to Lieutenant Spellman three times. And he still had questions.

"I'm still trying to figure out how you knew Sturges was the pyro."

He couldn't figure it out because I hadn't told him. I'd only told him about getting the list of patients from Mimi in an attempt to clear them all. I wasn't about to tell him any more either, at least not until Marvin Shapiro got there. Where was he, by the way? I'd called him over an hour ago.

I settled back into the soft pillow on the examining table. We were waiting for the X rays to come back on my head and my hand. My hand had been salved and bandaged, a chemical ice pack laid loosely on my head, and blood drawn for the requisite HIV test that was necessary as a result of Thomas Sturges and I having exchanged so much bodily fluid.

"I interviewed his mother, Virginia," I explained once again. It wasn't the whole truth, but it was enough of it for now. "Plus, Sturges wasn't the least bit reticent to talk about it once he thought he had me trapped. Elmore wanted to get him into a mental hospital, and he just wasn't going to have that. So Elmore had to go. One thing led to another.''

Spellman sat in the chair across from me and scribbled a few more notes. The curtain slid open and Dr. Sidney Hughes, the police psychiatrist, walked in. Hughes was gray-haired, tall, stately, the very picture of well-educated Southern manhood. In short, a real snot.

"How is he?" I asked.

"Completely dissociated, definite fugue state, borderline catatonia," Hughes said. "Hasn't said a word. Doesn't respond to voice, either command or conversation."

I sat up a bit on the table. "He's certifiable, isn't he? Insane, I mean. He won't have to stand trial or anything."

Hughes shook his head. "Not a chance. I don't think we can even get him in for a hearing. We'll commit him to MTMHC for observation. It's doubtful he'll ever come out."

I grimaced. Middle Tennessee Mental Health Center, the old Central State Asylum, was the state mental hospital out on Murfreesboro Road. It wasn't the best place in the world, but he'd be safe out there. And the world would be safe from him.

Pretty good trade-off, I figured.

"I feel kind of sorry for the guy," I said. "Imagine the abuse it takes to turn you into what he was."

"I feel sorrier for the people whose houses he burned," Spellman said.

"I feel sorry for him," Hughes commented, "because he got too close to you. That was some clip you gave him. His nose was completely broken, not to mention one of the nastier human bites I've ever seen."

Spellman smiled. "Stop grinning, Howard," I ordered. "I'm not proud of that. He scared the bejeesusing hell out of me. Nearly killed me in the process."

"I know that," Spellman said. "It's just the thought of you rolling around the front yard with somebody's neck in your jaw. Mr. Intellectual Investigative Reporter becomes Back-Alley Barroom Brawler. You know, Harry, this private-investigator shit might take yet on you.''

"I wish it'd never happened."

Sidney Hughes turned to Spellman, his voice like an announcement over the PA system. "Lieutenant, it's getting late. I'll file my report in the morning and we'll have the commitment papers drawn up for the hearing as quickly as possible. Do you anticipate any problems with the district attorney's office?''

Spellman shook his head. "I think this one'll be pretty straightforward.''

As Hughes left with a "Good night, gentlemen" the emergency-room resident walked in with a folder of X rays under his arm. "I've examined your film, Mr. Denton, and I don't see any evidence of fracture. You seem pretty lucid. No sign of concussion. I think I'll let you go on home this time. But watch that head, okay? That's quite a bump you've got.''

"I promise."

"I'll have some papers for you to sign, releases and such. Then you can go.''

It would be the second set of release papers I'd signed in less than sixteen hours. If you die, do they make you sign a release before your soul can leave your body?

"No problem," I said.

"And if you're up for company, there are two people outside here who insist on seeing you.''

I looked at Spellman and shrugged. "Sure, send them in.''

Marvin Shapiro walked in thirty seconds later, Lanie trailing behind him. I sat up on the edge of the bed; she came over silently, her face stark and white, and wrapped her arms around me.

"I hope Lieutenant Spellman has advised you of your constitutional right to have an attorney present during all questioning," Shapiro yammered.

"C'mon, Marv," Spellman said, "he's a witness, not a suspect."

"Yes, and as my employee, attorney-client privilege extends to him on all actions connected with this case."

"Don't worry, Marvin. The lieutenant has only asked me what happened tonight with Sturges. None of Dr. Elmore's other clients are involved."

"Good," Marvin said. "I hope we can close this awful business down. The media will want some account of this, but I insist that all of Dr. Elmore's clients be kept completely out of it."

Spellman stood up, snapped his notebook shut. "Chill out, Marvin. Everything's going to be just fine." Then he looked at me. "You'll probably have to testify at the hearing, at least file a deposition."

"Okay," I said. "I'll cooperate with you any way I can."

"Let me know where you are, Harry."

"Right, Lieutenant."

Spellman pulled the curtain to as he left and I scooted down off the table.

"Are you all right?" Lanie asked. It was the first thing she'd said.

"For a man who's been nearly killed twice in one day, I think I'm going to live."

"Oh, God, Harry. This is awful."

"Yeah," I said. "It's awful. But it's also over."

"I was so afraid. . . ." she said, shaken. "When I heard about your car, and that poor man."

"It's over, Lanie," I said, squeezing her shoulders with my arm. "We move on."

"Listen, Harry," Marvin said, "I know you've had some expenses with this one. The car and all."

"Not to mention my office."

"Yeah, so just draw up an invoice and submit it to the estate. With the heirs' permission, I think we can compensate you for your losses. Not to mention your bill."

I looked down at Lanie. "Yeah? I got your permission on that one?"

"Of course," she said. "You dope." She almost smiled.

I signed the papers to relieve the hospital of any liability for letting me go home, then walked out with Lanie and Marvin into the cold night air. The sky was black and clear, and even over the harsh, sulfurous parking lights I could see a blaze of pinpoints in the sky. I breathed in deeply, the sharp intake of dry air burning my lungs and making my head pound.

It felt great to be alive.

"Can I give you a lift anywhere?" Marvin asked.

I stared across the parking lot of the Metro Nashville General Hospital, which sat on a rise next to the morgue. In the farthest corner of the lot, beneath a tree just to this side of the morgue, a black Porsche sat with a vanity plate that read DED FLKS.

"No, uh, actually, Marvin, I think I got a ride."

"You sure?" Lanie asked.

"Yeah, I'm fine."

"Great," Marvin declared. "I'm outta here, guys. Why don't you drop by my office, work out a few last-minute details tomorrow?"

As Marvin disappeared Lanie turned to me, the light reflecting off her eyes and face. "Harry, I'm so sorry about all this."

"Me too. But I'm glad you're going to be okay. Things should work out well for you now."

"Maybe," she said. "I'm awfully scared. I'm sorry, too, that things went all, well, all wrong with us. I mean, we could always, you know, if you wanted . . . We could try again."

"Shhh," I said. "It's late and we're both tired. Both had the hell beat out of us. Let's call it a night."

She put her arms around my waist and hugged me, then backed away and smiled. "How will you get home?"

"Don't worry. I've already called a friend."

"If you're sure."

"Yeah, I'm sure. Go on, I'll talk to you tomorrow."

As my ex-wife walked to her car and, I was sure, out of my life permanently, I turned and started across the parking lot to the morgue. I heard the sound of Lanie's car as she sped quickly out of the lot and to the safety of her condo in the suburbs. She wasn't made for the inner city this late at night.

But strangely, it was beginning to feel like home to me.

I strode quickly over to the bulletproof steel-and-glass fortress-size front door of the morgue. Through the thick glass, Marsha stood at Kay Delacorte's desk in a pair of jeans and a ski parka, the phone to her ear.

I hit the buzzer. She turned and squinted for a second, then said something into the phone and put it down. Her face was drawn and tense. She came to the front door and pushed a door bar, and a massive amount of steel gave way at her efforts.

What the hell, I thought, she was that kind of woman. Move steel when she took a mind to.

I stepped in, the door whooshing shut behind me. She stood in front of me, looking down at me, her brow furrowed, her eyes dark.

"What am I going to do with—"

I leaned forward and kissed her, softly, gently. It was the first time I'd ever done that in her office. Luckily no one else was around.

"You finish with Virginia Sturges?" I asked.

"She's in the cooler," Marsha said. "What's left of her. I just checked her in. I'll do her tomorrow morning."

"Then do me a favor," I asked. "Would you please take me home? I'm exhausted."

"I could use a drink," she said. "I've got a special bottle of wine at home."

"Great," I said. "I'll open the door for you when we get there. I've got keys now, you know."

I wrapped my arms around her waist and held her for just a moment. There would be a lot of damage to repair, starting tomorrow. But for the rest of this night all I wanted to do was hold and feel this woman. Yeah, no getting around it; it was great to be alive.

"Let's go," I said.

Together we walked out into the cold, clear, beautiful night.

Harry James Denton's search for the killer of his college sweetheart's husband leads him into the parts of Nashville no one sings about unless they are singing the...

DEAD FOLKS' BLUES

by

STEVEN WOMACK

**Published by Ballantine Books.
Available in your local bookstore.**